MURDER AT THE BUNHOUSE CAFE

Will Cameron

KLH Publishing

Murder at the Bunhouse Cafe

For Karen
Always for Karen

PROLOGUE

They Approached From All Directions

It was a chilly morning in late February, and they approached the Partick Bunhouse Café from all directions. Some walked south down Byres Road, others came west along Argyle Street, most came east along Dumbarton Road. A couple descended from buses, one was dropped off by car, and another had taken the subway. Sixteen trainees in total headed towards the café that morning, with one of them completely unaware that they were approaching the scene of their own murder.

Julie Campbell was already crossing Partick Bridge, around ten minutes from the café. Smartly dressed, she found it strange to wear business clothes again, but she wanted to make a good impression right from the off. In her early forties, she told herself the walk would do her good, but her legs were already aching, and the day hadn't really started yet.

James Halliday was from Cornwall and in his early thirties. He had woken up that morning in a stranger's bed in Govan. He had no idea what had happened the night before, but on lifting his head from the pillow, he knew he had to get to Partick, regardless of how he felt. He mumbled a bye to whoever was still sleeping and jumped on the subway. Exiting Kelvin Hall station, he immediately headed for the coffee shop across the road.

Passing that coffee shop was Gideon Semanyo, excited and happy. From Ghana, he had been in Glasgow for nearly two years, and with his asylum claim finally settled, things had been going well for him. He was told some TV people would be at the café, and he had put on his best clothes for the occasion. He looked forward to it. Gideon loved meeting people.

Mary McNair hated meeting people. As such, it was nerves, more than a lack of fitness, that made her feel out of breath as she approached Partick Cross. A native Glaswegian in her late twenties, she was often asked why she was so quiet, and she didn't know why she was so quiet; she just was. She tried to put all her insecurities out of her mind and walked determinedly forward. The sooner she got there, she told herself, the sooner it would all be over with.

Andy McLean thought it was all a load of bollocks. As he got off the bus outside Kelvingrove Art Galleries, he crumpled up his ticket and threw it on the ground, before quickly realising he might need it for expenses. He stooped, picked up the ticket, uncrumpled it, and put it in his pocket. He had got on the bus in Yoker, not far from the shipyard where he had worked most of his life. Now, in his late fifties, he shook his head. A trainee? At his age? Aye right, it really was a load of bollocks.

Ahmed Farooq got off the bus just behind Andy McLean. In his mid-twenties, he had come from Syria via the English Channel, his legs spread apart on the side of a dinghy as if he were riding a horse. He had wanted to go to London, but was put on a bus and told he was going to Glasgow. Beggars can't be choosers, they said. As it turned out, Ahmed now loved Glasgow and saw ending up in Scotland's largest city as God's will. What God wanted, God got.

Danny Wilson had been unemployed for God knows how long and had been on more training schemes than he cared to remember. Twenty-five years old, he always thought about getting out of Glasgow and going somewhere really, really far away, like Australia, the US, or Wales. However, like most things, he always talked about it, but never got around to actually doing it. Still, he was looking forward to today. At the very least, it should be a laugh.

All sixteen trainees had been told to arrive at the café at 9:00 a.m. sharp. No ifs, no buts, for this was a very important day. Not only would they be meeting their fellow trainees for the first time, but they would be meeting the media. As the light grey sky began to darken and threaten rain, the trainees slowly filtered into a disjointed wave moving towards Bunhouse Road.

Mohammad Sayyid had been a good boy since he arrived from Afghanistan, well, sort of. At least, he hadn't murdered anyone. He strode down Bunhouse Road with his happy face, hating the people around him. If only they knew, but of course, they could never know. He glanced to his right and saw a really nice-looking girl on the other side of the road. She looked across at him, and he smiled a beaming smile.

The nice-looking girl was Kelly O'Connor. Twenty-one years old, she stumbled and glared accusingly down at the pavement. She wondered what day it was and if any hotties would be going to this café thing. There had to be at least one, surely. Hopefully, that weird, old guy on the other side of the road, smiling at her, wasn't going to the café. Then a thought about the night before came into her mind. No, she didn't, did she? She couldn't have. She feared she did.

Brenda Finnie needed a drink. Usually, at

this time in the morning, Brenda would still be in bed nursing a hangover. Under that bed was a hammer, a baseball bat, and an axe. Instruments of reassurance and self-preservation ever since an ex-boyfriend tried to set her alight while she was still asleep. That ex-boyfriend was now doing life for the murder of some other poor lassie who hadn't woken up in time. Brenda really needed a drink.

Umar Olowe from Nigeria turned into Bunhouse Road, still not quite sure if he was going the right way. He glanced nervously around him and was comforted by seeing a few other people walking in the same direction. Tall and unsure of himself, he was still getting used to Glasgow and the fact that everyone kept calling him 'Big Yin'. He was told it was a friendly term, but he still wasn't sure. He just hoped he was going the right way.

Jess Whittaker felt like murdering someone. From a small village near Fort William, she was not happy at all about having to go to this café thing. The more they made it sound like this big wonderful opportunity, the more she wanted to stay in bed and eat cheese. So much was going on in her life right now. Drama. She sighed and watched the woman with long jet-black hair in front of her going down Bunhouse Road, wondering if she, too, was going to the café.

She was. Linh Nguyen was from Vietnam.

She wasn't the tallest of people, but she felt even smaller compared to the tall woman in front of her. Linh was determined to excel on this course. She was determined to get on in her new country. She was determined about everything, even though she could barely speak a word of English.

The tall woman in front of Linh was Tegan Rees. Tegan was Welsh, and every time she spoke, people would say she sounded just like that character out of *Gavin and Stacey*. Tegan was not quite sure why she had agreed to go to this café. No matter, what was the worst that could happen? Anyway, she fully expected people to say she sounded just like that character out of *Gavin and Stacey*. Tegan had never seen *Gavin and Stacey*.

Russell O'Neill sat in the back of his parents' car, studying all the people walking down Bunhouse Road. His mother turned round from the front passenger seat and asked, for the umpteenth time, if he had his sandwiches. He said yes, all the while wondering, for the umpteenth time, why his mum thought he would need sandwiches when he was going to work in a café. Whatever. He studied the people once more and saw another black person. *I mean, that must have been like three he had seen.*

The third black person was Zande Mhkize from Zimbabwe. She was pleased to see she wasn't the only person of colour heading in the direction of the café. She wanted to be a lawyer, but was told there were no vacancies for lawyers at the moment. In the meantime, they said she could learn how to make sandwiches. OK, she shrugged. Being a lawyer and knowing how to make sandwiches could be a really useful combination.

The uneven wave of various people meandered down Bunhouse Road, edging towards the Partick Bunhouse Café. Standing outside the door of the café on the corner of Old Dumbarton Road was Siobhan Sutherland, wearing a smile and a clipboard. Siobhan was assigned to liaise between the trainees and the DSS, as well as with anyone else the trainees wished to liaise with.

Across the pavement from Siobhan was a small group of already bored photographers, cameramen, and journalists setting up. Gideon was the only one to acknowledge them, giving a small, excited wave. As all the trainees arrived, Siobhan ushered them into the function room, where five rows of six wooden chairs were arranged on a dark red, cheap-looking carpet in a dark red, cheap-looking room.

Curiously, along a far wall, eleven formally dressed men and women stood as if part of a police line-up. They all wore bright, insincere smiles as the trainees trudged in through the door. More than one trainee wondered if the line-up was some kind of welcoming cabaret act.

Once she was confident that all the trainees had arrived, Siobhan briefly introduced herself, as she had already met them during their initial assessment at the job centre. Her first job on this day was as compere, introducing the opening act, namely, their team leader, Alistair Carmichael.

Alistair had chosen to sit at the back, a move calculated to make his entrance a little more dramatic. Once introduced by Siobhan, he got up and ambled forward, trainee heads turning round as if to see the recipient at an awards show. Once Alistair finally arrived in front of the trainees, after what seemed like a couple of weeks, he smiled loudly and clapped his hands together, making a couple of trainees jump in the air.

Alistair spoke in a loud, resonant baritone voice. 'First of all, I'd like to thank you all for being here today...isn't it exciting?' He paused and looked upwards as if trying to find the right words. 'I don't think I'm exaggerating when I say we're launching something quite special here this morning, which is why we have the world's press standing across the street.' The world's press was perhaps a slight exaggeration since the furthest any journalist had come was Kilmarnock.

Some trainees looked at Alistair with curiosity, others with amusement, some with contempt. Andy McLean was of the latter variety. He turned to the diminutive Asian woman sitting next to him, and, with his hand over his mouth, muttered, 'Is this guy for real?' Linh didn't understand what he said.

'Now,' Alistair continued, 'in order to please our paparazzi pals, we'll shortly go outside and have a group photo done in front of the café. Those of you who don't mind talking to the press can stay outside. For those more intelligent individuals who do mind, come back inside. I promise there will be no hard feelings. For those who choose to stay outside, the journalists will probably want to ask you some mundane questions about the training program, about yourself, where you're from and so forth. If a journo asks you a question you don't want to answer, don't answer it—end of. After the questions, you can all come back inside, and we will have breakfast ready for you. Then, we can all properly introduce ourselves to one another.' Mary McNair died a little inside. 'Now, before we head outside, does anyone have a question?'

Andy McLean put his hand up.

'Yes, young man?'

'How do we claim our travel expenses?'

'Siobhan will explain that all in good time. OK, enough questions, it's time to meet the press.'

The sixteen trainees slowly got up and even more slowly made their way outside to stand in front of the café in the chilly morning air. The smartly dressed men and women who had been standing against the wall came out after them and proceeded to stand in front of the trainees. It turned out they were local dignitaries, a variety of people from the DSS, the Scottish Parliament, Westminster, and community leaders. They stood, their insincere smiles blocking the view of the trainees, until the press asked them to move out of the way, which they reluctantly did, slowly shuffling to one side. So, the sixteen trainees stood shivering in the morning cold, in front of the Partick Bunhouse Café.

Two months later, that same group photo would appear in several newspapers, but for an entirely different reason.

CHAPTER 1

Nothing

She wasn't there, and in her place was nothing. As DCI Mike Patterson felt Stephanie's absence beside him as he always did on waking up, Patterson couldn't help but glance to his left just to make sure she wasn't there. She wasn't. As always, Stephanie wasn't anywhere. Not in bed, not on the settee, not at the kitchen table, not in the garden, nor when Patterson arrived home or left for work. Stephanie was nowhere.

It was the 2nd of May 2011, two years since Patterson's wife had died. Of course, for Patterson, for him, life dripped onwards, and the clock edged relentlessly forward. He now sat at the kitchen table, eating his Shreddies and drinking his coffee, listening to that ticking clock, which only seemed to add to the silence. Nowadays, no matter where Patterson was, noise often reminded him of silence.

The phone rang. At half-six on a Monday

morning, he guessed who it could be, and putting the mobile to his ear, he was proved correct. It was Acting Detective Sergeant Brian McKinnon.

'Morning sir, you wouldn't happen to know where the notes on the Chalmers case are, do you? I went into your office but couldn't find them.'

'They're in the bottom left-hand drawer of my desk. Brian, was it really necessary to phone me up at this time just to ask that? I'll be in the office shortly.'

'Oh, I know, it's not that I'm phoning about; a body has been found at the Partick Bunhouse Café.'

'The Partick Bunhouse Café? And where exactly is the Partick Bunhouse Café? And please don't say Partick.'

'It's on Bunhouse Road.'

'Of course, and where exactly is Bunhouse Road?'

'Right next to the Kelvin Hall, just off Argyle Street, next to Partick Bridge.'

'Have Jack or Claire been informed?'

'Both. They're on their way.'

'OK, I'll be there myself within the hour, and get yourself down there as well, you're Acting DS remember? Oh, and don't forget to put those notes back, or else.'

Patterson clicked off the phone. Did he really say "or else"? God, he was turning into a grumpy old man. After Stephanie's death, he had been determined not to become bitter and resentful, quietly protesting against the injustices of life by answering everyday questions with sarcastic replies and withering put-downs, but it was hard. Still, he chided himself for being short with McKinnon.

For one thing, McKinnon had stepped up to the mark in becoming an Acting DS. Even if he still thought it necessary to do every menial job, such as typing up a report on the Chalmers case that should really be left to a more junior colleague.

Regardless of that, Patterson would hate for McKinnon to think he wasn't appreciated; he couldn't be more appreciated. Thankfully, McKinnon's full promotion to Detective Sergeant was only a few weeks away from becoming permanent.

As Patterson rose from the kitchen table, he vowed to be as nice as possible to everyone that day—to be as far away from the grumpy old man he had just been on the phone with McKinnon. Above all, no sarcastic remarks. Ten minutes later, aware of Stephanie's absence at the door, Patterson left home.

Looking up, Patterson saw the sky was a sombre grey, with occasional slats of silver passing charcoal clouds. At this time in the morning, Summer seemed as far away as it was at the start of the year, yet the days were slowly getting longer, and Patterson knew it would get warmer as the day progressed.

Soon, Patterson was turning his car into Bunhouse Road. He had not only been unaware of this Bunhouse Café but also of Bunhouse Road, even though, seeing it now just off Argyle Street, right next to Partick Bridge, as McKinnon said, he must have passed it a thousand times. It was one of those roads where there never seemed to be any reason to go down. You could happily live your entire life without being aware that Bunhouse Road existed.

Further down, the road was cordoned off. The yellow tape crossing the road, like bunting, hung to announce that the police were having a party. Patterson parked up by the side of the road, ducked under the tape, and walked towards the crime scene. The dark sky was slowly transforming into a slightly lighter shade of grey, but it was still quite chilly this early May morning.

As Patterson put on his protective polythene suit, he surveyed the Partick Bunhouse Café. On first impressions, it didn't look like much, occupying a depressed-looking building at the end of Bunhouse Road. Its windows seemed dirty, and the location didn't seem particularly appetising either. If Patterson had been starving and saw this place, he would probably pass it by to go somewhere else.

On the plus side, it was just up from the new Transport Museum on the Clyde, which had taken over those duties from the Kelvin Hall, and maybe it was not that far a walk from the Kelvingrove Art Galleries and the busy Argyle Street. Yet, you still had to make an effort to find this café more than it would naturally find you.

As Patterson continued to put on his protective suit and be unimpressed by the café exterior, Detective Inspector Claire Pettigrew, who had seen Patterson arrive, came out to meet him.

'Claire,' said Patterson, smiling. 'How are you this morning?'

Patterson's early morning cheeriness took Pettigrew by surprise, and she looked at her DCI for an additional moment, wondering where the grumpy old man she was used to had gone.

'Morning, sir, fine, thanks. The body is inside.'

Patterson nodded, still smiling and looking at the surroundings. 'I must say I've seen a few dives in my time, but this must be up there with the best of them. The victim didn't die of food poisoning, did they? I mean, could they have at least not given the windows a clean?'

'The café isn't open yet, it's being refurbished,' said Pettigrew. 'It's not due to open until July, I think.'

'Well, I hope they get a move on. I'm not sure two months is enough to turn it into a place people would like to eat. Then again, I suppose it could be quite pleasant in the summer, having panoramic views over the...River Kelvin.'

Patterson immediately checked himself for being sarcastic, remembering his earlier vow.

'Quite,' replied Pettigrew as she walked towards the entrance in an effort to encourage Patterson to do the same. Patterson eventually took the hint and, walking through the entrance after Pettigrew, found himself standing in a surprisingly large open space. They had knocked down a couple of walls so that the adjoining units on either side of the café building now comprised one big open-plan interior. The whole place strongly smelled of paint, wood and varnish. There were workmen's tools lying all around, paint-splattered white sheets covering the floor, which confirmed Patterson's view that there was still much to do in terms of refurbishment.

There were booths along the walls with tartan banquettes covered in thick, clear plastic sheeting. Yet, apart from that, nothing seemed to have beeen done at all.

The crime scene manager, DS Tom Doolan, came across. ‘Morning, Inspector, another bad one, I’m afraid.’

‘Morning, Tom,’ Patterson replied to the crime scene manager's familiar refrain of every murder being ‘another bad one, I’m afraid.’

‘The body is through here, sir.’ Pettigrew led Patterson across the café floor and through a path of tables and chairs to a wide door with "Disabled Toilet" written in large letters above a universal wheelchair sign.

‘Disabled?’ asked Patterson.

‘It’s the disabled toilet, but from what I can gather, the victim isn’t.’

Inside the toilet, at first glance, it was bright and spacious, although that space was currently filled with a multitude of specialist officers. A photographer was taking photos from different angles, while other forensic officers went about their respective tasks.

A body lay next to a toilet, its head hidden by a shiny silver toilet bowl.

Detective Sergeant Jack Simpson stood looking down at the body, but on looking up and seeing Patterson, he came across.

‘Morning, sir,’

'Jack,' Patterson said loudly, 'how are you today?'

Simpson glanced at Claire, who, with nothing but a raised eyebrow, managed to say, *I know.*

'Fine, thanks, and yourself?'

'Excellent, Jack, excellent. I had a good night's sleep and I'm in good health, what more could one ask for?'

Simpson nodded, gave a half-smile, and both officers turned round to see McKinnon arrive.

'Morning, everyone,' said McKinnon. A lot less cheerily than Patterson.

Patterson walked forward to get a better look at the body and found himself looking down at a slim, black man who appeared to be in his early twenties. He wore a short-sleeved white T-shirt printed with the letters "LA". A relatively small splash of red on the left side of the T-shirt added to its artistic nature. There was a small dried pool of blood around his left hand. His head lay between the side of the toilet bowl and one of the long white plastic supporting handrails. His eyes were staring upwards while his left arm was slightly raised and lazily draped over the toilet bowl, as if around the shoulder of a drunk friend. The man's mouth was slightly open, and his expression appeared one of surprise. He had very short hair, almost but not quite a shaved head. At the end of the light denim-clad legs, a pair of white Nike trainers stuck upwards from the blue speckled plastic floor.

'Do we know who he is?' Patterson asked, keeping his eyes focused on the body.

'His name is Gideon Semanyo.' Simpson showed Patterson a driver's licence, which connected the name to the face. 'As you can see, it looks like he's been stabbed. His wallet was in his back pocket, complete with money, so robbery probably wasn't the motive.'

'Probably,' agreed Patterson.

'He had over three hundred pounds on him,' Simpson added.

'So robbery was almost certainly not the motive. No phone?'

'No phone. Apart from the money, all he had on him was a set of keys.'

Simpson lifted up a set of keys inside a clear plastic evidence bag. Patterson studied the keys through the plastic.

'That looks like a car fob, but there's no car manufacturer badge on it.'

'Maybe it's a replacement,' said Simpson.

'Maybe,' said Patterson. He handed the keys to McKinnon. 'Brian, go outside and see if you can find the car this fob is for. Be careful how you handle them.'

McKinnon took the bag with the keys inside and left.

'Do we know what he was doing here? I mean in the café.'

'He's one of the trainees,' said Simpson.

'Trainees?'

'Yes, as I was saying,' said Pettigrew, taking up the explanation, 'the café is being refurbished. It's being used as a kind of training program for the unemployed from Partick Jobcentre.'

'You seem very well informed, Claire.'

'It was all over the news a couple of months back. Politicians and councillors see it as a way of getting the unemployed to refurbish different buildings in the area. This café is seen as a template, or something like that. No expense spared, apparently.'

'No expense spent, more like,' muttered Patterson, remembering the initial impression the café gave. 'And the refurbishment of a café was deemed important enough for the local news, was it?'

'Apparently,' said Pettigrew. 'I got the impression they were using it as some kind of PR exercise.'

'Yeah,' said Simpson, 'That's what I thought.'

'You saw it too, then?' Patterson asked Simpson in surprise.

'Like Claire said, it was all over the news. Couldn't miss it.'

'I assume it must have been a slow news day. In any case, I don't think they're going to like this PR,' Patterson said quietly. 'No sign of the murder weapon?'

'Nothing so far,' answered Pettigrew.

'Well, I presume this being a café, there's a kitchen, so it's possible the knife came from there. We'll need this whole place searched top to bottom once Tasmina has finished. Ah, speak of the devil,' Patterson said as he saw the forensic pathologist, Tasmina Rana, come through the doorway.

'Morning all.' She walked over to where the body was. 'Need some more time?' Her question was directed towards the crime scene photographer.

'Another couple of minutes, Tasmina, ' he replied.

Tasmina nodded and then turned to Patterson, 'And how are you today, Mike?'

'Excellent, Tasmina, excellent, yourself?'

'Excellent. Couldn't be better,'

Tasmina, always happy and upbeat, and Patterson, determinedly happy and upbeat, were in agreement that the world was a quite lovely place, even with a dead body lying at their feet.

Rana's mood did darken a little as she looked around and added, 'The politicians won't like this, someone being murdered at their precious little café project.'

'Don't tell me,' said Patterson, 'you've heard of this place as well?'

'Aye,' said Rana, 'it was all over the news a while back. Couldn't miss it.'

'So I'm beginning to believe,' said Patterson. 'I must have been busy that day, missing this major news story of a local café being refurbished.'

Rana was about to reply when the photographer came over.

'All done, Tasmina, ' he said, and Rana bent down towards the body, laid her instrument bag beside the victim and began her work.

'Who found him?' asked Patterson.

'The caretaker, when he came to open the place up this morning,' replied Pettigrew.

'What time?'

'Six,' said Pettigrew.

'It opens at six, even when being refurbished?'

'Aye,' said Pettigrew. 'Presumably, the kitchen and toilets still need to be cleaned, and the place looked over, and of course, it needs to be opened up for the trainees.'

'So, we believe the victim wasn't disabled?'

'Not according to the caretaker,' said Pettigrew

'So, what was he doing in the disabled toilet?'

Pettigrew shrugged.

'So, where's this caretaker now?' asked Patterson.

'He's in the main café area.'

'I best go and talk with—'

Patterson was interrupted by a woman appearing in the doorway.

'Oh God, no! Gideon!'

The woman tried to go towards the body but was stopped by Simpson. She stood staring towards the young man, her hand on her mouth. Simpson gently turned her around and led her out through the door, as she continued to try and turn her head to see the body.

'How the hell did she get in?'

'Sorry,' said DS Doolan, appearing in the doorway. 'My bad.'

'My bad?'

'My fault,' clarified the crime scene manager.

Patterson glared at him, not only for letting the woman trespass an active crime scene, but for his assault on the English language. He took a deep breath. He was being that grumpy old man again.

As Simpson led the sobbing woman out of the toilet, Patterson followed. He saw an elderly man sitting in a booth on the other side of the café, whom he presumed was the caretaker.

'I'll take it from here, Jack,' said Patterson as he led the woman to a booth by the side. She sat down on a polythene-protected seat, which gave a rustling and then a whoosh as air was squeezed out. Sitting down beside her, Patterson studied her as he waited for the woman's sobbing to subside.

Siobhan was in her mid-forties with dark hair and green eyes. On first impressions, she came across as intelligent and businesslike. Her trim figure, along with a clear complexion, indications of someone who took care of herself. She wore little make-up, no lipstick, and she knew she suited that fresh, natural look. She looked even fresher wearing a green and white polka dot dress. Eventually, Siobhan became a little calmer and looked at Patterson as if emerging from a daze, wondering who he was. Patterson answered the unspoken question while he took out his notebook and pen.

'I'm DCI Patterson, Partick CID. Can I ask your name?'

'Siobhan Sutherland, I'm the liaison officer.'

'Liaison as in...?'

'I'm the go-between for the trainees and the DSS. I generally assist them with things like paperwork, any queries they have or help they need regarding benefits, or their job search.'

The woman spoke in short bursts as she continued to regain her breath and composure.

'The trainees still do job search?' asked Patterson.

'Yes, even though they're trainees, they're still job seekers.'

'How many trainees are there?'

'Sixteen, well...I suppose there's fifteen now.'

'And Gideon was one of the trainees?'

'Yes,' said Siobhan, shaking her head. 'Gideon was from Ghana. He was one of the nicest people you could ever meet.'

'You knew him well?'

'Quite well.'

'Gideon wasn't disabled?' asked Patterson.

'No.'

'So, do you have any idea why he would be in the disabled toilet?'

Siobhan shrugged. 'I really don't know. I—'

McKinnon came over. 'Sorry to interrupt, but there's no car I can find for the fob.'

'OK,' said Patterson. He turned to Siobhan. 'Do you know if Gideon had a car? We found a car fob with the set of keys he had.'

'No,' said Siobhan, shaking her head, 'I don't think so. I'm sure he walked here from his flat.'

Patterson handed the bag with the keys inside back to McKinnon. 'Thanks, Brian.'

Patterson watched McKinnon return to the toilet and turned his attention back to Siobhan. 'You were saying about Gideon being in the disabled toilet?'

'Just to say, I think he may have gone in there from time to time. Maybe he preferred it, I don't know.'

'OK. You were saying you knew Gideon quite well?'

'Quite well,' replied Siobhan, 'as much as the other trainees, I suppose.'

'Have you any idea who could have done this to Gideon?'

'Of course. Don't you?'

'Why would I know?' asked Patterson, confused by her answer. 'Who do you think it was?'

'The far-right, of course.'

'You think the far-right did this?'

'Isn't it obvious? After all the threats—'

'What threats?'

'Sorry, but I presumed you're from Partick police station.'

'I am, listen, you'll have to row back a bit, assume I don't know anything. What's this about threats?'

'There have been threats made against the trainees. I received letters addressed to me at Partick DSS. I reported them to Partick police station that's why I thought you'd know.'

'But why would anyone, the far-right, threaten the trainees?'

'Isn't it obvious? This training program aims to integrate immigrants, asylum seekers, and refugees into local training opportunities. Some have objected to that. You see, there was a lot of publicity when this café project was announced.'

'So, I gather,' said Patterson.

'Initially, we were delighted with the publicity, but then we received letters, threatening letters addressed to me.'

'Just letters'

'Just letters.'

'A lot?'

'Two.'

'Two letters? And both addressed to you personally?'

'Via the DSS office in Partick, yes.'

'How did they know to contact you personally?'

'My position is publicly available online as the liaison officer.'

'So, what sort of threats were made?'

'They just said we better stop what we are doing or else there will be consequences, they used the n—word a couple of times.'

'And you believe the threats came from right-wing extremists?'

'Who else?'

'Have you still got these letters?'

'I told you I handed them over to Partick

police station.'

'Who did you deal with? Which officer?'

'DS Easdon.'

'Did you get a crime number?'

'Yes, I don't think I have it on me, but I could get it.'

'No, no, it's fine. I know Grant, DS Easdon, and you say you haven't heard anything since?'

'No. After the first letter, DS Easdon instructed me not to open any others and to contact him immediately if any more arrived. Only one has. Of course, we advised everyone at the DSS office. One of your fellow officers came and took it away.'

'And when did this happen?'

'The second letter arrived about two weeks ago, I think the first was over a month ago. I can't believe they actually went through with it.'

Patterson was surprised he hadn't heard anything about the letters, but decided to find out about them when he got back to the station.

'OK, so, tell me more about Gideon. You said he's from Ghana?'

'Yes, he is, was, an asylum seeker. His claim was settled about nine months ago. He's been in Glasgow for about two years, I think.'

'His driving licence gave his address as

Laurel Road. That's just off Crow Road, isn't it?'

'I believe so, I know he lives somewhere near Crow Road. All the trainees live locally. Otherwise, they wouldn't be registered at Partick Jobcentre.'

'Do you know if Gideon lived with anyone or alone?'

'He's on his own, I think.'

'No partner?'

Siobhan shook her head. 'Not that I know of. At least, he hasn't mentioned anyone.'

'What about family?'

'No, they're all in Ghana. That's to say, what's left of his family. I believe he lost his parents and his elder brother in a war, but he may still have some other family members alive.'

'Was there any particular job Gideon was training for?'

'He was training to be a barista. He went to Glasgow City College twice a week as part of his training, as did all the trainees.'

'Barista?' said Patterson. 'You mean someone who makes coffee?'

'Yes,' replied Siobhan, giving Patterson a quizzical look.

'Are all the trainees learning to be baristas?'

Patterson wondered why they couldn't just say the person who makes coffee? Why the fancy title? Not for the first time that morning, Patterson checked himself for being a moaning old git.

'Oh no, they're learning all sorts,' said Siobhan. 'Most are learning to be catering assistants. There's a huge demand in the city for catering assistants at the moment. Others are focusing on customer service.'

'So when was the last time you saw Gideon?'

'It would have been Friday, Friday afternoon.'

'What's the normal routine for Friday afternoon?'

'Well, usually, we have lunch at midday. Start again at one. I teach a few things about job search, you know, such as how to look for work or what to do at interviews, that kind of thing, then at half two we have a break for fifteen minutes and then the trainees fill out all the paperwork they have to do until they leave at half-four.'

'What's the paperwork?'

'Travel expenses, questionnaires, surveys —the DSS loves a survey—plus job search documents. I also like to use Friday afternoons as a kind of bonding session for the trainees. Some of the trainees have been unemployed for a while, so they may lack confidence. I feel it helps everyone to socialise and have a bit of a laugh. It's my favourite time of the week.'

'And Gideon was there on Friday afternoon?'

'Yes, he was his usual bubbly self, laughing and joking around. He was just the sweetest, sweetest guy.'

Siobhan dabbed her eyes again with a tissue.

'So on Friday afternoon, all the trainees were here?'

'Everyone. I think. Oh, no, hold on, Linh had to leave early to go to the dentist. She's from Vietnam, she's training to be a catering assistant. Oh, and Tegan Rees—some drama going on at her flatshare she had to get back for, and there was someone else who left early...that's right, Zande Mhkize, but all the rest were here.'

'And did anything unusual happen on Friday? Or during the week. Did you notice anyone hanging around outside that you haven't seen before, for instance?'

Siobhan thought for a moment and shook her head. 'No, not that I can think of.'

Patterson nodded.

'I take it, in general, the trainees, being unemployed, haven't much money.'

'No, they get their social security and then ten pounds on top of that for coming here, plus their travel expenses, of course.'

'So not a lot?' said Patterson.

'No,' Siobhan agreed.

'In that case, if I said Gideon had over three hundred pounds on him, would you be surprised?'

'Three hundred pounds? Yes, I would be surprised.'

'And you have no idea why he should have so much money on him?'

Siobhan shook her head. 'No idea.'

'Do all the trainees have access to the kitchen?'

'Of course. They can go in whenever they want. The catering trainees are in there all the time.'

'So, I presume there's a kind of teacher chef as well.'

'Yes, our chef de cuisine, Eddie. He teaches basic catering, along with how to be a barista and general customer service.'

'So...he's the only teacher then?'

'Yes.'

'Is Eddie in today?'

'Yes, he's usually in about now. Why?'

'Oh, it's just in case he can spot if there is a knife missing from the kitchen.'

'Oh, right, of course.'

'So, will the other trainees also be arriving soon?'

'Yes, they usually start at nine and finish around four. Would you like me to try and contact them to tell them not to come in?'

'No, it's probably best to have them all here this morning so we can ask them some questions.' Patterson thought for a moment. 'Why are you here so early?'

Siobhan hesitated.

'I...sometimes come in early on Monday morning to get a head start; there's always so much to do.'

Patterson nodded, but something else crossed his mind. 'How did you know it was Gideon who was murdered?'

'How do you mean?'

'When you entered the toilet, you said "Oh god, no, Gideon", how did you know it was Gideon, even before you got a chance to properly see who it was?'

'I'm not sure to be honest...Oh, of course, Jim the caretaker told me when I arrived.'

'OK, Siobhan, that's all for now, you've been very helpful. If you could stick around until the trainees arrive. In fact, is there any room where the trainees can go, so they're not trampling over the crime scene?'

'There's a function room next door. It can be accessed from outside.'

'That sounds perfect. Would you mind going outside and directing the trainees there when they arrive?'

'No, of course not.'

'And I would prefer if you didn't mention to any of them about what has happened, just yet. If anyone asks, just say there has been an incident and I'll explain it once they're all here.'

'OK, well, I'd better get out there now then,' said Siobhan, 'they should be arriving any minute.'

'Great, I'll see you in a bit.'

Siobhan nodded, and Patterson headed back to the toilet to hear what the pathologist, Rana, had to say.

CHAPTER 2

The Caretaker

Tasmina Rana was just standing up, having done her initial assessment. She walked over to Patterson slowly as if still thinking something over. Patterson didn't need to ask a question before Rana started talking.

'It appears pretty straightforward, he died from a single stab wound to the heart.' Tasmina put her hands on her hips and looked back at the body as she talked. 'The knife was thin, with a very sharp blade, around five inches long, almost like a paring knife or something similar. Death would have been more or less instantaneous.'

'Time of death?' asked Patterson.

'Hard to say exactly, but more than 48 hours ago.'

'More than 48 hours ago?' asked Pettigrew, who had come over to hear what Rana said. 'So he was here all weekend?'

'Almost certainly,' said Rana. 'There's no sign of the body being moved, and rigor mortis is well set in; his blood has settled...He's definitely been lying there for around two days. If you want a calculated guess, I'd say he died late Friday night or even earlier, say, Friday afternoon.'

'Any other injuries?'

There are some nasty cuts, slices to be exact, to the palm of his hand; most likely as he tried to grab the knife when it was plunged into him. Other than that, there's nothing external apart from a small bump on the back of the head, probably due to him falling backwards and hitting his head on the floor.'

'So he was stabbed and then fell backwards?'

'Yes. The scenario I see, going by the position of the body, is that he would have been standing in front of the toilet, facing his attacker, was stabbed once in the chest, and then fell backwards, his legs giving way, and he ended up lying as he is now.'

Tasmina peeled off her gloves. 'There's a good chance I can get the autopsy done tomorrow, and I can tell you more then.'

'OK, thanks, Tasmina,' said Patterson, as he thought of Gideon being here all weekend. He turned to Simpson and Pettigrew, who were also contemplating this.

'This place is closed for the weekend, so that would be why he wasn't found until this morning,' said Simpson.

'It begs the question, though,' said Patterson, 'just when on Friday was Gideon murdered. As I understand it, most of the other trainees were here until around half- four.'

'Which also makes one of the other trainees a possible suspect for Gideon's murder,' said Pettigrew.

'Perhaps. Who closed the place up on Friday?' asked Patterson.

'The same person who opened up this morning, the caretaker,' said Pettigrew. She nodded in the direction of the elderly man Patterson had noticed earlier. 'His name is Jim McLintock.'

The caretaker, in his mid-to-late sixties, stared at a polystyrene cup he held, slightly tipping it one way and then another.

'OK, we'll need this whole place sealed off and searched to try and find that murder weapon. Make sure the search includes the surrounding area and the Kelvin embankment if necessary. Brian, do you think you can arrange that?'

'Sure, no problem,' said McKinnon, who immediately left to get on with it.

'The other trainees should be arriving

soon,' said Patterson. 'There's a function room next door, so I've instructed Siobhan to direct the trainees there. They'll need to be interviewed. Of course, we're especially interested in what happened on Friday afternoon.'

'How many trainees are there?' asked Simpson.

'Fifteen,' replied Patterson, 'sixteen minus Gideon. I'll go and have a word with Mr McLintock.'

Patterson walked over to where the caretaker sat, still swirling his drink, lost in thought. He looked up as the detective approached.

'Jim?' asked Patterson, and the man nodded. Patterson sat down beside him. 'I'm DCI Mike Patterson, Partick CID. I'd just like to ask you a few questions.'

Jim gave another slight nod and shifted in his seat.

'I guess this must be quite a shock for you,' Patterson began.

'Aye, you could say that.' There was a strong smell of soap and deodorant, and Patterson noticed that the caretaker's white shirt was neatly pressed, almost new, while his thick grey hair glistened with some kind of gel; the man obviously took pride in his appearance.

'Did you know Gideon well?' Patterson

asked as he put his notepad on the table.

'You still use them, then?' the caretaker asked. He had a polite Glasgow accent, possibly one that had mellowed with time.

'What's that?' asked Patterson.

'The notebook,' the caretaker explained, 'I thought ye'd all have some kind of techy thing nowadays, an electronic notepad or something.'

'Some officers use electronic notebooks. I'm more old-fashioned in my ways. I find these electronic notepads too fiddly. So?'

'So, what?'

'Did you know Gideon well?'

Jim shrugged. 'Kind of. I know all the trainees well, but aye, I suppose you could say I knew Gideon more than most. He was easy to talk to, was Gideon.'

Patterson scribbled in his notebook, the caretaker trying unsuccessfully to make out what the small writing said.

'Actually, can I just confirm your name?' asked Patterson.

'Jim McLintock.' The caretaker spelled out his last name.

'And where do you stay, Jim?'

'Gardner St. 56 Gardner St.'

'Have you been the caretaker long?'

'Since they started doing the café up, about four months now. They officially began the refurbishment in late February. There was this big hoo-ha with the press and everything. I wisnae here that day, though. Started the next day. The place is due to open on the first of July.'

'Have all the trainees been here since late March?'

'Aye, surprisingly; it's the same lot who started then who are still here now.'

'And as caretaker, what is it you do exactly, Jim, what do your duties involve?'

'Main thing I do is open the place up in the morning and then lock it up at night. I stay for an hour or so in the morning, sweep up if it's needed, clean anything that I missed the day before, make sure there's loo rolls, that kind of thing. Then, at night, when everyone is gone, I empty the bins, sweep and mop. I don't do any heavy cleaning, mind.'

'You wouldn't want to,' said Patterson, 'what with that nice white shirt you've got on.'

'Aye, well. I like to keep smart. Always have done. I know it's just a wee job, but I like to look professional, no matter what I do.'

'Were you in the services by any chance?'

'How'd ye guess? RAF maintenance for

eight years, down in Lincolnshire, mostly.'

'So you stay for an hour or so in the morning, after you open up?'

'Aye, I usually leave about just after seven, then head over to Castlebank Primary, do a bit of cleaning there, and then go to an office near the top of Byres Road for the same thing.'

'You're keeping busy, then?'

'That's it. It's shite money but ye do like two or three wee jobs and it all adds up.'

'You'll be a keyholder here, I take it?'

'Aye, I'm the main keyholder. I think the DSS has got another set somewhere; this is their gaff, but aye, I'm the main keyholder.'

'Where do you keep the keys over the weekend?'

'In my flat. Put them in the kitchen drawer. They were there all weekend, as per usual, if yer wondering.'

'Do you live with anyone?'

'Naw, the wife died a few year back. Cancer.'

'Sorry to hear that.'

'Aye, well, there's just me and I don't really go out much the weekend either. I mean, sometimes I'll go and see Thistle if they're at home, but that's about it.'

'So you lock this place on Friday and no one has access to the café till Monday?'

'Aye. The place is always, usually just as I left it on Friday.'

'And there was absolutely nothing different you noticed when you arrived this morning? Like, a window being open, nothing out of place?'

The caretaker reflected for a moment.

'Cannae think of anything, naw. Everything was just as it always is, apart from…the obvious. As I said, I live in Gardner Street, so it's no' that far. Twenty-minute walk, if that. I usually have a wee cuppa and a sit down before I start proper. I arrive, walk around the outside, make sure the place hasn't been broken into or vandalised or whatnot…'

'You don't check the place before you sit down?'

'There's usually no need to. Everything's the same each morning.'

'The front door was locked? Back door? Absolutely nothing different?'

'Front and back doors were locked. There's a keypad just inside the front door; I need to enter a code after I enter so the alarm doesnae go off and alert you guys. I did that, and then I sat down, had a coffee, and then got up to check everything. I know I should have probably checked everything before I sat down, but anyway, that's my routine. After my coffee, I went into the kitchen—everything was fine—I went into the toilet and...' The caretaker shook his head. 'I saw Gideon lying there. Even then, I didnae immediately clock he was dead. I thought he must have been drunk or something, somehow got locked in, then I saw the blood stain on his shirt and his eyes, but I still checked for a pulse and breathing just in case. Nothing, so naturally I called the police immediately. Poor Gideon.'

'Going back to last Friday afternoon. Were you the last to leave?'

'Aye, and everything was just the same as always. On Friday morning, I opened up as per. Left and came back about half-two, cleaned some stuff. The last of the trainees had left. I did my usual checks and then locked up; must have been about five when I left.'

'Did you check the toilets before you left?'

'Aye, of course.'

'And there was nothing untoward?'

'You mean like a dead body lying there? Nah, Gideon wisnae there.'

Patterson wasn't convinced.

'You did check the toilets? You're absolutely sure about that?'

'Absolutely. I always make a point of checking every toilet. Male, female, and the disabled.'

'Jim, you need to be truthful with me. Did you definitely check the toilets before you left?'

Jim picked up his polystyrene cup and twirled it around again, before shaking his head. '...OK, naw, I didnae check the disabled toilet. No-one uses it much. I checked the other toilets, but not the disabled. How was I to know somebody had been murdered?'

'Jim, I need you to tell me the truth. Final time, you're now saying you definitely didn't check the toilets before you left on Friday?'

'Naw.'

'So, when was the last time you went into the disabled toilet on Friday, what time?'

'Probably about half two. Just after I arrived. Cannae mind exact..'

'Could Gideon or someone else have gained access to the café over the weekend?'

'Don't see how. I told ye, even if someone had a key, there's an alarm as well, a code you have to punch in within a couple of minutes after opening the door. No one knows that except me. There are two other doors with keypads like that, one in the kitchen and one in the function room.'

Patterson looked around.

'What about the workmen? Doing this

place up? What time were they here on Friday?'

'Workman? The workmen aren't here on a Friday. They're only here Tuesdays and Wednesdays when the trainees are at college. That's why it's taking so long to do the place up.'

Patterson looked at his notepad and what he had written.

'OK, that's all for now, Jim. We're taking witness statements in the function room later, so if you want to make your way there now, an officer will interview you shortly. I'd appreciate you not telling the trainees what has happened just yet.'

'Aye, no problem. I'm sorry about not checking the toilet.'

'As long as you're being honest, that's all I want.'

'Oh, one other thing. When Siobhan arrived this morning, did you tell her it was Gideon that had been stabbed?'

'Aye, of course. Why?'

'No matter.'

'Still hard to believe Gideon is dead. He really was a nice guy. One of the best.'

As the caretaker talked, Patterson watched as the first of the trainees walked past the window, with Siobhan calling them over and directing them to the function room.

'I really should be getting to my other work,' the caretaker said.

'I'm afraid you'll have to stay here until you give a statement to my fellow officers. I'm sure your other employers will understand if you give them a call.'

'What about this place?'

'This is a crime scene now, so you won't be required to do any cleaning for some time. As I said, if you could go to the function room and wait with the others, that's fine.'

'No probs.'

Patterson watched the caretaker get up and walk through a grey door marked 'Function Room'.

Patterson stayed sitting for a moment, thinking things over. Was it possible that Gideon was murdered when the other trainees were present on Friday afternoon? If so, Pettigrew was right. The murderer could well be one of the other trainees.

CHAPTER 3

Breaking Bad News

Patterson walked across to the door he had seen the caretaker go through. Walking through it himself, he was suddenly confronted by numerous eyes staring back at him as if he were a professor late to give a lecture.

The trainees sat in silence, but their annoyance was conveyed through facial expressions and body language. Chairs had been arranged in five rows in the centre of the room, rather like the day the trainees had first arrived at the café, two months earlier.

The windowless function room had a kind of staleness that often affected spaces which sometimes hosted social events. It was like a shabby alcoholic with a permanent hangover. The walls had been unwisely painted red, which, added to the dark red carpet, gave the room a claustrophobic feel.

There was a sound system haphazardly

piled up on a slightly raised platform positioned in front of the trainees, along with a large screen monitor and a cheap, lonely-looking electric keyboard. Folded-up tables and chairs leaned against the other walls.

Patterson, his mind still turning over what he had learned about the murder so far, wasn't prepared for having all these eyes trained on him. As such, a sliver of anxiety passed through him. Instinctively, Patterson refocused on the task at hand and the grave news he now had to impart.

Seeing Siobhan sitting in the chair nearest to him at the end of the front row, he walked up to her and bent down, talking in as quiet a voice as possible.

'Are they all here?'

'Yes, they're all here,' Siobhan replied in the same quiet tone.

'And you haven't told them anything?'

Siobhan shook her head.

Patterson straightened up and walked onto the raised platform. Looking at the trainees, he was struck by the variety of faces—black, white, Asian, Middle Eastern, young, old, with roughly half female and half male. Patterson could well have been giving a college lecture, and he himself resembled how many would envision a lecturer looking.

DCI Patterson was a man in his early fifties, tall with a slim build. He had an intelligent, kind face and wore silver-rimmed glasses. His short grey hair was neatly combed to one side, and he had a slightly nervous, self-consciously stooped-over posture. That day, he wore corduroy trousers and a sleeveless V-neck jumper that could have come from the fifties. He had recently been wearing the regulation shirt and tie that Superintendent Dunard expected of him, but had fallen back into his old ways of wearing his preferred old ways attire.

Still, the trainees stared back at him, naturally curious as to what was going on, which Patterson acknowledged as he began.

'OK, I understand you all must be wondering what's happening, and I thank you for your patience. My name is DCI Mike Patterson from Partick CID.'

Part of the reason Patterson had told Siobhan not to reveal anything was that he was interested in the reaction of each trainee to what he was about to say. So far, looking across the variety of faces, he couldn't discern anything; they all seemed genuinely bemused as to why Patterson was there and what had happened.

Patterson was about to continue when the door he had come through opened again, and in walked Pettigrew and Simpson, who both smiled and sheepishly moved to a side wall to unsuccessfully try and be inconspicuous. The college lecturer continued.

'I'm afraid I've got some very bad news to convey,' Patterson said, still studying the faces. 'Gideon Semanyo, Gideon, your fellow trainee, was found dead this morning.'

This brought the gasps Patterson had expected, with a few trainees, both male and female, putting their hands to their mouths, and some bursting into tears. However, some didn't react, including the tall black man, Umar Olowe, and the small Asian woman, Linh Nguyen. A man, possibly in his late fifties, Andy McLean, also didn't react and instead sat with his arms crossed, as if he'd just been told the coffee machine wasn't working.

Patterson quickly surmised why the small Asian woman didn't react when the young woman next to her, Kelly O'Connor, turned and mouthed slowly, 'Gideon's dead.' This now brought a reaction from the Asian woman, who put her hand to her mouth, repeating, 'Gideon dead?' Kelly O'Connor nodded, with tears in her eyes.

'Gideon was found dead? You mean here, at the café?' asked James Halliday, his West Country accent only just apparent in his speech.

'Yes, and I'm afraid I have even more disturbing news. It appears that Gideon was murdered.' There was another round of gasps as if the trainees were doing a Mexican wave of surprised reactions. Kelly O'Connor, apparently the resident translator, leaned over and explained once more to the small Asian woman what Patterson said. Once again, Linh raised her hand to her mouth, shaking her head. There was the sound of muffled crying and incidental talking, so much so that Patterson had to raise his voice.

'Now, I know this is all very upsetting, but if you'll just let me continue for a moment...' Patterson paused as the group of trainees was visibly and audibly upset. Still, the tall black man and the middle-aged man were the exceptions. Soon, the noise died down enough for Patterson to continue. 'Gideon was found in the disabled toilet by Jim, the caretaker, when he opened up this morning. It appears Gideon had been stabbed.'

There was still the sound of sobbing, but Patterson ploughed on.

'Now, as I say, I understand how upsetting this must be for everyone, but it's my job to find out exactly what happened to Gideon and, of course, to find out who could have done this. From what I have learned so far, it's possible Gideon's body could have been here all weekend.' Patterson noticed that several trainees looked at each other with confused expressions.

'We will need to talk to all of you. So, my colleagues—Patterson looked towards Pettigrew and Simpson—will shortly be interviewing each of you, and it's likely that at some stage in the next few days, you'll also have to come to Partick police station to give a formal witness statement. For now, I'd like to ask you as a group: do any of you have any information that could shed light on Gideon's murder?'

There was silence.

'No?' Patterson quickly realised it was best to just wait for the interviews. 'OK, do any of you have any questions?'

Andy McLean put his hand up. 'Do we still get our expenses?'

'You'll have to ask Siobhan about that, but I would expect the answer to be yes.'

Julie Campbell raised her hand. 'Is our training cancelled for today, then?'

'Yes, and almost certainly for the next few days, unless arrangements are made for you to continue your training elsewhere. Again, you'll have to ask Siobhan about that. For the moment, the café is an active crime scene. Now, which one of you is the chef de cuisine?'

A thin man, slightly grubby in appearance, put his hand up. 'That's me.'

'OK, I'd like you to come with me if you could. The rest of you: if you stay in here for the moment, and as I say, my colleagues will hold a quick interview with each of you. The sooner we get the interviews over, the sooner you can all go home.'

Patterson walked over to Pettigrew and Simpson. 'OK, each of you get a couple of those tables and set them up. You can start the interviews straight away. I especially want to know if any of the trainees saw when Gideon entered the toilet and if any saw Gideon leave the café. I want to make sure Gideon didn't leave the café and come back later at some point.'

Simpson and Pettigrew walked towards the folded-up tables and chairs against the wall and proceeded to set them up at different ends of the function room as Patterson left the function room with the chef de cuisine.

In the main café area, Patterson saw McKinnon, who was on the phone.

'Everything all right, Brian?'

McKinnon put his thumbs up as he continued the phone conversation.

Patterson turned to the chef de cuisine. He couldn't help noticing a slight smell of body odour, the kind that thrived in a world without soap.

'What's your name again?'

'Eddie.'

'OK, Eddie.' Patterson stopped outside the kitchen door. 'Thanks for your help. As I said earlier, it appears Gideon was stabbed, so it's possible the murder weapon came from the kitchen. I just want you to take a quick look around to see if, on the off chance, you notice a knife missing. Do you think that's possible?'

'Maybe. I have my own chef's knives, which I take away with me at the end of each day, but there are other knives in the kitchen, of course, so yeah, I might notice one missing.'

'Excellent. Now, the forensic pathologist said it was possibly a knife about five inches long, very sharp, almost like a paring knife, she said, though I'm guessing it could be any type of knife.'

'I'll certainly have a look. I know where all the knives are kept.'

'That's what I thought, and please don't touch anything. If you need to open a drawer, tell me and I'll open it for you,' Patterson said, putting on a pair of polythene gloves.

Eddie nodded, and they entered the kitchen together. As with the rest of the café and as with the chef de cuisine, the kitchen looked pretty grubby. Nevertheless, it was fairly spacious, and a large plate-glass window let in ample light from the far end, and gave a view of a fast-flowing stretch of the River Kelvin.

Patterson watched as Eddie slowly walked around the kitchen, first looking at the knives in two wooden stands that were full, as well as another batch of knives hanging from wall hooks.

Eddie then stopped in front of a speckled granite worktop with a wide metal drawer underneath.

'Some knives are kept in here,' he said, nodding down at the drawer.

Patterson pulled it open, and the chef bent down to carefully study its contents.

'No...as far as I can tell, all the knives seem to be there.'

The chef de cuisine walked across to another drawer beneath another worktop.

'Some knives are also kept in here.'

Patterson pulled the drawer open. Again, Eddie bent down and looked for a moment, and then looked back at Patterson.

'I can't be sure...but you know, it's just possible one of the knives could be missing from this drawer. I mean, maybe someone has stored it elsewhere without telling me, but it's a knife just like the one your...'

'...forensic pathologist.'

'...your forensic pathologist said. I always have two knives in here, which I use solely for peeling vegetables and the like, but there's only one knife that I can see. As I said, perhaps someone has placed it elsewhere, but I always put two knives in here, I'm sure...'

'What does the knife look like? '

'It's about five inches long, quite thin, and it has a green handle.'

'A green handle?'

'Yes, a bright green plastic handle. All the knives are colour-coded, like the chopping boards. The green knives are used for peeling and chopping vegetables. I have two of them, and only one is in the drawer.'

Patterson looked in the drawer at the other knife with the green handle and gingerly picked it up. 'So it would be exactly the same as this one?'

'Exactly the same, yes.'

Patterson put the knife back and closed the drawer.

'OK, that's excellent. Let's just have a look around and make sure the knife isn't elsewhere.'

They did so, looking in different places, above, below and behind appliances, but the knife was nowhere to be found.

Patterson escorted Eddie back to the function room. 'If you just wait here, my colleagues will interview you soon. By the way, did you stay on Friday afternoon with the other trainees?'

'Not me, every Friday, as soon as it's midday, I skedaddle along with Alistair, the team leader. We usually head to the pub. It's just the trainees that stay, and Siobhan.'

'OK, we'll still need to interview you, so if you don't mind staying for now.'

'Of course.'

Patterson watched as Eddie walked back into the function room.

This could be a significant development, thought Patterson. If the knife was indeed the one identified by the chef and taken from the kitchen, did that make this more likely to be a spur-of-the-moment killing or a murder that was planned in advance? And why was a knife taken from that drawer, rather than simply taking one that was already out in the open? Did the murderer want a smaller paring knife that was easier to conceal?

At the very least, it was very possible Patterson now knew what the murder weapon looked like, and that was a big plus.

CHAPTER 4

Interviews

Simpson and Pettigrew set up tables and chairs on either side of the function room, with sufficient distance between them so that the content of the interviews couldn't be overheard.

The order of who would be interviewed was simply determined by who was seated nearest to the set-up tables. For Simpson, that was those seated at the back left, and for Pettigrew, those sitting at the back right. Once interviewed, the trainees would be allowed to go home.

The first person to be interviewed by Pettigrew was Mary McNair, who, as was her habit, sat at the very end of a row near the back. Pettigrew's first impression of Mary was of a friendly, shy young woman who seemed like a younger version of herself.

Mary's testimony was to prove the template for all the other trainees' statements and what had already been said to Patterson by Siobhan. The last time Mary saw Gideon was on Friday afternoon. He was laughing and joking, and if anything, even more hyper than his usual hyped-up self. He had bought everyone doughnuts from the local bakery, which Umar had gone to fetch.

'Was Gideon in the habit of buying the other trainees doughnuts?' asked Pettigrew.

'Not often. It happened a couple of times before,' said Mary. 'You could say he was generous.' Mary's compliment was grudging, and Pettigrew got the impression Gideon wasn't Mary's favourite person.

'Were you not curious how he could afford to buy doughnuts for everyone?'

'A little,' said Mary, 'I mean, yes, some of us were curious how he could afford it, but we didn't ask. We just assumed Gideon had a job on the side or something.'

Mary said she didn't see Gideon enter the disabled toilet that day or leave the café.

'Was Gideon in the habit of using the disabled toilet?' asked Pettigrew.

'Sometimes, I think he just went in that toilet to get some privacy,' answered Mary.

Mary said that most of the trainees, like herself, left around half past four. Pettigrew didn't note anything unusual in what the trainees said or did, and all the testimonies of the trainees were more or less consistent. They didn't see Gideon enter the toilet or leave the café.

Likewise, Simpson's batch of interviews had a similarity between them. No one noticed anything unusual happen on Friday afternoon. It was just a typical day, when they sat around, filling out forms and drinking tea or coffee. However, Simpson was also surprised to hear that Gideon had bought everyone a doughnut from the local bakery.

'But that's what he was like,' said Danny Wilson. 'Gideon was one of the good guys. I'm telling ye.'

As with Pettigrew, no trainee interviewed by Simpson saw anything out of the ordinary, anything unusual, such as a stranger hanging around outside. Once the interviews were over, Pettigrew and Simpson joined each other in the now deserted function room.

'Anything of note?' asked Pettigrew.

'No,' answered Simpson, 'all their testimonies seem consistent. On Friday afternoon, they filled out paperwork, nothing unusual happened, no one saw Gideon leave, and that was that.'

'Aye,' said Pettigrew, 'I found them to be a

fairly normal bunch.'

'Me too,' said Simpson.

Walking back into the main café, McKinnon told Simpson and Pettigrew that Patterson had gone to Gideon's flat, so both officers decided they would head back to the station.

CHAPTER 5

Black

As Simpson and Pettigrew were starting their interviews, Patterson walked over to McKinnon in the main café area.

'Brian, any problems?'

'No, just getting everything organised. Obviously, Bunhouse Road will need to be closed off for quite a while. I've arranged a search team for the café, and forensics are in the kitchen.'

'Good, I'm just off to Gideon's flat. Have you got those keys that were found on Gideon?'

McKinnon went and got the keys, then handed them to Patterson.

'Thanks,' said Patterson, give me a call if you need anything.'

'Will do,' McKinnon replied as he went to speak with some other officers.

Patterson drove up Bunhouse Road and

onto Argyle Street, which led onto Dumbarton Road. The rush-hour traffic was gathering momentum, and a steady stream of buses and cars headed towards the city centre, with lesser traffic, including Patterson, heading in the opposite direction.

The busyness of Partick was centred around Merkland Square and the transport hub, which comprised a bus interchange, subway station, and mainline train station.

Partick was situated on the north bank of the Clyde, across from Govan on the south side. Like many areas of Glasgow, Partick began as a village before expanding and eventually being incorporated into the Burgh of Glasgow. Even more so than other areas of the city, Partick had a distinct mix of rich and poor areas, with the affluent area situated around Dowanhill and an area blighted by poverty near the riverside. That mix had, for the most part, persisted to the present day.

Dumbarton Road was the main thoroughfare of Partick. As its name suggests, in effect, Dumbarton Road ran from Partick, from Bunhouse Road in fact, all the way to Dumbarton, even if it took on a nom de plume or two along the way. Dumbarton Road in central Partick was home to a plethora of charity shops, pubs, bookmakers, banks, and restaurants, and it was always a popular area for many due to its cosmopolitan nature. It had good housing, mostly four-storey tenements that had stood the test of time and were expected to do so for many years to come.

In short, you could say Partick was smart but casual, in its atmosphere, architecture, and people.

Patterson turned right off Dumbarton Road into Crow Road and then, after a short distance, left into Laurel Street. Laurel Street was a relatively small street, slightly tucked away, as if keeping itself to itself, which was often the best policy for many streets in Glasgow. In the recently arrived early morning sunshine, it appeared pleasant, with a mix of housing: modern flats at one end and traditional red sandstone tenements at the other.

Patterson pulled up outside the street number corresponding to Gideon's address, which was a tenement entrance. Exiting the car, Patterson put on a pair of nitrile gloves and carefully removed the bunch of keys found on Gideon from the evidence bag. He held the car fob between his thumb and forefinger. Looking around, there were not many cars on the street. Patterson pointed the plastic fob in one direction and pressed. Nothing. He pointed it in a slightly different direction, but again, there was no sound or movement from any of the cars. He walked further up the road and pressed again.

This time, the indicators of a car flashed, along with the small thud of car doors unlocking.

The car was a metallic dark grey Porsche Boxster. A nice car, thought Patterson, if a little impractical and not exactly the type of vehicle you would expect an unemployed asylum seeker to have. Patterson opened the passenger-side door and sat inside. The interior smelled heavily of leather and lightly of pine from a hanging air freshener. It was very clean inside. He leaned over and looked around—nothing of note. In any case, it would be thoroughly checked out later on.

Exiting the car and locking its doors again, He walked back and stopped outside the stairwell entrance. The tenement was four storeys high with attractive bay windows. There were steep steps leading up to the stairwell entrance from the pavement. So steep, in fact, that it meant you couldn't live here if you didn't have reasonable mobility. For the most part, Patterson did and walked up the steps, albeit holding onto the side rail. He studied the keys again. In addition to the car fob, there were three small Yale keys and another fob, possibly for the front door main entrance.

Outside the main front door—on the wall to the right—there was a panel for a fob. Sure enough, when Patterson positioned the other fob next to it, the door buzzed and clicked open.

Gideon's flat was on the fourth, top floor, and it was a slightly out-of-breath Patterson who finally arrived in front of Gideon's door. The elegant silver and black nameplate stated Gideon Semanyo's name in full. Patterson picked out a key that was the most likely suspect to open the door and was rewarded for his calculated guess when the key turned first time and the door opened.

The immediate impression inside was of a showpiece flat. It was immaculate, or at least the hallway was, and the flat smelled pleasantly of nothing but fresh, clean air. Patterson pulled the small key out of the door, closed it, and gravitated towards the bright sunlight coming from a room straight ahead, which turned out to be a spacious living room. The central bay window was slightly open, supplying that air of natural freshness.

With the early morning sunlight streaming in, the whole room appeared pleasant, with everything painted in either cream or white. A cream leather settee sat in front of a spotless glass table, which featured a music magazine, the cover of which showcased a moody-looking man with dreadlocks. There was also a laptop which Patterson knew would have to be analysed.

Like the hallway, the living room was immaculately clean. It barely looked lived in. A huge painting of an African sunset dominated one wall. On the wall opposite, a large mural depicted three African women carrying pots on their heads. This painting was done in bright, vibrant colours with the women dressed in yellow, blue, and red, and their figures reflected on the ground. Another wall had a print that was simply large black letters on a white background, boldly stating the word *Black*.

Patterson walked across to the bay windows and looked out, seeing the ever-constant spire of Glasgow University proudly atop Gilmorehill. Looking down, he saw the Porsche Boxster in the street far below. A thought struck him: did this road get so busy that it was necessary for Gideon to park so far from his close entrance?

Patterson walked back through the hallway and into the bedroom. It had a king-size bed with a yellow, red and green duvet. Again, this room was spotless. African trinkets were dotted around the room. On one wall was a print of an African village at sunset. The golden rays lit up stick figures like it was an African L.S. Lowry.

Patterson pulled open the drawer of the bedside cabinet, and it was filled with condoms and some banknotes. Patterson estimated there was just around £200. He closed the drawer and opened up a wardrobe built into the far wall. The clothes looked new, and indeed, many still had shop labels on them.

Patterson walked through to the bathroom was finished in grey marble tiling. Again, it was spotless. Almost too clean and tidy, thought Patterson. Towels were neatly folded over the shower rail. Was this really the flat of a single young man? This was more like a hotel room that had just been serviced. Unless Gideon had OCD, it was all very curious.

Having seen enough, Patterson left the flat and headed back to the station.

CHAPTER 6

White

Back at the station, Patterson entered his office to begin the preparatory work for the upcoming investigation. So far, that Monday morning, there had been no further development. The only lead they did have, which could be very significant, was the letters threatening the trainees.

Patterson went along to see DS Easdon to ask about them. Easdon was a competent enough officer, but nothing more, and it hadn't been a surprise when Siobhan said she hadn't heard any follow-up since she handed the letters over.

DS Easdon was a small, compact man with short fair hair and glasses. From a distance, he could easily be mistaken for a schoolboy. With Easdon by his side, Patterson went down to the evidence room.

Easdon opened the two letters and placed them side by side on a table.

'We had them analysed for fingerprints but they're completely clean apart from the liaison officer's prints. You can see from the envelopes that they were sent from the city centre, G1. I got the impression it was just a crank and nothing more.'

Patterson looked at him. 'You'll have heard about the murder?'

Easdon looked down as if studying the letters again, sheepishly avoiding eye contact.

'Yes, I heard,' he said quietly. 'As I said, there was nothing to follow up. It was two letters. We thought it best to wait to see if another letter arrived and take it from there.'

In one sense, Patterson could understand Easdon's argument, but he knew if the press found out, there would be trouble. Patterson looked at the letters once more. Both messages were printed on primrose-yellow A4 paper and were identical. They read:

'Stop the cafe program now and stop employing n—s. If you don't, n—s will pay. You have been warned.'

On each, there was a rather childish pencil drawing of what looked like an AK-47.

The envelopes were addressed to Siobhan Sutherland, Liaison Officer, c/o Partick DSS, gave the address of the DSS office in Partick and were sent second-class.

'Did you inform Dunard about them?'

Easdon hesitated, then slowly shook his head. 'No. Honestly, it was a couple of letters. I told Siobhan to be vigilant, but there was nothing else to follow up on.'

'You know you could be in for a bollocking or worse?' asked Patterson.

'I know,' said Easdon.

'And I'll have to tell Dunard about it.'

'I know,' Easdon repeated, in a quiet voice.

'OK,' said Patterson, feeling slightly sorry for his fellow officer. 'I suppose there wasn't much else you could do. Thanks, Grant.'

Patterson headed back upstairs to his office.

As soon as Patterson sat down, Dunard called and confirmed Patterson was the Senior Investigating Officer, and the murder of Gideon Semanyo was of absolute priority. There was an urgency in Dunard's voice which alerted Patterson that this case could be troublesome. Why was that? Patterson was denying the obvious. A young, black man, an asylum seeker, had been murdered, and racial tensions could arise because of it. That was surely why Patterson had an uneasy feeling about the murder of Gideon Semanyo.

His thoughts were interrupted by the phone ringing again.

'Hello?' Patterson answered.

'DCI Patterson? Hello, It's Ken Edwards from the West End Chronicle. How are you? Listen, I'm getting reports that there's been a murder on Bunhouse Road. I wonder if you could confirm this?'

'How did you get this number?'

'I'd just like you to confirm if you could, whether—'

Patterson put down the phone. Yes, he definitely had a bad feeling about this case.

McKinnon came in and said everything was organised at the café. Divers were on standby to search the River Kelvin if no weapon was found beforehand. The formal statements from the other trainees were arranged to be taken on Wednesday. McKinnon said he would also return to the café later to ensure everything was proceeding correctly. Patterson nodded, wondering how he had coped before without McKinnon's additional assistance as Acting DS.

Ten minutes later, Patterson exited his office and entered the investigation room, where his fellow detectives were at work. He wiped the whiteboard clean and asked for attention.

'OK, everyone, it's Monday morning, and we have a new murder investigation to begin. The victim's name is Gideon Semanyo. Gideon was murdered at the Partick Bunhouse Café, which is, believe it or not—Patterson looked at McKinnon—down Bunhouse Road. If any of you are unsure where Bunhouse Road is, it's just next to Partick Bridge, and for those of you who weren't at the crime scene this morning, I'll fill you in on what we know so far. The Bunhouse Café is being refurbished—'

Suddenly, Patterson felt unsure of everything. He felt out of breath, and the room started to spin.

'OK, get on with what you're doing. I just—remembered— something.'

Patterson went unsteadily back to his office, shut the door, and sat down. What was that? A panic attack? He hadn't had one of those in such a long time, but he suddenly felt pole-axed by anxiety.

Pettigrew came into his office and shut the door. 'You OK, sir?'

'Yes, fine, fine, just had a bit of a turn, that's all.'

'Do you want me to take over the briefing?'

'Eh? No, no, it's fine. Just give me five minutes; I'll be all right.'

Pettigrew seemed unsure but turned and left the office.

Patterson took deep, steady breaths and eventually started to feel a little calmer. Where had that come from? He had felt a shiver of anxiety when walking into the café function room earlier that morning, but thought nothing more of it. Patterson continued to sit, gathering his composure, and eventually, the anxiety faded to a point where he felt confident enough to go back outside. He poured himself a beaker of water from the dispenser and stood once more in front of the whiteboard.

'OK—where was I?—Yes, the refurbishment of the…Partick Bunhouse Café is being used as a kind of training program…for the DSS. For the sake of convenience, I'll simply call the Partick Bunhouse Café, the Bunhouse, from now on. Anyway, the trainees are learning to be catering assistants, provide customer service, or become baristas. A barista is someone who makes coffee.'

Pettigrew wondered once more if Patterson was all right.

'Gideon was one of sixteen trainees there, a Ghanaian national who, I believe, had been in this country for around two years. He was working as a trainee barista. Until we know differently and until we have the autopsy, Tasmina believes Gideon died from a single stab wound to the heart. There were no other visible external injuries apart from cuts to the palm and fingers of his left hand, where Gideon had probably tried to grab the knife. The crime scene photos will be arriving soon to give you a better idea of exactly how and where Gideon was found.'

Patterson took a sip of his water. He felt much better, which made him wonder again where that anxiety had suddenly come from.

'As for the time of death, Tasmina gives a preliminary estimation of Friday afternoon or possibly early evening. That's interesting for a number of reasons, the main one being that all the trainees were still at the café up until around four, four-thirty on Friday. So, it's possible that Gideon was murdered when the other trainees were still at the café. If not, the murder took place just after the trainees had left.'

Now that Patterson was immersed in the details of the case, any anxiety he had felt had gone completely. He looked around the investigation room, which always reassured him because he had a team he fully trusted. Partly, a result of him having the final say on who joined his team. Patterson turned towards the whiteboard again.

'Now, first of all, I want to find out all we can about Gideon Semanyo. Jack, Get in touch with the Home Office. Find out exactly when Gideon first claimed asylum, when his claim was settled and any other info you can glean. His family also needs to be informed. I'm told he has no relatives here, but he still has some family back in Ghana. Nevertheless, double-check if there are relations in the UK we don't know about.'

'Claire, I want you to find out all you can about what Gideon has been doing in recent weeks. I visited his flat, and he seemed to be doing all right for himself. In fact, a little too well for himself. Not only did he have a very nice flat, but also a very nice car, which must have cost a few bob. I also found around £200 in his bedside cabinet, plus we know he had £300 on him when he was murdered. Not what you would expect from someone on benefits. Therefore, it's very possible that Gideon was working on the side, although even with a job, say, with a food delivery company, he would have had to deliver a considerable number of pizzas to sustain the lifestyle he appears to have had. So was he engaging in any criminal activity? That's the only explanation I can think of, and if so, that could be connected to his murder. Leanne, I want you to find out about his movements leading up to the day he died, which, as said, is most probably Friday. He goes to college on Tuesdays and Wednesdays. Find out which one and head over there. Has anything happened at college? What does he do at night?

Who does he visit? Was he a regular at a bar or club? Find out what you can.'

Patterson knew DI Leanne Davies was particularly good at carrying out this type of task.

'Graham and Jill, I want the CCTV gathered from all roads leading to Bunhouse Road. That means Argyle Street, Dumbarton Road, Sauchiehall Street, Old Dumbarton Road—every road. If someone entered that café and murdered Gideon, I want them caught on CCTV. Start with Friday evening and work backwards.'

CCTV was, as always, one of the most tedious but crucial parts of any investigation. The more officers on this task, the better, but for now, Patterson knew DC Graham Murray and DC Jill Garvie would do a thorough job.

'Now, we do have one significant lead. The liaison officer, Siobhan Sutherland, received a couple of threatening letters warning the DSS to stop the program or involving immigrants participating in it. This is because the group of trainees has a number of individuals from overseas, such as Gideon. Some have accused those from overseas of taking opportunities away from locals. Hence, Siobhan believes a far-right group is behind these threats, which is a perfectly logical conclusion. This is especially the case since there was significant publicity about what the trainees were doing at this café. So, the sooner we can determine if a far-right extremist, either an individual or a group, is behind the murder of Gideon, the better.'

Patterson turned to DI Luke Ogilvie and DC Thomas Black.

Luke and Thomas, I want you two to ask around regarding this possibility, find out what you can. I'll arrange for a counter-terrorism officer to arrive at some point, but in the meantime, we can conduct our own investigation on this matter.'

'Scott, we need to go over Gideon's social media. There was a laptop at his flat we need to retrieve. See who he was in touch with and if he personally received any hate messages. I also want background checks done on all of the trainees. Organise yourselves into groups and take three or four each. I want as much information about them as possible. Claire and Jack conducted initial interviews with them this morning, and we'll get their thoughts shortly on what they learned if—'

A tall woman walked in through the swing doors from the corridor.

She had short black hair, a stern countenance, and wore a long, thick green coat.

'Yes, can I help you?' asked Patterson.

The woman looked around the room.

'Sorry, I'm looking for Chief Inspector Dunard.'

'He's on the next floor up, through the swing doors, first door on the left.'

The woman nodded but didn't leave, continuing to look around the room.

'Is there something else?' asked Patterson, hoping she would take the hint.

The woman did take the hint, gave a tight smile in response, and then disappeared back out through the door.

'How hard is it to get off on the right floor?' Patterson asked himself as much as his fellow officers.

'Lift's broken down,' said DC Garvie.

'Since when?'

'Since about half an hour ago.'

Patterson shook his head before continuing.

'OK, I'll let her off. Anyway, as I was saying, Claire and Jack have already had a brief interview with the trainees. Jack, what did they say?'

'They more or less all said the same thing. On Friday, they finished their usual work at the café about midday, which was the norm. They went into the main café, had lunch, and then, from one o'clock onwards, did some job search, filled out the paperwork they had to do. They all left, more or less around the same time, which was half past four. A few of them mentioned that Gideon seemed in good spirits, which, apparently, was also par for the course.'

'Claire, what about you? Did anyone say anything we didn't know already?'

'No, can't say they did. Just as Jack found, all my interviewees were pretty consistent. Friday afternoon, they sat around filling in forms, questionnaires, surveys and the like. Apparently, the DSS loves surveys and questionnaires. No one noticed Gideon go into the disabled toilet, but he was known to do so from time to time. No one saw him leave the toilet or café, perhaps for obvious reasons as it turns out.'

'It's still good to know he didn't leave and gain entrance to the café later somehow,' said Patterson. 'So for either of you, no trainee drew your attention in any way?'

'I suppose there was one trainee who came across as very nervous,' said Simpson.

'Who was that?' asked Patterson.

'Umar Olowe. He's from Nigeria and is in his early twenties. He was sweating profusely and stuttering when I interviewed him. Though I think that may have been his nature rather than for any particular reason.'

'Actually,' said Pettigrew, 'a couple of trainees I spoke to mentioned Umar. They said that if I wanted to know anything about Gideon, I should talk to Umar since he was Gideon's best friend. One said he followed Gideon around like a lost puppy.'

'If you mean the tall, black man,' said Patterson, 'I did notice when I announced Gideon had been murdered, he was one of those who didn't react, which, if he was Gideon's best friend, is a bit odd. Anyway, did no one else grab your interest, Jack?' asked Patterson.

'Not particularly,' said Simpson. 'I believe some probably didn't like Gideon as much as they made out, but apart from that, it seems Gideon was actually quite popular.'

'One thing,' said Pettigrew, 'I did find slightly strange is that on Friday afternoon, Gideon bought everyone doughnuts from the local bakery. He gave Umar money to go to the local Greggs at the top of the road. So, it does seem he did have some money to spare.'

'Yeah,' said Simpson, 'I forgot to mention that.'

DC Billy Pearson popped his head round the door.

'Sir, Chief Inspector Dunard wants to see you.'

'Thanks,' said Patterson. 'We'll leave it

there. Does anyone have any questions?' When met with silence, he said, 'OK. Let's get on with it.'

Patterson returned to his office first and then walked up the stairs to Dunard's office. He knocked on the door and entered to see Dunard sitting behind his desk, with the woman who had earlier asked for directions sitting in one of the two seats before Dunard's desk.

'Sit down, Mike,' Dunard nodded towards the empty seat next to the woman.

'Mike, this is Gillian McKenzie, she's the local councillor for this area.'

Patterson nodded but could sense a slight coldness in the woman's manner towards him. She continued to look towards Dunard as if she was in a huff with Patterson.

'Gillian is here regarding the murder of Gideon Semanyo. Gillian, this is DCI Patterson, who I've just made the senior investigating officer on the case.'

The councillor finally turned towards Patterson. It was as if she wanted to smile but couldn't quite manage it. As such, Patterson settled for receiving a slight grimace.

'Yes,' Gillian began, 'I've just heard about what happened. It sounds terrible. I thought I'd hear first-hand how the investigation is going.'

'Well, there's not much I can tell you, at this stage, the investigation has barely started, as you can imagine,' said Patterson. 'One of the trainees who was working at the Bunhouse Café was stabbed.' That was as much information as Patterson was prepared to give the councillor at that time.

'That's what I heard. I'm led to believe that he was an asylum seeker,' said Councillor McKenzie.

'I believe so,' said Patterson. 'We're still checking all the details at the moment.'

The local councillor perceived Patterson's reluctance to divulge any information. 'I can assure you, anything you tell me will be in the strictest confidence. I attended the launch of the café's refurbishment, and I've been working closely with the Scottish Parliament to bring this project to fruition. We're all very proud of it. I know some asylum seekers are an important part of the program.'

'Yes...well, we'll keep you updated with everything. Naturally, the café will be shut for a while as we carry out our investigation.'

Although she didn't say anything in reply, Patterson still sensed that Gillian seemed dissatisfied with his answer and wanted him to say more. Dunard appeared to sense it as well, since he echoed Patterson's words.

'As my DCI says, there's really not much we can say at the moment, Gillian. However, we'll certainly keep you up to date as much as we can, and if there are any developments we'll—'

The councillor appeared to ignore Dunard's statement. 'So you can confirm this young man was one of the asylum seekers?'

Patterson decided to allow her this one fact.

'We believe Gideon Semanyo was an asylum seeker, yes.'

'Gideon Semanyo? You mean he was a man of colour?'

'If you mean was he black, the answer is yes. We are still trying to contact his family in Ghana. That's our priority right now.'

'Ghana?' You mean he's from Ghana?' Every new fact about the murder victim seemed to shock the councillor. 'So, if I understand you correctly, a black asylum seeker from Ghana has been stabbed, murdered right here in Partick?'

Patterson stifled a sigh as best he could. Could this woman not take a hint? Could she not take a hike? It was Dunard who again acted as Patterson's backup.

'Councillor, as my inspector says, we really can't tell you much information at the moment. The investigation has just begun. I, or my inspector, will be making a statement to the press later. So if—'

'You have to understand that if this is a young black asylum seeker from Ghana who's been murdered, the implications for the African community in the city could be huge.' The councillor said with an admirable sense of drama.

Patterson and Dunard glanced at each other. Any suspicions that this councillor could be trouble were confirmed.

'Councillor,' said Patterson. 'We fully understand the implications, but we are rather busy at the moment, so—'

'I appreciate that, and I certainly don't want to take up any more of your time than necessary,' said the councillor, almost managing a genuine smile. 'However, if this is a young black man who was murdered, an asylum seeker, there will be a lot of concern that there could be a racist motive behind this poor man's murder. The far-right has been very active in Glasgow recently.'

Patterson tried to placate her further. 'Of course, we'll be looking into that possibility, but it's still far too early to say what the motive is, and so far, there's no indication this is a racial murder or that the far-right is behind it.' Patterson knew this was a slight, possibly a full-on fib, considering threats had been received by letter. However, he was not prepared to divulge this to the councillor.

'Of course,' the councillor continued, 'and I don't want to labour the point, but you must understand we now have many migrants in the area, many of whom are people of colour. They'll still be very concerned that this man could have been murdered because of his skin colour.'

Patterson shifted in his seat. He had a lot to be getting on with, and this councillor was pure time-wasting. 'Let's not get ahead of ourselves. If the colour of Gideon's skin is a factor in his murder, then you can rest assured we'll follow that line of enquiry thoroughly. Until then, we'll keep all our options open.'

Dunard also wanted the councillor to take her leave, but realised he had to be more direct for that to happen.

'Councillor, I thank you for your visit, but I'm sure you'll understand we have a lot to be getting on with.'

The councillor still didn't move or make any indication that she was about to move. Patterson and Dunard couldn't resist glancing at each other once again as Dunard tried to press the point once more.

'As I say, we'll keep you up to date with any developments and if you—'

Instead of getting up to leave, the councillor spoke again, her words coming out fast as if this was what she had been dying to say.

'Chief Inspector, I feel there is something I must bring up with you. I happened to wander by accident into the inspector's investigation room this morning, and quite frankly, I was appalled.'

Dunard looked at Patterson and Patterson looked at Dunard, both wondering what the councillor meant.

'Quite frankly,' continued the councillor, 'well, there's no easy way to put this but...I was shocked that every officer I saw in that room... was white.'

Patterson smiled, not quite knowing what the councillor meant and felt the need to ask.

'Sorry, I don't quite get your point,' said Patterson, not getting her point at all.

'That's what I'm worried about,' said Councillor McKenzie. 'There must have been around a dozen officers in that room, and every one of them was white. Without exception, they were all white.' She managed to make the word white sound like a criminal offence.

Patterson took off his glasses and pinched the top of his nose. He just knew this was going to be a difficult investigation. He put his glasses back on and took a deep breath. No, it was no use;

he had to lose his temper.

Dunard sensed this and leaned forward to interject before Patterson said something both of them would regret, but he was too late. In a raised voice, Patterson said, 'I'm sorry, I still don't understand. Why would you be appalled that everyone is white?'

The councillor now gave a genuine smile, which was far less appealing than her grimace. She didn't address her words to Patterson; instead, she turned to Dunard. 'You see, that's exactly the mindset I'm talking about.'

Patterson shifted in his seat. He wasn't sure quite how much more he could take of this councillor.

'Chief inspector,' the councillor continued, 'have you really got no diversity policies in place at all? How can you not have at least one officer who isn't white? I mean, just one? You know, when I think of it, since I came to this station, I've only seen one other person who wasn't white. One. And I believe that person was of Asian persuasion.'

'Asian persuasion?' asked Patterson, now becoming exasperated.

'I believe she was possibly of Pakistani origin. The point is, it's not good enough. Do you really think this is how you should be running a police station in this day and age?'

Dunard was about to say something conciliatory, but Patterson jumped in again; he was past caring.

'Councillor, I choose my team based on ability, not appearance. I believe I have one of the best investigation teams in the city, if not the country and I'm sure you'll see that with the investigation into Gideon Semanyo's murder.'

'I don't doubt it, Inspector, but we must look at the facts. We are now dealing with the murder of a young black man, an asylum seeker, to boot, from Ghana, and how will it look when every officer investigating that murder is white? At the very least, it's very bad optics.'

'Bad optics?'

'It looks bad.'

Dunard was strangely quiet, as if he had decided Patterson should do the arguing, and Patterson was only too willing to fulfil that role.

'Frankly, from my perspective,' said Patterson. 'I think what would really look bad is if we didn't find Gideon's murderer. That's why I have chosen my officers based on ability.'

'Oh,' said McKenzie, 'so you're suggesting that if you had a more diverse team, it wouldn't be as competent? I see. Quite frankly, I think that's a disgusting thing to say. You're honestly suggesting that somehow non-white officers are less competent than white officers—'

'That's not what I'm suggesting at all,' protested Patterson.

'—because if you are, I find that highly—' The councillor's voice had risen in volume, and now Patterson's did too as Dunard continued to look on in silence.

'All I'm saying is,' Patterson interrupted, 'that I have the best officers because they're chosen based on ability, not racial identity or any other superficial characteristic.'

'With all due respect, DCI Patterson, I find your unconscious bias rather disturbing. Although maybe I shouldn't be surprised by that attitude from a middle-aged white man.'

Sensing Patterson was going to explode, Dunard finally spoke up. 'Councillor, I have full confidence in my Inspector's ability and his team's ability. He's proven time and again how good he is at the job he does and—'

Not letting Dunard finish, the councillor finally stood up, shaking her head. 'Well, I want it put on record that I'm not happy.'

'I think that's already on record,' said Patterson, quietly.

The councillor glared at him, then addressed her next comment to Dunard. 'I'll be keeping a close eye on this investigation, Chief

Inspector. I want the far-right possibility properly investigated, and if I find out—'

'Don't make demands, councillor,' Patterson interrupted again, 'We'll carry out our investigation with the same professionalism as we always do.'

The councillor said a polite goodbye to Dunard but not to Patterson, then left the room.

Patterson shook his head. 'What an absolute idiot.'

'Nevertheless, Mike, we do have to try and keep these people on board.'

'Do we?'

'I don't like it any more than you do, but that's the way it is.'

'You're acting like she's important. She's a city councillor with nothing better to do than come here and talk nonsense.'

'That's as maybe...Anyway, how is the investigation going? Any leads yet?'

'As it happens, there is a possibility that the far-right is behind this murder. There had been threats made to trainees because they are incorporating refugees. However, having said that, there are some other factors which contradict that possibility.'

'Such as?'

'For one thing, it's possible that Gideon was murdered when all the other trainees were at the café. It raises the distinct possibility that one of the other trainees could well be the murderer. It's too early to tell at the moment, either way. Nevertheless, given the threats received, I would like a counter-terrorism officer to be part of the investigation.'

'I can arrange that,' said Dunard.

'Good,' said Patterson. 'The other trainees need to be checked out thoroughly as well. It could be that one of them has links to the far-right or there's a racist motive, even if, for the moment, it's still too early to tell.'

'OK. Well, keep me informed,' said Dunard. 'I'll be giving a statement tonight at six.'

'You'll give a statement?'

'Yes,' said Dunard, 'so tell me the moment there is any development.'

'I will,' replied Patterson, standing up. 'We can only hope my all-white investigating team doesn't hold us back.'

Dunard shook his head as Patterson left his office.

CHAPTER 7

Logistics

Patterson went back to his office to help set up the logistics of another murder investigation. Yet, he found it hard to concentrate. Councillor McKenzie had succeeded in intensely irritating him, and his determinedly happy attitude from the start of the day had taken a near-fatal hit.

It wasn't just that she had criticised everyone in his team for being white, crazy as that was, but she used phrases that got under Patterson's skin. *Bad Optics. Asian Persuasion.* They sounded like acts on *Britain's Got Talent.*

Yet, despite himself, he couldn't help wondering if McKenzie had a point. Was it wrong that everyone in his team was white? He hadn't really thought of it before. He hadn't thought of it because what he said was true. He simply judged everyone on ability, not their skin colour or anything else superficial. To do otherwise would be unthinkable.

He thought back to those who had previously applied to be on his team. Had he ever been guilty of unconscious bias? For whatever reason, not many people of colour—another phrase he hated—had applied to be on his team. He thought of one person he had interviewed recently, whom he had rejected. Yet, it was because she had come across as unsettled, and Patterson thought, in his judgment, she wouldn't have lasted long on his team before wanting a transfer. Skin colour hadn't come into his thinking. Why was he even asking that question? That councillor was an absolute pain. Yet, the fact remained that everyone on his team was white and that now irked him for some reason, and it irked him that he was irked. He tried to shake those thoughts from his mind and refocus on the investigation.

This was actually the part of an investigation that Patterson liked the most. At the very beginning, when it was all about constructing the framework to ensure the investigation ran as smoothly as possible. Soon, very soon, there would be mounting pressure to find the murderer, a pressure that would continue to increase with every passing day if he didn't get a result. Yet, for now, it was all about logistics, applying procedures that had, for the most part, worked before. Patterson often reflected that if he hadn't ended up in the police force, he would have got a job somewhere else that involved logistics—perhaps working out the routes for deliveries, that would be nice. Mind you, it was probably all done by a computer nowadays.

For the murder of Gideon Semanyo, he was initially following up on what he had said in the briefing. A priority was checking CCTV around Bunhouse Road. There weren't any cameras on Bunhouse Road itself, but there were several on the surrounding roads. Additionally, if necessary, buses, car dashcams, or shop CCTV could be obtained, and with some luck, yield results.

For the moment, Patterson was most eager to find out what the autopsy would reveal, particularly for the time of death to be determined. As he was contemplating this, Pettigrew entered the office. Patterson looked at her for an additional moment, conscious that she was white. He could kill that councillor.

Pettigrew noticed his lingering stare. 'Something wrong, sir?' She self-consciously touched her hair.

'Eh? No, no, sorry, just daydreaming.'

Pettigrew smiled, but her boss was still acting strangely. She tried to ignore his behaviour.

'I contacted the dealership Gideon bought his car from,' she began, 'a showroom on Maryhill Road. It's a second-hand car but still cost £15,000, and he paid in cash.'

'Cash?'

'Yep, they gave him a five-hundred-pound cash discount.'

Patterson drummed the desk with his fingertips. 'As I said before, even if he was working on the side, he'd have to do a lot of overtime for that kind of money.'

'So what do you think,' asked Pettigrew, 'drugs?'

'Got to be something like that. Yet his flat seemed clean. If he were dealing drugs or doing some similar activity, I would have thought there would be indications at his home. Apart from the money, I saw nothing else at his home to indicate drug dealing. We'll need the place thoroughly searched. Check his bank accounts and see what you can find.'

'Will do,' said Pettigrew and left.

Simpson came in. Patterson stared. White. Simpson was white. Patterson sighed, took off his glasses and ruffled the top of his head.

'Everything all right, sir?' Simpson asked.

'Fine, fine,' said Patterson, 'it's just been a long morning.'

Simpson nodded. 'I contacted the Home

Office. Gideon's parents are still alive, and he has a couple of siblings, so I'm trying to get in touch with the authorities in Ghana.'

'I was told his parents had been killed in a war.'

'Well, you were given wrong information on both counts. His parents are still alive, and as far as I'm aware, there is no war in Ghana. I'll double-check, but I'm sure that's the case.'

'So how come he was claiming asylum? What did the Home Office say?'

'They didn't specify. As you know, his claim was settled nine months ago, but he's been here for two years.'

'Anything else you found out?'

'He arrived in the back of a lorry at Felixstowe. There also appear to be discrepancies regarding his age. He told Border Control he was sixteen, but I believe the DSS now have his age as twenty-three.'

'Hmm,' said Patterson, 'it appears Gideon wasn't averse to telling a lie or two. Okay, Jack, work with Claire and keep trying to find out everything you can about him. Let me know when you've successfully contacted the authorities in Ghana.'

Simpson nodded and left. So far, the logistics of the investigation were going according to plan, and Patterson was happy. He was even managing to put that silly councillor out of his mind. The phone rang.

'Inspector Patterson? This is Nicola McLeary from the Lanarkshire Gazette. I wonder if you could confirm—'

'How did you get this number?'

'Are the reports—'

'There will be a statement at six by the Chief Inspector.'

Patterson put the phone down. Dunard giving a statement was another sign of the importance this case was taking. Still, Patterson had to admit that Chief Inspector Dunard giving the statement would be good optics.

Patterson contacted the media department, informing them that they could expect a high volume of enquiries, some of a 'sensitive' nature, and provided an outline of the Gideon murder to help them be better prepared. To be fair, they knew the drill already, and there was nothing they had to handle now that they hadn't handled before. Initially, they would attempt to conceal Gideon's nationality and race for as long as possible.

The rest of the afternoon and evening went smoothly enough. Soon, the first day of a new murder enquiry was over, and it was time for Patterson to return home. As he rose from his chair, his body ached. He knew, even more than usual, that the sooner the murderer of Gideon Semanyo was caught, the better it would be for everyone.

CHAPTER 8

Coming In From The Cold

Patterson arrived home around nine. It had been a long day, as was usually the case with a new investigation. As always, after putting his papers on the hall side table, he went into the living room and lit a candle for Stephanie. He then went into the kitchen, where he mercilessly stabbed the polythene cover of a lasagne ready meal and placed it in the microwave. As it began to turn and hum on the glass turntable, Patterson slumped down at the kitchen table, pulled the laptop towards him and switched it on.

The café murder had made the news, though it was only reported that a twenty-three-year-old man from Glasgow had been murdered. Dunard's press conference had been short and impressive for what it didn't reveal rather than what it did reveal. Dunard urged the public not to speculate online about the details of the murder. Despite the phone calls to his mobile that day, which suggested that certain journalists knew more than Dunard had officially disclosed, caution seemed to take precedence over anything else. Patterson still feared that there would be some kind of media frenzy once it was generally known that the murder victim was a black asylum seeker from Ghana.

Patterson took his meal out of the microwave, peeled off the plastic cover and emptied the steaming lasagne onto a plate, which he placed on the table with the laptop pushed to one side.

As he ate his meal, he thought about the café a little more. Everyone except him seemed to be aware that this café was being used as a training program for Partick's finest unemployed.

Patterson pulled the laptop back towards him and went onto YouTube. He typed in "Partick Bunhouse Café" on the off chance that there would be a video associated with the training program. He was surprised when numerous videos appeared. Most were news reports dating from the day the café refurbishment was launched. Patterson clicked on the first news report from the local evening news.

The report began with the group of trainees standing outside the café, looking cold and miserable. One of the exceptions was Gideon, who wore a warm, beaming smile in his smart white shirt and colourful tie. There was some preamble by the reporter that gave general information about the café before it cut to the last person Patterson wanted to see, Gillian McKenzie. She launched into a heartfelt monologue about how this training program would serve as a template for a future where all members of the community, from near and far, could work together to build a better Glasgow.

There were vox pops with the trainees themselves. The first, appropriately enough, was with Gideon Semanyo. It was helpful to Patterson to see the murder victim when he was alive. At the very least, he knew what the others meant when they said he was always happy and laughing. He almost, but not quite, matched Councillor McKenzie for bubbliness.

Yet, Patterson wondered whether the prominence Gideon had been given could have actually contributed to his murder. In many ways, he did seem the star of the show.

'Yes, I'm training to be a barista. I hope to find a job very soon once the training is over. I'm so happy to be here.' His English was very good, and he already had a slight Glaswegian twang to his voice.

He spoke confidently to the camera, and the camera loved him in return. The news report then cut to Danny Wilson, who, to his credit, was a little more subdued.

'Aye,' he began, 'I'm pleased. It gives me something to do during the day, know?' Interview over.

It then cut to another trainee, a smartly dressed middle-aged woman, Julie Campbell. 'Yes, I'm learning customer service, which will always come in handy. Everyone seems nice so far, from what I can tell.'

There were various shots of the café again, which they said, rather optimistically, would be transformed into one of the city's top eateries. Patterson paused for a moment. He switched off the laptop, stood up and placed his empty plate in the sink.

Walking through to the living room, he sat down on the settee and switched on the television, but Patterson's mind inevitably drifted back to the case. He knew it would be like that until the case was, hopefully, solved. What intrigued him most at the moment was Gideon's good financial situation. Although he had bought doughnuts for the other trainees, Patterson suspected his wealth wasn't something he advertised. He walked to work and back instead of taking his flashy car. The car fob even had the make of car removed, unless it was a replacement. The car itself had been parked up the street, not directly outside his tenement close. These were just a few details, small signs, but for Patterson, they could be significant signs.

Patterson pondered again that if Gideon was involved in illegal activity, it could well be linked to his murder. Drug dealers in the city didn't take kindly to newcomers trespassing on their turf. Yet, Patterson knew there could also be something else behind Gideon's murder. In fact, wasn't he ignoring the obvious? Could this simply be a hate crime? The fact that Gideon was one of the few trainees to be interviewed on the local evening news elevated that possibility up by a couple of notches.

Patterson flicked through the TV channels with the sound down. There was nothing on. Of course, there was nothing on. There was never anything on. Silence. Stephanie. When his wife died, for the first few months, he had managed to make the memory of Stephanie overcome the absence of Stephanie, but now her absence had long since come back with a vengeance.

He then remembered the panic attack he had had that morning. It had been a while since he had felt anxiety so severe that he had to walk away from a situation. And now, as he sat on the settee, listening to the silence, what did he feel? What was this ache, this emptiness he now felt within and around him?

Loneliness.

Perhaps, it wasn't just the absence of Stephanie that had again become apparent in his life; it was the absence of anyone.

The strange thing was, he couldn't remember ever being lonely in recent times. Of course, he had never been lonely with Stephanie; even in her wildest, darkest moments, he had never felt lonely. He always knew she was the woman he was meant to be with—his soulmate. Even before Stephanie, loneliness had never been an issue; he had always been someone who could bear his own company.

Now, though, it seemed different, and it was hard, even strange to admit, but…it would simply be nice to have someone to talk to when he got home. Someone to flick through the silent TV channels with and complain about there being nothing worthwhile to watch, and how people said barista instead of someone who made the coffee. There was no doubt about it. He felt lonely, and he didn't like it, not one little bit. Then again, maybe it was a good thing. Maybe emotions were coming back into his life after the overwhelming numbness of grief. Like the tingling of hands or feet in front of a warm fire after being out in the cold for so long, perhaps feelings were returning, and that included anxiety…and loneliness.

Patterson decided he would go to bed with a book and switched off the TV. You could never be lonely with a book. He turned towards the space beside him. 'Well, I don't know about you, but I think I'll have an early night.'

'Yeah?' Patterson answered, *'I think I might join you.'*

'Excellent,' Patterson answered, 'the more the merrier.'

Patterson stood up, blew out the candle for Stephanie and went upstairs to bed.

CHAPTER 9

Jason King

Early on Tuesday morning, the police discreetly released a statement about the Bunhouse murder, including the fact that the 23-year-old man murdered was Gideon Semanyo, an asylum seeker from Ghana.

Knowing this statement had been released, Patterson arrived at the station nice and early on Tuesday morning to avoid any media scrums he expected outside later. At eight o'clock, he strolled into the main investigation room and stood in front of the whiteboard.

On that board was now pinned a photo of Gideon Semanyo, smiling and alive in his white shirt and tie, as well as unsmiling and dead in a crime scene photo. The names of the fifteen other trainees were listed on one side, along with a small map of the area, a floor plan of the café, and a photo of the café exterior.

'Morning, everyone, I hope you all slept

well. I just want to go over your tasks for the day and to mull over some of what we learned yesterday.'

His team was seated behind different desks around the room. Patterson felt no anxiety at all and was so focused on the case that he never even noticed everyone in his investigation team was white.

'Throughout tomorrow, Pettigrew and Simpson will be taking witness statements regarding what happened last Friday. All the trainees are coming in on Wednesday, I'm right in saying that, aren't I, Claire?'

'Yep, the trainees usually go to college on a Wednesday, but it's been cancelled so that they can give their statements. We have arranged for half to come in this morning and half this afternoon.'

'Good,' continued Patterson, 'Let's see if we can learn anything more than we know already. As for the far-right extremist angle, Dunard has informed me that a counter-terrorism officer is also arriving later today. Now, as for yesterday, Brian, you were looking into what was found on Gideon's laptop. Anything of interest?'

McKinnon shook his head. 'No, actually. Gideon was surprisingly unengaged with the internet. He mainly used it to communicate with family and friends back in Ghana. We've found nothing relevant to the investigation. No one was sending him threatening emails.'

'Claire, you were looking into his bank account. Anything?'

'He had just under £16,000 in his account. That includes a £5,000 cash deposit he made two weeks ago.'

'Cash deposit? Presumably, the bank asked questions?'

'Yes. Gideon said he had sold a car online to someone who paid him £5,000 in cash. This was true. Gideon had sold a car through an online car marketplace. Once the bank saw he had all the relevant documents and receipts, they were happy. I contacted the person he sold the car to, and she's a legitimate buyer, a young woman who's very happy with her purchase. '

'It still begs the question, where did he get the money to buy his previous car?' asked Patterson. 'He must have an income stream we're still unaware of.'

'And it is actually quite possible he has more money stashed elsewhere,' said Pettigrew.'

'Why do you say that?' asked Patterson.

'Because if you have £16,000 or more in your bank account, then you're not entitled to any unemployment benefit. The fact that he has just under £16,000 could indicate that he has put additional money elsewhere rather than keep it in his bank account. Additionally, there is no record of where he obtained the £15,000 to purchase his new car. He didn't withdraw it from his account, so it must have come from elsewhere. I'll be following that up.'

'OK. Good. Everyone, just get on with what you were doing. I'll be going to the autopsy later and hopefully we'll find out exactly how Gideon died and when he—'

Patterson stopped as his attention was drawn to a man putting his head round the door from the corridor.

'Oh, I'm sorry,' the man said, smiling broadly as he walked further into the room, the swing doors shutting behind him. 'I'm looking for Chief Inspector Dunard. I was told by the chappie downstairs that he was around here somewhere, though it would appear I have taken a wrong turn.'

His accent was a curious mix of upper-class Scots and upper-class English. He had a distinct handlebar moustache and wore an open-neck yellow shirt with a large collar, a red kipper tie, and trousers that, although not the full flares of earlier times, were still quite wide.

'He's up the next flight of stairs, go through the doors along the corridor and it's first on the left.'

The man gave a theatrical salute and a wide smile. 'Thanks ever so much.' He turned and left the room.

'Is Dunard having a fancy dress party I don't know about?'

'Did you not recognise him?' said Davies.

Patterson shook his head. 'Should I have?'

'That's Zach Andrews. He's the MSP for this area.'

'If he's a member of the Scottish Parliament, then why is he dressed as Austin Powers?'

'He's known for it,' said Davies. 'He's quite the character. He loves all things from the seventies.'

'Does he indeed? Oh, how I miss the days when politicians were serious individuals. Anyway, what was I saying? Yes, I'll be attending Gideon's autopsy later, and we'll hopefully learn Gideon's time of death. Does anyone have any other information we may not have mentioned yesterday?'

Simpson spoke up. 'I've managed to contact the authorities in Ghana, They said they'll contact the family. Apparently, Gideon still has a large family in Ghana and was planning for relatives to visit Glasgow later this year. Oh, and as I thought, there is no war in Ghana as Gideon claimed.'

'OK, well, at least his family will know what's happened. Will Gideon be repatriated?'

'I believe so. It's all being arranged now.'

An officer popped his head round the door.

'Dunard wants to see you.'

'Does he indeed,' said Patterson with a sigh, and turned back to his team, 'OK, you all know what you have to do. I'll catch up with you later.'

Patterson left the investigation room to go upstairs.

CHAPTER 10

Zach Andrews

Patterson went upstairs and entered Dunard's office. The same man who, in colourful clothes, had earlier wandered into the investigation room, asking for directions, now sat in front of Dunard's desk. As Patterson entered, the man turned around with the same broad smile he had downstairs and continued to smile at Patterson as he sat in the vacant chair.

'Mike, this is the MSP for this area, Zach Andrews. He's just paying a visit to see how the investigation is going.'

'Naturally,' said Patterson with a slight sarcasm in his voice, which Dunard hoped the MSP wouldn't pick up on.

'I was just telling Zach,' said Dunard, 'the investigation is in its early stages, so there's not much we can say at the moment.'

'I heard,' Andrews said, his broad smile

being suddenly replaced by an expression of concern, 'that the far-right may have been behind poor Gideon's murder.'

'That is one possibility, though we're still following a number of leads at this stage,' replied Patterson.

The MSP turned to Dunard with a quizzical look. 'I'm sorry, but weren't threats made to the trainees by the far-right, or did I hear wrong?'

Patterson wondered how Andrews knew threats had been made but before he could deny it, Dunard confirmed it. There was a leak somewhere within the station, or perhaps with the DSS.

'No, you're right,' said Dunard. 'Threats were made to the training group, which we're currently looking into.'

'So,' Andrews continued, 'we most probably have an act of murder committed by the far-right on our hands. I always feared this would happen.'

'As I said, extremism is just one avenue of enquiry we're following at this time,' said Patterson. It's not certain that there is even a racist motive behind Gideon's murder.'

The MSP shifted in his chair and carefully stroked his long moustache. Patterson didn't like judging people before properly getting to know them, but he couldn't help thinking Zach Andrews was an idiot.

'Of course, and I grant you I'm no expert,' continued Andrews with a small chuckle, 'but I would have thought a black man being murdered after threats had been received from the far-right would make the far-right the number one suspect, or am I being naive?'

'No, it's not naïve at all,' said Patterson amicably, 'threatening letters were received that indicated they were from extremists; however, we don't know exactly where the letters originated from. They were not signed by any group. Certainly, it could be an extremist acting independently—a lone wolf if you like. A counter-terrorism officer is arriving later to help us with that line of enquiry. However, Gideon's murder could just as easily be unrelated to the threats received. For the moment, we feel it's best to rule nothing out, especially since some aspects of this murder don't add up with the far-right being involved.'

'Such as?' asked Andrews.

'Such as...well, if an extremist organisation were involved, they could easily have murdered Gideon in any number of places less risky than the café. It's quite fortunate, from the murderer's point of view, that Gideon's body wasn't discovered until two days after his murder.'

'Perhaps they were trying to make a statement,' said Andrews.

'That's a possibility,' replied Patterson, all the time wondering why he was wasting time discussing this case with a Jason King lookalike. 'But, at the same time, an organisation didn't identify itself in the letters; if they were making a statement, then why not identify their organisation in the letters? It's just my opinion,' said Patterson, modestly, 'but I feel Gideon's murder could just have easily been carried out by a fellow trainee.'

Andrews shook his head and laughed again.

'You don't agree, Mr Andrews?' asked Dunard, on behalf of his DCI, whom he correctly sensed was not too enamoured with this MSP.

Andrews let out an exaggerated sigh before speaking, as if he were talking to a child. 'As I said, far be it for me to tell you how to do your job—'

'Quite,' Patterson cut in.

'Quite,' repeated Andrews, 'but if you will allow me to make an...observation.' Andrews crossed his legs, brushed some imaginary fluff off his green trousers, and looked towards the ceiling, 'that surely the far right should still be the prime suspects here and not his fellow trainees.'

'You could say that,' said Patterson patiently. 'But, again, at this early stage of the enquiry, we're looking into every possibility.'

'Of course, you are,' said Andrews, still smiling as if Patterson had just relayed a slightly amusing anecdote.

'Is there something bothering you?' asked Patterson, sensing Andrew's scepticism.

'I'll be blunt with you, Inspector, the fact is I almost get the impression you don't want it to be the far-right.'

'Don't want it to be the far-right? Just why would I not want it to be the far right?' said Patterson, realising his earlier assumption that this man was an idiot was the correct one. Had these politicians nothing better to do than visit police stations and annoy detectives?

'Oh, don't get me wrong, inspector, I'm certainly not suggesting you sympathise with the far-right.'

'I'm glad to hear it,' replied Patterson, now realising idiot wasn't a strong enough word to describe this man. Cretin, yes, cretin, thought Patterson, would be a far more apt description.

'I'm just saying,' Andrews continued, 'you appear foolishly stubborn in not concentrating on the far-right when, from what I can see, they're clearly the number one suspects. Instead, you tell me you're investigating this man's fellow trainees, many of whom, I believe, are themselves asylum seekers like poor Gideon. You know, a large number of my constituents are deeply concerned about this murder, especially the African community. They are worried that extremists have a cell operating right here in Partick and quite frankly, I don't blame them.'

'A cell? It's correct that some other trainees are asylum seekers, or ex-asylum seekers, to be exact. As I have already said, we have a counter-terrorism officer arriving later today to help us pursue that line of enquiry, but as I've also said countless times already, far-right extremism is just one avenue we're pursuing, and at this early stage, we're ruling nothing—'

'For goodness sake, man!' Andrews exclaimed, almost shouting. 'The evidence is right there! As I say, I've been concerned for some time that the far-right has been getting a foothold in this city, as have many of my fellow MSPs. I'm sorry if I'm getting emotional, but I've been fighting extremism all my life. When I hear you talk about investigating Gideon's fellow trainees, it worries me that you're not taking the racism angle seriously enough. Look at the evidence, man!'

Patterson's evaluation of the man had gone from idiot to cretin to slightly deranged.

'You talk about evidence, Mr Andrews,' said Patterson, taking off his glasses and pinching the top of his nose, his default action when trying to control his anger. 'Just what evidence are you talking about?' he asked, as Dunard had once again fallen into mute observer mode.

'The evidence that threatening letters were received from the far-right, followed by the murder of a young black man. Is it really that difficult to put two and two together?' said Zach in an exasperated voice.

'We can perhaps assume these letters are from the far-right, yes, but assumptions aren't evidence,' said Patterson as he put his glasses back on. '

'Yet you're telling me you're still looking at one of his fellow trainees as the possible murderer? I mean, dearie me,' said Andrews, shaking his head.

'As I've already stated countless times, ' said Patterson, through gritted teeth, 'we're pursuing all avenues at this stage in the investigation. Now, if you'll excuse—'

'What could make you possibly believe the murderer would be one of his fellow trainees?'

Patterson was loathe to reveal more than was necessary to Andrews, yet couldn't resist enlightening the MSP on some facts.

'It's quite possible some other trainees were present when Gideon was murdered. That not only complicates things but also means the other trainees are suspects just as much as the far-right. Plus... certain aspects of Gideon's lifestyle are in question. It's very possible Gideon was working on the side or involved in some illegal activity, and that could well turn out to be a factor in his murder. '

'Ah,' said the MSP, laughing once more and shaking his head, 'now we're getting to it.'

'Getting to what?' asked Patterson, wishing Dunard would say something to make Andrews leave. Instead, Dunard just looked on at the two men sparring as if he was watching TV.

'Victim blaming.'

'Victim blaming?' asked Patterson, looking at Dunard, confused.

I'll be honest with you,' Andrews said, turning to Dunard, 'the reason I came down here this morning is because someone informed me that the police were casting aspersions on this young black man, and now I find that is true. Can I remind you this man had travelled thousands of miles, on his own, as I understand it, all the way from Ghana, to escape a war.'

Patterson wondered, not for the first time, how some people seemed so well-informed about this case.

'Actually, there isn't a war in Ghana at this time,' said Patterson, quietly.

'There is always a war in Africa!' said Andrews, raising his voice again, which now prompted Dunard to intervene, albeit meekly.

'Listen,' said Dunard, 'this is getting us nowhere. Mr Andrews, I understand your concerns, but I think my DCI—'

'Superintendent, frankly, I don't feel Gideon is getting the professional police investigation he deserves. Just because the murder victim isn't white, it doesn't mean he doesn't deserve as much consideration as anyone else. If you stubbornly refuse to investigate the far-right—'

'Mr Andrews,' said Dunard, 'My inspector has already told you we have a counter-terrorism officer arriving later today to help us with that line of enquiry. I must also warn you not to cast aspersions on my officers again. I have 100% confidence in Inspector Patterson. Ask anyone, and they'll tell you he is one of the best detectives on the force. So, if that is all, the inspector and I have a lot to be getting on with, as I'm sure you do.'

Patterson stared at Dunard. The mouse had roared, albeit for a minute.

Andrews stood up and said defiantly, 'This isn't over.' He glared at Patterson, who just smiled as the politician turned without saying anything further and left the office. He predictably closed the door louder than was necessary.

'What an insufferable man,' said Dunard.

'Yes, insufferable is the word. Thanks for sticking up for me, although it took you long enough.'

Dunard glared at him.

'Only joking,' said Patterson.

'Of course, I'll stick up for you,' said Dunard. 'However, as I've said already, it really would help if you caught who did this as soon as possible.'

'Isn't that always the case?' said Patterson.

'Aye,' said Dunard, 'Anyway, what are your plans for today?'

'I'm just off to the autopsy to see if Tasmina can tell us anything new.'

'Well, keep us up to date with everything. This case seems to be attracting more than one imbecile to my office.'

'So I noticed,' said Patterson, getting up and leaving. He had always known this investigation would be trouble.

CHAPTER 11

Time of Death

Patterson visited the Glasgow City Mortuary at the Southern General Hospital. The Southern General was a huge, sprawling collection of buildings on the south side of the river that gave the impression of having just fallen out of bed.

Entering the mortuary always meant being hit by a claustrophobic smell of chemicals. Patterson entered to see the pathologist, Tasmina Rana, busy as always, dictating notes to her assistant. Rana always appeared like a nugget of busyness. She could be standing still, looking vacantly into mid-air, and she would still give the impression of being busy. Her dictating notes was a promising sign for Patterson, as it usually meant he had arrived at the tail end of events and didn't have to observe any of the actual autopsy. Rana confirmed this by looking up and exclaiming, 'Mike, perfect timing as always.'

'I'll take that to mean you've just finished,' said Patterson.

'That's exactly what I mean. At least, just about. I'll be with you in a couple of minutes.'

Patterson nodded, looking at the body of Gideon, most of him covered by a sheet on the central table. His uncovered face, like so many of the dead, wore an expression of serenity and peace. Patterson wondered whether there was a spiritual reason behind that.

Rana eventually came over, smiling, holding her clipboard.

'OK,' she began, 'first things first, cause of death is as expected, a single stab wound, which punctured the heart and would have caused almost instantaneous death. The weapon would have been approximately 5 inches long, featuring a thin blade matching the description of the missing knife from the café kitchen. If that isn't your murder weapon, then I can confirm it is very much one like it.'

'That's good to know, for a start.'

'It is. The entry wound is on his left side and came from in front and slightly to the right. The knife was thrust into his side, indicating that the assailant was probably right-handed. There are cuts to the inside of his fingers and the palm of his left hand, as said before, most probably when he tried to grab the knife. As for the time of death, I would also confirm it was sometime around Friday afternoon. Generally, in line with my initial estimate, although slightly earlier of around three to five pm.'

'No surprises?'

'I don't know if you can call it a surprise exactly, but the earlier blood tests we've got back show Gideon had a significant cocktail of drugs in his system. Cannabis and ketamine, mostly, plus evidence of earlier drug taking, including amphetamines. When he died, he was pretty high.'

'An addict?'

'I wouldn't go that far, though, taking drugs was a regular occurrence. There's no evidence of any harder drug use, certainly no needle marks on his arms or the rest of his body. He also hadn't eaten much on Friday. In fact, all we found was an undigested pastry, possibly a doughnut. I would say he died very shortly after eating that item.'

'That could be very helpful. We have witnesses who saw him eating a doughnut around half two. If he died shortly after that, it also suggests you're correct about the time of death.'

'Almost certainly. Given that information, I would certainly put his time of death between three and five pm.'

'Would it have been noticeable he had taken drugs?'

'To those who know the signs, perhaps. Others would have thought he was just very hyper.'

'That also ties in with what we know...but he would still have been coherent?

'Oh yes, but as I say, he would have appeared fidgety, nervous, hyper, quite annoying, in fact.'

Patterson nodded. 'Anything else?'

'No, that's about it really. There are still some other lab results to come back. I'll let you know the results later.'

'Okay, Tasmina, thanks for that. This information could indeed be very helpful.'

'Glad to be of service, as always.'

'And you always are,' Patterson said, smiling as he left the room.

CHAPTER 12

Annabelle Pearce

Patterson left the Southern General and returned to the station, all the while wondering about Gideon's lifestyle. Drugs were maybe not a direct factor in how Gideon died, but they could be an indirect factor in why he died. An indication of the company he kept, how he spent his spare time and, with that, possibly an indication of something more.

As Patterson entered Partick Police station, he saw with dismay the lift engineers talking to one another outside the elevator on the ground floor. Shouldn't they be getting on with their job instead of standing about chatting? After chastising himself for being a grumpy old git again, Patterson was tempted to say something, but decided against it. Besides, what did he know about repairing lifts? Perhaps they had encountered an issue they had never seen before. A one-off. A problem that would go down in the annals of lift-repairing history. With a sigh,

Patterson pushed through the swing doors and walked up the stairs.

The investigation room was a hive of activity when he entered. This impression was not so much a result of what Patterson saw as an underlying buzz he instinctively sensed. Nevertheless, after checking up on what everyone was doing, he found there were no new developments. He walked into his office and no sooner had he put his jacket on the back of the chair and sat down than the phone rang. It was Dunard.

'Mike, you're back. Could you come and see me ASAP?'

'Don't I always?' Patterson got up and headed for the stairs once again, walked up to the next floor, and entered Dunard's office.

A slim blonde woman was sitting in front of Dunard's desk. Patterson feared the worst. Who was it this time? Another politician asking if they had caught the murderer yet? Was it a member of the public just passing who thought they'd pop in and see how the investigation was going? Perhaps it was a councillor politely enquiring whether he could change his skin colour in time for the next press conference? Or someone asking if there was any way he could possibly become a little bit younger? *I hate to ask, but it would make things so much easier...*

'Mike,' began Dunard, 'this is Annabelle

Pearce from the counter-terrorism unit in Govan. Annabelle, this is DCI Mike Patterson, whom I was telling you about.'

Of course, Patterson had completely forgot that a counter-terrorism officer was arriving. He politely shook hands with Pearce and sat down in the chair next to her. On first impressions, Annabelle Pearce didn't look like a counter-terrorism officer, though he wondered what he had expected a counter-terrorism officer to look like. Her blonde hair and small stature gave the impression of a woman who worked in an office. She was wearing a nice dress and smelled... flowery. Or was it that Patterson had been expecting a man? Was that sexist? Was he now sexist as well as racist?

'As you mentioned, Mike,' Dunard continued, 'with the possibility of an extremist organisation being behind Gideon's murder, it's best to bring in a counter-terrorism officer.'

'Rest assured,' said Pearce, 'I'm not here to take over your investigation. I'm simply here to see if I can perhaps provide additional information on certain far-right groups that may be involved and, of course, give any other assistance I can.'

Patterson noted her voice was harsher than he expected, given her appearance. Or was he now classist as well as sexist and racist?

He got the initial impression of a woman who had worked hard to achieve her current position—someone who had grown up without the benefits of a wealthy family and had succeeded through sheer hard work and intelligence. Patterson wasn't sure if this was a good thing or not. She was also slightly younger than he expected. In her late thirties, perhaps. Or was he now being ageist? Was he ageist, as well as classist, sexist, and racist? He was running out of ways to be prejudiced.

Although there was an outward friendliness in Pearce's manner, Patterson detected a hard interior; Maybe not the toughness of an MI5 agent, more like a receptionist at the health centre who wasn't afraid to say no, but still that hard centre was there. Patterson decided he didn't like this person, which was strange because he knew he was being irrational. He wasn't one to dislike people for no apparent reason, unless it was Zach Andrews. Yet, he couldn't deny it; he was immediately on guard with this Annabelle Pearce. He suspected she was a wolf in floral-smelling sheep's clothing. Ideal for a counter-terrorism officer, perhaps. Whatever. For now, he was open to playing the game of superficial mutual cooperation.

'Of course,' said Patterson, trying as best he could to keep his wariness of Pearce out of his voice. 'I wouldn't think otherwise.'

'Can I ask just why you think the far-right may be involved?' said Pearce.

'There were direct threats made to the DSS, who are overseeing this training program, via a couple of letters sent. The trainees include a number of individuals from outside the UK, including three from Africa. I glanced over the letters myself. Both letters are identical. The N-word was used, and they talk about how the training program should be shut down, or that no...outsiders should be involved. There was a drawing AK-47—that's a machine gun.'

'I know what an AK-47 is,' said Pearce, 'and it's an assault rifle, not a machine gun. I'd like to see those letters as soon as possible. So why would they know about this café and the training program in the first place?'

Dunard took up the explanation.

'There was considerable publicity regarding its refurbishment and the involvement of asylum seekers in the training program, which is based at this café. Politicians and councillors view this refurbishment as a kind of template to utilise the skills of new arrivals to the city. They wanted as much publicity as possible, and by all accounts, they got it.'

'In addition,' Patterson continued, 'Gideon Semanyo himself was an asylum seeker, from Ghana. His claim was settled about nine months ago. I watched TV news reports on the café, and Gideon was interviewed more than once.'

As Patterson spoke, Pearce stared at him with intense hazel eyes; something which he found unnerving.

'And the threats have only been by letter? No emails, notes through letterboxes or anything else?'

'Not as far as I'm aware,' said Patterson. 'You're best talking to Siobhan Sutherland; she's the liaison officer for the trainees. I'll give you her details later. She reported the letters, brought them to the station, here, and I spoke to the officer who dealt with it, but there was no follow-up.'

'That's unfortunate,' said Pearce, smiling. 'Any threat from extremists has to be taken seriously.' Her tone was like that of a parent admonishing a small child. Patterson found it even harder to conceal his irrational dislike for her.

Dunard, knowing Patterson better, sensed his antagonism towards Pearce and spoke to try to deflect Pearce's attention. 'Do you have any initial thoughts yourself about who could be behind this murder, Annabelle, if it does turn out to be the far-right, that is?'

'There are a few likely candidates. As I said, I would like to see the letters first. The wording can be a giveaway. Certain groups have a fondness for particular words and slogans. Some specific groups will always say 'Alba' instead of 'Scotland,' and some will always reference the Knights Templar, or they'll talk about patriots, that kind of thing. Though I have to say, it's rare for these groups to actually act on their threats; for the most part, they're trying to intimidate. It's not unknown for them to carry out a murder, but rare.'

'These messages were very short,' said Patterson. 'For the record, my own feeling is that there could well be an entirely different reason behind Gideon's murder than extremism. I suspect Gideon had been dealing drugs or involved in some other illegal activity. He could have come into contact with some bad individuals. However, at this stage, we're open to all possibilities, as I've had to explain to quite a few people already. Are there a lot of extremist groups in Glasgow or Scotland, Annabelle?'

'There's enough,' said Pearce, 'they've been more vocal in recent years, what with the influx of immigrants. They are more prominent at anti-immigration rallies, but they also conduct much of their recruiting through specific bars, nightclubs, gyms, and other establishments. Rest assured, if there is a specific far-right group behind this, then we'll soon find the perp.'

'Perp?' asked Patterson.

'Perpetrator.'

Patterson knew full well what perp meant, and Dunard looked at Patterson, knowing full well that Patterson knew full well what perp meant, but it was clear it was another word that annoyed Patterson. He couldn't help taking off his glasses and pinching the top of his nose. I mean, really, thought Patterson. Perp. It was like those football pundits who called a penalty a pen. 'Yes, for me, Clive, it was never a pen.' Was it really that difficult to say the whole word? Would saying those extra letters result in falling down in an exhausted heap?

Inspector Pearce, much to Dunard's relief, didn't seem to notice Patterson's annoyance and continued talking.

'I'll make some enquiries straight away to see if there is a specific group that could have carried out this murder. Word gets around quite quickly between the main groups, and the ring-leaders are well-known to us, but you say, Mike, despite the letters, you're not entirely convinced an extremist group could be behind this murder?'

'Not at the moment,' said Patterson, putting his glasses back on. 'It's not just the drugs angle. I've just been to the autopsy, and the pathologist puts the time of death as Friday afternoon—last Friday—between three pm and five pm, which means there is a good chance some of the other trainees were present when Gideon was murdered in the disabled toilet—that's where he was found. Plus, if an extremist did murder Gideon, it means they managed to get into the café without anyone noticing, murdered Gideon in the toilet, then managed to leave, again without anyone seeing them. In my opinion, on balance, and given what we now know so far, Gideon's death is either drug-related or it's possible another trainee murdered him.'

'But, if, as you say, it was drug-related, wouldn't the murderer still have had to enter the café unseen, the same as an extremist?' asked Dunard.

'I suppose,' said Patterson.

'Unless,' said Pearce, 'one of the other trainees is already a member of an extremist group. That way, they could have a ready-made accomplice inside the café. If you could provide me with a full list of all the other trainees as soon as you can, and anyone else who was at the café that day, I can check that out as well. I take it this café isn't open to the public yet?'

'No, it's not due to open until the first of July. We're currently conducting our own background checks into the other trainees, but of course, you may have additional resources that could be useful in that regard. To date, we haven't found any indication that any trainee is linked to extremism. '

'Do you really think Gideon could have been dealing drugs?' asked Dunard.

'Gideon had a relatively expensive car, and a good wad of banknotes was in his bedside drawer and on his person when he died, plus there's evidence of cash payments he made into his bank account, which leads me to suspect he could have been dealing in drugs, yes. If he was, I have an idea that he could have went into the disabled toilet, which he apparently did regularly, to make phone calls related to his dealing. However, no phone was found on him, so the murderer almost certainly took it away. That also suggests a potential drug connection. As I said, I'm thinking he could have got on the wrong side of a current drug dealer.'

Patterson turned to Pearce. 'Anyway, I'll make sure you get all the relevant documents, including those letters, to help bring you up to speed with the investigation, and if there is anything else you want, just let me know.'

'I've set Inspector Pearce up in a room on the second floor, just along from the investigation room,' said Dunard. 'I know the main investigation room can get a bit crowded.'

'Good,' said Patterson, then turning to Pearce, 'I'll introduce you to the rest of the team now if you like, so they know who you are.'

Patterson stood up, followed by Pearce. 'I'll keep you informed of any developments,' Patterson said, turning back to Dunard, and the two officers left to go downstairs.

CHAPTER 13

The Most Likely Scenario

With Pearce by his side, Patterson walked down the stairs into the main investigation room and stopped in front of the whiteboard, with Pearce standing beside him.

'Everyone, if I can have your attention for a moment...'

Everyone duly stopped what they were doing and looked at their DCI.

'This is Inspector Annabelle Pearce from the counter-terrorism unit in Govan. She'll be working alongside us on the Gideon Semanyo case. Chief Inspector Dunard has allocated her an office just along the corridor, so if you have any questions or you find anything you think might be relevant to her side of the investigation, you know where to go.'

Patterson looked over at DC Cathy Evans.

'Cathy, I'd like you to stop what you're doing for a moment and help Inspector Pearce settle in, if you could show her where everything is, bring her up-to-date with all that we have been doing and give her anything she needs. While I'm here, I'll bring you all up to date on the autopsy findings. Patterson turned to Pearce, 'If you'd like to take a seat for a moment, Annabelle.'

Pearce sat down, and Patterson picked up a marker pen, went over to the whiteboard and wrote 'Time of murder between three and five pm.'

'That precise?' said Jenkins.

'Yes,' replied Patterson. 'Tasmina thinks that Gideon died late Friday afternoon and believes she can put the time of death within those two hours. Gideon died from a single stab wound to the heart, most probably from the knife we have already identified. So, this makes it all the more likely that Gideon was murdered when the other trainees were still at the café. As I understand it, all the trainees had left the café by half-four. The caretaker left just around five.'

'But how?' asked Davies. 'Apparently, no one saw anything unusual or mentioned someone who shouldn't have been there. Let alone finding a body in the toilet.'

'It was the disabled toilet. No one really went in there apart from Gideon,' said Patterson.

'As I see it, it probably means Gideon was lying there dead while the trainees were unaware of the fact. In fact, let me give you my interpretation of what could have happened, and feel free to interject at any time. OK, so we now know for certain that Gideon was stabbed on Friday afternoon in the disabled toilet between three and five o'clock last Friday. His body lay in the toilet until Monday morning, when it was found by the caretaker. No one mentioned seeing a stranger in the café on Friday afternoon, which suggests the murderer of Gideon may well have been a fellow trainee unless, of course, someone did manage to sneak in undetected.'

'What about Siobhan Sutherland, the liaison officer?' asked someone.

'And the caretaker,' said Pettigrew.

'True,' said Patterson, 'we also need to take those two into consideration. At the same time, we can eliminate, for now at least, three trainees who had left the café early that Friday, namely Linh Nguyen, Danny Wilson and Zande Mhkize—so adding two and taking away three leaves fourteen people who were in the café around the time Gideon was murdered. That is the twelve trainees plus Siobhan, the liaison officer, and Jim, the caretaker. Just to say, the chef de cuisine, Eddie McKenna and Alistair Carmichael, the team leader also left at midday.'

'So, what if,' said Simpson, 'someone else did sneak in earlier and waited until Gideon went into the toilet?'

'Which still implies the murderer knew Gideon went into the disabled toilet from time to time. Anyway, for now, I'd like to concentrate on determining the most likely scenario,' said Patterson. 'Apart from Gideon, there are a few of the trainees who went into the disabled toilet from time to time, but rarely. However, so far, no one has reported seeing anyone, including Gideon, go into that toilet on Friday afternoon. So, in my opinion, the most likely scenario is as follows. Gideon was either stabbed late in the afternoon when the trainees were still there or possibly just after the trainees left. No one saw Gideon leave the café, so it's more likely that as the trainees left, no one realised Gideon was lying dead in the toilet. Jim McLintock, the caretaker, has admitted that he didn't check the toilet before closing up for the weekend. I suspect whoever murdered Gideon also knew that the caretaker wasn't in the habit of checking the disabled toilet at the end of the day, which again points to someone who knew the routine at the café.'

'That's taking one hell of a risk though, is it not?' said Davies. 'Hoping no one else goes into the toilet during that time, and why did Gideon not shout out when he was stabbed?'

'Presumably, because he didn't get a

chance. It was a knife plunged into his heart. He tried to grab the knife, but it wasn't enough. Anyway, that's the most likely scenario, and the one we should be working with while, of course—he looked at Annabelle—keeping all other options open. OK, I just wanted to put that out there, that's all for now, keep on with what you're doing and remember what I said about Inspector Pearce. Give her all the help she needs.'

DC Evans walked over.

'Cathy, as I said, give Inspector Pearce here all she needs. She'll need to see those threatening letters, which are in the evidence room, and she'll require a list of the trainees and their details. If there is anything you're unsure about, then tell me, OK?' he turned to Pearce, 'I'll see you later. Annabelle.'

Pearce smiled and said thanks, and Patterson left the two officers talking as he went back to his office.

CHAPTER 14

Time Would Tell

Patterson left the station on Tuesday around eight pm. It had been another long day, and Patterson was eager to get home. On the way there, he decided to stop at the supermarket to pick up some groceries and a couple of newspapers.

Home was silence as soon as he walked in the door, but there were times when that silence was welcome and this was one of those days. Despite the time, he made a proper dinner—mince and tatties—and sat down on the settee after lighting a candle for Stephanie, then began to eat. He felt tired, but it was a kind of mental and physical exhaustion that made his eyes close, before he would jolt awake, time and again. He sat up, stretching his eyes and his body, trying to shake off the fatigue, and, after finishing his dinner, picked up the newspapers.

There were several stories about the Bunhouse Murder, as it was now known. Many of the later editions had revealed Gideon Semanyo, a 23-year-old asylum seeker from Ghana, was the victim of a senseless stabbing that had 'left a city shocked'. Most newspapers had an accompanying photo of all the trainees standing outside the café for the group photo, on the first morning they arrived.

Inevitably, one of those quoted in the news articles was Councillor Gillian McKenzie. She said she had been warning for some time that the immigrant community would become a target of right-wing extremists, but that no one had listened.

In another paper, the Bunhouse Murder was front-page news, featuring three separate articles on the actual murder, along with related stories about far-right extremism. One article had the headline, 'Has the far-right taken over Glasgow?' Numerous community leaders said they had raised the same concerns as Gillian McKenzie that far-right extremism wasn't being taken seriously enough, and this murder was the end result. Zach Andrews also made an appearance to say that he feared what the future held, and if the police didn't do what they were paid to do, racial murders would become a regular occurrence in the city.

Patterson got a name check a couple of times, and not in a good way. Councillor McKenzie said that institutional racism within Police Scotland was also a major concern and that she would be raising the issue in the city chambers. In her experience, she said, Police Scotland, were male, pale and stale.

Patterson switched on his laptop. As expected, most news outlets had the same take as the newspapers. What struck Patterson most of all was just how much of the media had conclusively decided that this was a racist murder carried out by far-right extremists, despite it being far from certain, this was the case.

Councillor McKenzie, who appeared to have spoken to every news organisation going, announced that there would be a protest march against far-right extremism on Saturday. Patterson tried to dismiss her antics, but an underlying annoyance, even anger, simmered on a low heat as he listened to her speak.

Patterson switched off the laptop and leaned back on the sofa, the fatigue still fighting to gain dominance over his consciousness. He sensed that almost a hysteria was building in the media, and in part it was because certain people, such as Gillian McKenzie and Zach Andrews, had an agenda. At the same time, he knew the best way to stop everything getting completely out of hand was to find the murderer as soon as possible. Yet, at that moment, he was floundering to work out how best to do that.

He felt so tired. He thought about what he had to do the next day and remembered he had arranged to meet his informer, Billy, at Partick Library in the morning. His thoughts started to fall asleep, but now and then, questions would shake him awake. Was it really the far-right that murdered Gideon? Was he being wilfully blind? Or was it another trainee? Or was it someone, or something else entirely? *Who knows*...Patterson thought...*who knows*, his eyelids slowly shutting out the light, *who*...*knows*...*time would tell*...Patterson's head drooped to one side... *time would tell*... he slowly slumped to one side and fell fast asleep on the settee.

CHAPTER 15

Engaged

Partick Library, situated on Dumbarton Road, was one of those buildings that quietly went about its business without any fuss and had been doing so since 1925. For many, it was a building they passed every day but never entered. Yet, if anyone asked, people would always know where Partick Library was.

Walking through its entrance situated between two thin marble columns, the library had the same revered quietness of a church, the outside noise of Partick miraculously reduced to a whisper within an instant of the impressively thick swing doors gradually whooshing to a close.

Patterson had arranged to meet Billy at eleven o'clock inside the library. Yet, having arrived early, he took the opportunity to look around the bookshelves. On a whim, he checked his wallet to see if he had his library ticket and was delighted to see he had, so he headed to the various bookshelves, wondering what he would find. In doing so, he was instantly transported back to his childhood, and by the time he would leave the library, he had four books tucked under his arm. Reading remained one of the consistent pleasures in his life. A pastime that eased the loneliness which seemed to peek into his life with ever more frequency of late.

Patterson sat at a table tucked away in a corner behind one of the clean pine shelves before pulling one of the two seats slightly out, so Billy would see him when he arrived. When Billy did arrive, Patterson was surprised to see just how smart he was. Billy wore grey trousers, a clean white shirt and a navy blue jacket. Patterson couldn't remember if he had ever seen Billy not dressed in his traditional tracksuit and trainers.

'Hello, Billy,' Patterson said as his informant spotted him and sat down. 'Off to a job interview?' Patterson wondered if Billy had a court appearance, but was trying to be polite.

Billy didn't answer, and only smiled as if Patterson was making a joke. Nevertheless, he seemed a little uncomfortable with what he was wearing, constantly tugging at his jacket sleeves, feeling his collar and patting down his trousers.

'Morning, Inspector, Ah huvnae been here

since I was a kid.'

'You should come more often. You get all sorts of books here, and all free to read. Have you not got a ticket? I could get you a ticket.'

Billy shook his head 'Naw, yer fine honest. I just huvnae got the time for reading...So what is the reason you wanted to meet?' asked Billy, as if he was in a rush to get somewhere.

'I'm investigating the murder at the Bunhouse café. You'll have heard about it?'

'Oh aye, all over the news, it is. They're saying it's Nazis behind it.'

'Aye, well, don't believe everything you see in the news. Have you heard anything yourself about it?'

'Can't say I have. You don't think it's fascists yersel' then?'

'I have my doubts. Have you had any dealings with them? Extremists, I mean? The far-right?'

'Naw. I know a few nationalists, right enough, but mostly patter merchants, though. At least, they're no' the kind that go around murdering people.'

'So what about the victim? Heard anything about him?'

'The asylum guy?'

'Aye, his name's Gideon Semanyo from Ghana. I suspect he may have been involved in drug dealing, not sure what exactly. I want to know for certain if he was or not. The drugs squad don't have anything on him, but he was probably still new to the game, under their radar. I was wondering if you had heard anything about that?'

'Can't say I have, but I can ask about if ye want.'

'Do that, see if anyone knows anything. As I said, he's a twenty-three-year-old Ghanaian, been here for two years. I'm curious whether his involvement with drugs could have something to do with his murder.'

'That's a possibility. There's a lot of newbies coming in, treading on toes.'

'Well, anything you can find out about him would be good.'

'OK, Inspector, I'll do my best.'

'So how are you keeping yourself, Billy?'

'No bad, actually...I've got a bit of news.'

'Oh aye?'

'I'm engaged.'

'Engaged?'

'Aye, it's a bit of a whirlwind romance, you know how it is.'

'That's great news. Is that why you're all dressed up?'

'All dressed up? Oh aye, well, Lorraine likes me to look smart.'

'Lorraine? Is that the lucky lady?'

'Aye, I'm thinking of going to college, n'aw.'

'It's all happening. Doing what at college?'

'Huvnae decided yet.'

'Well, if you need any help with anything, filling out forms, a reference, or if any lecturers need arresting, just give us a buzz...Anyway, I'm afraid I have to get going.'

'Me too,' said Billy.

Patterson and Billy stood up at the same time. Patterson discreetly handed Billy some banknotes, which he put in his inside pocket.

'I'll get back to you as soon as I can about that, Inspector.'

'Fine, see you, Billy. Hey, you suit the new look by the way.'

Billy gave an embarrassed half-smile.

Patterson watched Billy exit the library, then checked out his books. It was always good to go to the library and learn something new, though learning that Billy was getting engaged was a genuine surprise. Once he had his books checked out, Patterson headed to his car for the short drive back to the station.

CHAPTER 16

The First Witness Statements

As Patterson was meeting Billy at Partick Library, back at the station, Simpson and Pettigrew were beginning the first of the formal witness statements of the trainees, which were scheduled to take place throughout the day.

The first trainee Simpson interviewed was Danny Wilson. He was slight in stature, with a wiry build and a happy-go-lucky personality. He wore a dark green bomber jacket and faded jeans and entered the interview room smiling, as if looking forward to the experience. The interview itself turned out to be straightforward and a template for the day. Danny said he liked Gideon; he was a good laugh. He had even met him a couple of times outside the café when they went for a game of snooker. On Friday, he saw Gideon go into the disabled toilet once or twice, but Gideon often went into the disabled toilet; Danny assumed it was for privacy.

'Really?' asked Simpson.

'Aye, well...you know.'

'We do know,' said Simpson, 'We suspect Gideon often went into that toilet to make phone calls to do with his drug dealing. We believe he was dealing drugs outside the café, so you can tell us the truth, Danny, you won't get into trouble.'

'Aye, well...you know,' repeated Danny. 'What could I do about it?'

Simpson probed some more, but there wasn't anything Danny said that was of particular interest. In any case, Danny had left the café at midday on Friday, before Gideon was murdered. Simpson finished the interview and moved on to the next interviewee, Brenda Finnie.

Brenda Finnie walked unsteadily into Interview Room Two, as if she had a drink in her, and she would sporadically break into a fit of uncontrollable giggles. Despite this, Simpson pursued his questioning, but, as with Danny Wilson before her, there were no revelations. She said she didn't like Gideon that much; he seemed a bit of a chancer, and she avoided him whenever she could. She hadn't seen Gideon enter the toilet that day nor leave the café.

Pettigrew's first interviewee was James

Halliday. On first impressions, he seemed friendly and a nice guy, and before the interview started, Pettigrew asked what had brought him to Glasgow.

'I met this girl, woman I should say, when I was up here for a stag weekend with some mates. She invited me to stay, and I did. Big mistake,' he said, smiling. 'Still, I liked the city, still do, and she's now living down south, so it's all good.'

Pettigrew then asked about Gideon and if anything unusual had happened on Friday, and James said no. He really liked Gideon and had been very shaken by what happened. Gideon was always laughing and joking, but he seemed even more hyper than usual on Friday.

'Why do you think that was?' asked Pettigrew.

'No idea,' said James.

'You know he took drugs?'

'...Yeah, I knew. Never into it myself, though. Alcohol and coffee are my drugs of choice.'

As Pettigrew was writing down some notes, James added, 'You know you wouldn't be half bad if you lost some weight.'

'You think? That's kind of you to say so,' said Pettigrew, smiling. 'I'll remember that next time I'm on the treadmill. It'll give me a little morale boost.' She had heard enough comments in her time not to react. Still, her initial impression of James being a nice guy had slowly turned into a realisation that he was an arsehole, something this comment confirmed. As for the interview, James didn't have any major revelations.

The interviews that followed for both officers were also routine. Ahmed Farooq, Tegan Rees, Linh Nguyen, with her interpreter, Mohammad Sayyid, and Zande Mhkize all had the same story—that nothing unusual happened. No one had seen Gideon go into the disabled toilet and no one had seen him leave the café. Likewise, no stranger had been seen entering the café or loitering outside.

Simpson then interviewed Julie Campbell. Simpson was impressed by her, though he couldn't quite put his finger on why. Perhaps it was because she exuded the air of someone intelligent and confident. In truth, she was indeed intelligent but far from confident.

She may have had every reason to be confident, but a series of misfortunes and injustices in life had eroded the confidence that should have been there naturally. From losing her job as a well-paid secretary for a highly respected legal firm to ending up in a relationship with a charming man, whose charm cloaked a much darker and abusive nature.

Now, after being unemployed for nearly a year and, thankfully, single, she was desperate to get any work, or at least get back into a work routine. Hence, she even jumped at the chance to train as a catering assistant.

Simpson went through the formalities at the start of the interview, and Julie went through the formalities of the answers. She had filled out the paperwork on Friday afternoon, chatted with others, and didn't see or hear anything unusual.

'We believe, Julie, that Gideon may have been conducting drug deals over the phone from the café. Were you aware of that?'

'No...' Julie hesitated but didn't expand on her thoughts.

'You don't seem surprised.'

'I'm not. I did get the impression he was up to something, but I didn't know what.'

'We suspect that's why he often went to the disabled toilet, making phone calls so he wouldn't be heard by others. Did you see him go in there?'

'Yes, quite a few times, but I thought he just went in there for privacy or to talk to others.'

'Who else went in there?'

'A few, but I didn't see anyone go in on Friday.'

'Who did you see go in at other times?'

'There was his friend, Umar, he used to follow Gideon everywhere, though. Danny used to go in as well, that's Danny Wilson, and two of the girls used to go in there a lot, though I don't know what they went in for.'

'The two girls?'

'Kelly and Jess.'

'Not Tegan?'

'No, Tegan's a nice lass. She sounds just like —'

'—her out of Gavin and Stacey, yes, I know,' said Simpson, having interviewed her on the Monday. 'So you think Kelly and Jess went in there for some other reason than talking?'

Julie smiled. 'It's not for me to say. It was just gossip. I'm sure there was nothing to it.'

'So tell me what the gossip was.'

'Well, I don't know how to put it. Jess is a bit of a wild one, to say the least, not too precious about spreading it about, if you know what I mean.'

'You think she might have had sex with Gideon in the toilet?'

'That was the rumour.'

'And Kelly?'

'Not sure. She might have, but she's all right, is Kelly.'

Simpson thought it possible that some animosity between the females was influencing what Julie was saying about Jess. It could indeed be just gossip. Then again, perhaps not.

'Do you know any reason why anyone would have harmed Gideon?'

'None, whatsoever. I admit I didn't much like him myself, but Gideon was harmless enough.'

'You didn't see Gideon fall out with anyone? Arguing with anyone?'

'No, not really. Danny and Andy used to take the mickey out of him, but it was more banter than anything serious.'

The rest of the interview didn't provide any surprises, and Simpson left it there. Outside, he met Pettigrew, who had just interviewed James Halliday.

'Claire, you're interviewing Kelly O'Connor later, aren't you?'

'Yes, why?'

'I've just interviewed Julie Campbell, and she says the rumour was that sometimes Kelly or Jess had...intimate relations in the toilet with Gideon. It could just be gossip, you know how it is, but ask Kelly about it, and I'll ask Jess. Let's see what they say. Anything interesting turned up your end, so far?'

'Nope, they all generally have the same story. They all thought Gideon had left the café early since he disappeared around three, three-fifteen.'

'Which suggests he could have been lying dead in the toilet from that time onwards, and while the trainees were still there.'

'And which further suggests one of the other trainees could have been responsible.'

'But who?' asked Simpson.

'Ah,' replied Pettigrew, 'that's the big sixty-four thousand dollar question, isn't it?'

'It is. So who have you got next?'

'Russell O'Neill. You?'

'Andy McLean.'

'Right, I'll see you later, then,' said Pettigrew, smiling, and both officers went their separate ways.

CHAPTER 17

Moses Price

After meeting Billy at the library, Patterson returned to the station and had just sat down in his office when the phone rang. Patterson answered it with a sense of foreboding, which proved justified when Dunard asked to see him.

'Seriously?' asked Patterson.

'Yes, seriously,' Dunard responded, seriously. So, once again, Patterson trundled up the stairs, knocked on Dunard's door, and entered.

A tall, slim black man stood up as Patterson walked into the room, politely buttoning up what appeared to be an expensive jacket. Patterson's first impression was of a professional businessman, possibly a salesman. Patterson's second impression was that this was his replacement.

'Mike, come in and take a seat,' Dunard said, and both the young man and Patterson sat down. Patterson waited for Dunard to say the inevitable—but he didn't.

'Mike, this is Detective Constable Moses Price. He's just been transferred up from the Met. Moses, this is DCI Patterson, your new boss.'

Patterson nodded and smiled, though he was slightly surprised, as any new team members were usually discussed beforehand and only then agreed upon with Patterson's final word. For the sake of not embarrassing the young officer, Patterson tried to hide his surprise, only glancing at a smiling Dunard, which was still enough to alert Dunard to what his DCI was thinking.

'Moses comes highly recommended, Mike. We're lucky to have him.'

'I'm sure we are,' said Patterson, turning to Price. 'What made you want to come to this barren outpost of all places?'

'My partner's stationed here. She's a fellow officer from Glasgow. I met her while she was transferred down to London for a time.'

'Where is she now?'

'Central division.'

'Oh, right. What's her name? Just in case I know her.'

'Lucy McColl, Detective Sergeant.'

Patterson shook his head. 'No, can't say

I know the name, although it's not surprising with so many officers in the city. So, when did you find out about your transfer to Glasgow?'

'Actually, it was all a bit of a last-minute thing, real–'

Dunard interrupted. 'Yes, Moses had been planning to come to Glasgow for a while. I've just been given an extra allocation of cash to recruit more officers, so when Moses's superior said he was available, I jumped at the chance. Otherwise, I would have let you known sooner before Moses arrived, naturally.'

'Naturally,' said Patterson, but something didn't seem right. Nevertheless, he still didn't want to say anything in front of Price and was glad to have an extra officer to work with. His previous requests for additional staff had always been fobbed off with some reason involving cutbacks, cutbacks, or possibly cutbacks.

'Do you know Glasgow at all?' Patterson asked Price.

'A little. I've visited Lucy a few times since she came back here. I like what I've seen so far.'

'Aye, I suppose once you get used to the accent and the cuisine, there's worse places.'

Price smiled, and Patterson looked across at Dunard, who was also smiling, albeit with a more awkward version.

'Right, well, I'd better take you down and introduce you to the team,' said Patterson.

'Before you go, Mike, are there any updates on the case?' asked Dunard.

'I've put a few feelers out to find out for certain whether Gideon was dealing drugs or not. I'm just waiting for one of my contacts to get back to me. I'm also waiting for Pearce to get back to me about whether she has found any evidence of extremist involvement, but in general, there are no new developments.'

'OK, well, keep me informed. I always like to know what's going on,' said Dunard.

'You and me both,' replied Patterson, shooting Dunard a look, and the two officers left for downstairs.

CHAPTER 18

No Evidence so far

Patterson walked into the investigation room with Price by his side.

'Everyone, I'm pleased to announce we have a new member on the team; this is DC Moses Price. He's come up from London to be with us and his girlfriend, who lives in Glasgow. I'd like you all to make him welcome.' He turned to McKinnon. 'Brian, if you'd do the honours and show Moses the ropes, and bring him up to speed with the current case.'

Patterson turned back to Moses, 'If you could start by helping us study CCTV in the area, that'd be great. I know it's tedious work, but we need as many bodies as possible on this. We have to know for certain that Gideon didn't leave the café and come back at some point, as well as ensure no one else approached the café who could be a suspect. That means identifying certain individuals whenever possible and establishing their origins and destinations. I'll catch up with you later.'

Patterson then walked along the corridor to see Inspector Pearce. He knocked on the door and entered to see her studying some papers on her desk.

'Ah, Mike, I was just coming to see you. I didn't know if you were back yet.'

Patterson sat down. 'Any news?'

'Not really. I've been studying the letters that Siobhan received, and I haven't been able to link them to any specific group I'm aware of. They're very...bare as you indicated. In fact, I find it unusual that no extremist organisation has claimed responsibility. Usually, that would be the case; publicity for any group is a valuable currency.'

'So what do you make of that?'

'Not sure. Of course, it could be that they are wary of being traced, but the possibility of publicity—call it advertising if you like—usually outweighs the risk of detection.'

'So you have no clue who could be behind these letters?'

'Not at the moment. The wording doesn't give any clues as to any group I've dealt with in the past. There are three or four active extremist groups we are particularly aware of, and the types of threats they send via email or post—these don't match. I also have a good undercover contact within a well-known organisation, and he says he hasn't heard anything about any activist being involved in this murder. He would have usually heard a whisper if that had been the case.'

'Is this contact reliable?'

'100%. He also says he's never heard of this café. I understand this training program may have been big in terms of local news, but it wasn't so big to attract attention from further afield; at least no informant in any extremist group I've contacted had heard of it.'

'So what's your thinking?' asked Patterson, not knowing if he should be pleased that his own thoughts about the far right not being involved were being vindicated or whether he should be disappointed that a possible lead was a probable dead end.

'Like I say, at the moment, there is no evidence of an extremist group being involved in the murder of Gideon, but I'll keep probing in case I've missed something. If this is an extremist or racial murder, then it is more likely to be a lone wolf rather than an organised group. As for the trainees, none have shown up on any of our watchlists.'

'OK, Annabelle, in a sense that's good to know. How are you settling in, by the way?'

'Fine, it's not that different from Govan. I've brought my own coffee machine in, though.' She nodded in the direction of a machine on a cabinet behind the door.

'Ah, so I see,' said Patterson, looking across at the small but expensive-looking cafetiere. 'Very wise.'

'Yeah, no offence, but the coffee in your investigation room is rank.'

'I can't disagree with you there.' Patterson stood up, then paused. 'Tell me, Annabelle, if this isn't an extremist killing, what are your thoughts on who could have committed the murder? Your hunch, I mean?'

'My hunch?' Pearce cupped her cheeks in her hands, leaning on the desk with her elbows. Patterson was surprised by how cute she looked, or perhaps, was surprised that he noticed how cute she looked.

'My hunch tells me it was one of the other trainees,' Pearce continued. 'But who, though? I haven't the foggiest.'

'But then how do you account for the letters?'

'It's feasible that someone could have made threats, but the actual murder may be something entirely separate.'

Patterson nodded, 'Aye...I think you could

be right, OK, see you later.' Patterson left Pearce's office as she got up to make a new pot of coffee.

CHAPTER 19

Snap

Simpson and Pettigrew continued taking witness statements, and it was more of the same. Andy McLean told Simpson that, yeah, he was still upset by Gideon's murder. Gideon didn't deserve what happened to him. He said nothing unusual happened on Friday afternoon. It was the usual routine of filling out paperwork and waiting to go home. The only slight difference was that Umar went to the bakery to get doughnuts for everyone, which Gideon had paid for. That was around two. Andy hadn't seen Gideon enter the toilet or leave the café.

'Thinking back, to before Friday afternoon,' asked Simpson, 'did Gideon ever get in a fight, or fall out with anyone?'

Andy thought for a moment before shaking his head. 'No, everyone got on with Gideon. He was that kind of guy; he really was. I mean, there was a lot of discontent sometimes, but in general, everyone got on with everyone else.'

'What do you mean by discontent?'

'Just, you know, a lot of us are only at this training program cos if we didn't go, we'd lose our dole money.'

'But you're learning skills, are you not?'

'What? Making sandwiches and coffee? Oh, aye, we're learning skills all right.'

'It's better than nothing,' said Simpson, smiling.

'Maybe so, but it's not what we were promised. We were told we would be learning things like carpet fitting, painting and decorating, plastering, but naw, we're being taught how to make a cappuccino.'

'So a lot of the trainees aren't happy?'

'Aye, well, it's better now.'

'What's changed?'

'Ach, nothing really; I guess ye just get used to it. Alistair, the team leader—as he's called—gave us a wee pep talk. Anyway, what can ye do; it is as it is.'

Simpson wrapped up Andy's witness statement, not learning much that was new.

Pettigrew's first interview in the afternoon was with Russell O'Neill. Russell entered the interview room, asking where he should sit, and gave the impression that he needed permission to do anything.

Russell was quite small in stature. He had short black hair, with a very straight fringe which looked like his mum had put a bowl on his head and cut round it, but which was actually the current trend amongst teenagers. He had an unhealthy pallor; if Pettigrew were a doctor, she would have prescribed him a lot more sunlight. As Russell seemed very nervous, Pettigrew tried to relax him by indulging in some small talk.

'Did you manage to find the station easily enough?' she asked.

'Oh, yes, I've seen it many times on passing. My mum wanted to drive me, but I didn't want her to wait outside. I told her I didn't know how long this will take.'

'Well, it shouldn't take that long,' said Pettigrew. 'We're just trying to get a better picture of what happened on Friday afternoon. We appreciate your cooperation.'

'It's nothing,' said Russell, and he blushed.

Pettigrew thought this blushing was endearing and realised she was interviewing a very shy young man.

'Did you know Gideon well?'

Russell shook his head and shifted in his chair. 'No, we hardly talked. I don't think he liked me.'

'Oh, why do you say that?'

'Why what?'

'Why do you think Gideon didn't like you?'

'Dunno, I could just tell. I tried to talk to him a couple of times, but he just turned away. Some people are like that.'

Pettigrew couldn't disagree. 'We believe Gideon was involved in dealing drugs, Russell. Do you know anything about that?'

'Drugs? No, I don't know anything about that.'

'No? I believe quite a few people in the café knew, but you didn't hear anything yourself?'

Russell looked down at the table. 'I suppose I might have heard something, but I thought it was just talk.'

'So you *did* hear that Gideon could have been dealing drugs?'

'Yes, but like I say, you don't know who to believe at times.'

Pettigrew paused for a moment. There was something about Russell that intrigued her.

'How did you get on with the other trainees?'

'How do you mean?'

'Just how did you get on with them? Did

you like them? Talk to them? Apart from Gideon, I mean.'

'I got on with some. I went to the function room sometimes with a few of them. Mohammad, Brenda, Julie, Mary, Tegan....'

'What about the other girls, Kelly and Jess?'

'What about them?'

'Did you know them well?'

'Not really. Jess was like Gideon; she just ignored me. Kelly was all right, though. She's always kind to me.'

'In what way?'

'Well, she talks to me, for a start.' Russell smiled shyly and blushed again. 'Yeah, I like Kelly.'

'But not Jess?'

'Nah, not my type,' said Russell, sitting up in his chair and looking at his hands.

Pettigrew nodded and thought for a moment. She then asked about Friday afternoon, and was given the same answers the others had given. Nothing unusual happened, and Russell didn't see Gideon leave the café. Pettigrew brought the interview to a close.

The next interview for Simpson was Jess Whittaker. Jess was striking in her appearance.

Taller than Simpson, her brunette hair ran almost the whole length of her back. She had very dark eyes, and regularly pouted her full lips as if it were a nervous twitch, and perhaps it was. Her face was slim, matching her body; her high cheekbones made her look both more attractive and more unhealthy. There were a few additional lines under her eyes, which were possibly a sign of too many late nights. She entered the interview room as if she were a child preparing to serve detention.

'OK, Jess, sorry to drag you all the way down here; it's just a formality, but there are one or two things we wanted to go over with you again, as with all the trainees.'

Jess didn't answer, but looked at Simpson for the first time, as if to say, *You really are an idiot, aren't you,* and she did this successfully every subsequent time she looked at Simpson. Simpson ploughed on, regardless.

'First of all, Jess, we suspect that Gideon was sometimes using the café and especially the disabled toilet as a kind of office out of which he did some drug dealing over the phone. Were you aware of that?'

Jess didn't reply at first, but eventually sighed and said, 'I can't recall exactly. Gideon was always going into the disabled toilet.'

'Were you aware he was dealing drugs?'

'Yes, I knew. I'm not into all that myself; it's bad for my skin.'

'Do you know what drugs he was dealing in?'

'Small stuff. Ketamine, I think, a bit of coke, mostly hash.'

'And you never received anything, yourself—drugs, I mean?'

'I may have taken a bit of hash now and then, but that's all. If he was offering, that is, but nothing else.'

'You mean you smoked the odd joint in the toilet?'

Jess hesitated. 'Might have done.'

'Yes or no?'

'Yes!'

'Jess,' said Simpson, 'again, I'm not trying to get you into trouble, I'm only trying to find out as much as I can about Gideon and what happened to him, so there's something else I need to bring up with you. I was told that you and Gideon were more than friends. That you used to have sexual relations with him in the disabled toilet.'

'Sexual relations? Who the hell would say that? That's disgusting!... I mean, OK, we screwed a couple of times, but that's all.'

'Just a couple of times?'

'Yeah, just a couple of times. I liked Gideon; he was a nice guy, always up for a laugh. Not like some.'

'Did you ever meet outside the café?'

'Nah, I liked him, but not that much.'

Simpson decided to move on.

'On Friday, did you see anyone go into the toilet, apart from Gideon?'

'Yeah, I did, as a matter of fact. I saw Mary go in.'

'Mary? Mary McNair?'

'Is that her second name? Then yeah, Mary McNair.'

'You haven't mentioned this before.'

'I wasn't asked.'

'Do you remember what time you saw Mary go into the toilet?'

'I think it was around three, no, hang on, just after maybe—about a couple of minutes past.'

'How do you remember the time so precisely?'

Jess shrugged. 'Cos I looked at my watch. I was wondering how long we had to go before we could leave, and I looked at my watch, then I looked up, and Mary was going into the toilet, all sneaky-like.'

'All sneaky-like?'

'Yeah, I don't know how to explain it; she is just always really sneaky. She's a right weird one, is Mary. Really quiet—sneaky quiet.'

'So just to be sure, you're saying you definitely saw Mary McNair enter the disabled toilet just after three.'

'Yeah.'

'OK, did you see anyone else go into the toilet on Friday?'

'Nah, just Mary.'

'When was the last time you saw Gideon in the café?'

'I'd say about half two, he bought us all doughnuts; he was like that was Gideon—really generous, I don't think I saw him much after that.'

'You didn't see him leave the café?'

'Nah, I didn't.'

Simpson asked some more questions and then brought the interview to a close. This new information about Mary could be the breakthrough they were looking for. He first wanted to have a chat with Pettigrew.

Pettigrew, meanwhile, was in the midst of

interviewing Kelly O'Connor. Kelly was another interviewee who Pettigrew found very friendly at first. Yet, when Pettigrew first saw her, for some reason, the word that came to mind was not friendly, but fluffy. More than anything, Kelly O'Connor was fluffy. She had fluffy blonde hair, fluffy cheeks and a fluffy smile. In turn, fluffy could be replaced by wholesome and innocent. She looked like the kind of woman you would find on the cover of a puzzle magazine. She never stopped smiling—ever.

As Pettigrew led Kelly from the reception to Interview Room One, Kelly seemed fascinated by her surroundings. She asked Pettigrew a variety of questions, as if Pettigrew were a tour guide at the Louvre. Kelly sat down and leaned eagerly forward, waiting for Pettigrew to start asking questions. As Pettigrew began to speak, Kelly suddenly became very serious, all the while managing to smile.

Pettigrew laid out, as she had with the other trainees, why Kelly had been brought to the station. She then asked one of the main questions she had asked of others.

'Were you aware Gideon was dealing drugs?'

'Not sure, but it wouldn't surprise me,' said Kelly. 'Gideon had his fingers in all sorts of pies.'

'And it doesn't bother you that Gideon was

dealing drugs?'

Kelly shrugged. 'Well, it's not like he was doing anyone any harm, is it?'

'Well, actually, yes,' said Pettigrew. 'Dealing drugs can do a lot of people a lot of harm.'

'Ach, as I understand it,' explained Kelly, 'it was just a few amphetamine tablets here and there.'

'He was dealing amphetamine tablets?'

'I think so, that's what I heard, at least.'

Pettigrew delicately began her next line of questioning. 'Kelly, we have to try and find out how everyone got on or didn't get on with Gideon. There have been suggestions that you were very close to Gideon, in fact, that you went into the disabled toilet and had sex with him. Is there any truth in that?'

Kelly looked shocked and didn't speak for a few seconds, but just stared at Pettigrew. Eventually, she blurted out 'That's a complete lie! Who told you that? I would never do anything like that with any man in a disabled toilet, well, any toilet, any public place. That's simply not true!'

'OK,' said Pettigrew, 'I just had to ask you about it. Let's move on.'

Pettigrew asked some more questions that she had already asked others. 'On Friday afternoon, did you see anyone, apart from Gideon, go into the disabled toilet?'

'Yeah, I did, actually.'

'Who was that?'

'Mary.'

'Mary McNair?'

'That's right, Mary. I saw her go into the toilet on Friday afternoon.'

'What time was this?'

'Must have been about three, no, hang on, I remember now. I looked at my watch; it was just after three, about a couple of minutes past.'

'Did you not think to mention this before?'

'I would have, but I only just remembered when I was coming here and thinking back to last Friday.'

'You're sure it was just after three? How can you be so precise?'

'I had my phone out, seen the time, and I looked up to see Mary go into the toilet.'

'Did Mary usually go into that toilet?'

'Come to think of it, I think that was the first time I saw her go in there.'

'So why did you think she went in there?'

'I suppose she wanted to speak to Gideon for some reason.'

'Gideon was in the toilet at the time?'

'Not sure, I presume so, he usually went in that toilet, and I hadn't seen him anywhere else.'

Pettigrew asked some more questions, but she was sceptical of the answers Kelly had given and brought the interview to a close. She escorted Kelly out of the building, watching her turn twice down the steps outside and give a small wave as if she had been visiting her granny.

Pettigrew walked back up the stairs to the investigation room and found Simpson.

'Hello,' Simpson said. 'I was just coming to find you. Was that Kelly O'Connor you were interviewing?'

'It was.'

'What was she like?'

'She was...fluffy.'

'Not a murder suspect then?'

'Oh, I wouldn't go that far, but she did have one interesting piece of information. She said she saw Mary McNair enter the disabled toilet on Friday afternoon.'

'Snap,' said Simpson.

'What?' asked Pettigrew.

'I just interviewed Jess Whittaker and she said the same.'

'What time?' asked Pettigrew.

'Two minutes past three, to be precise.'

'Snap,' said Pettigrew.

'You mean Kelly said she saw Mary enter at exactly two minutes past three?'

'Yep.'

'OK...that's a good thing, right?' asked Simpson.

'Absolutely,' said Pettigrew. 'We have two witnesses who saw Mary enter the disabled toilet at exactly the same time and right around the time we believe that Gideon was murdered.'

'OK...even better,' said Simpson.

'You don't believe a word of it, do you?' asked Pettigrew

'Not a word,' answered Simpson. 'You?'

'Nope, not a word. I would love to, but I got the distinct impression that Jess and Kelly were trying to get Mary into trouble, even to the point of making her out to be a murder suspect.'

'And even to the point of lying in a police interview. They almost certainly corroborated on their stories.'

'I'm afraid so,' said Pettigrew. 'Which actually suggests they themselves could have something to hide.'

'Quite possibly. Anyway, who have we got left to interview?'

'The talk of the steamie, Mary McNair,' said Pettigrew.

'The talk of the what?' asked Simpson, puzzled.

'It's a saying,' replied Pettigrew. 'Like the talk of the town. Who have you got left?'

'Umar Olowe, Gideon's best friend, apparently.'

'OK, two witness statements to go. Let's get them over with.'

With that, the two officers went their respective ways.

CHAPTER 20

Umar and Mary

As Umar Olowe walked into the interview room, Simpson, as with the other trainees, tried to put him at ease by indulging in some small talk, but he didn't get much of a response. Simpson wondered if Umar understood him, despite being told that Umar spoke and understood English well.

Sitting down, Simpson continued, 'Right, Umar, this is just a formal witness statement to help us get a better picture of what happened last Friday afternoon when Gideon was murdered.'

Umar still didn't give any reaction.

'Just to check, Umar, you fully understand what I'm saying?'

'Yes, I understand.'

Simpson remembered that Umar probably had a low IQ and formed that impression during his first interview, but now understood it more clearly.

Simpson started the questions and, as expected, received the same answers from Umar that he had received from the other trainees. Umar said he had filled out paperwork, nothing unusual had happened, and then he had left the café.

'What time did you leave the café?' asked Simpson.

'About half four.'

'That's quite late, isn't it?'

'Siobhan said I hadn't filled out a form correctly, so I stayed behind.'

'Did you sit with Gideon during the afternoon? I believe you were a good friend of Gideon.'

'I sat with him earlier, but then he went away. I think he went to the toilet.'

'So, at the end of the afternoon, you stayed behind to fill out forms, and you never saw Gideon leave the café?'

'Yes, I saw him leave the café.'

'You did see Gideon leave the café?' asked Simpson, surprised.

'Yes.'

Simpson paused for a moment, thinking again that maybe Umar hadn't understood him correctly. 'Just to clarify, Umar, you're saying you definitely saw Gideon leave the café on Friday afternoon?'

'Yes.'

'OK...what time was this?'

Umar thought for a moment. 'About quarter past, maybe half past three, I think.'

'That's quite early, isn't it? Aren't you supposed to stay until at least after four?'

'Usually, but this time Gideon just left.'

Simpson began to realise that Umar's command of English was much better than he had first given him credit for.

'But when I spoke with you on Monday, you said you didn't see Gideon leave the café.'

'I know. I didn't remember then. Now I remember. I did see Gideon leave the café.'

'But you didn't leave with him?'

'Like I say, I had to stay and do paperwork I didn't do right.'

'When Gideon left, did he say goodbye to anyone?'

'No, he just walks out.'

'Do you know which way he went?'

'He walked towards the main road, up the way.'

'Towards Argyle Street?'

'Yes.'

Simpson wondered about this. If Gideon did leave the café, as Umar said, how come he was found in the toilet on Monday morning? He must have come back later. But how? And why? Or was Umar mistaken? Or lying, and if so, why?

These questions went through Simpson's mind as he pressed Umar again on whether he had actually seen Gideon leave, but Umar remained adamant that he had.

Simpson asked Umar whether he was aware of Gideon doing drug deals at the café, and Umar said he wasn't. This seemed unlikely, since if the other trainees knew, surely Umar, his good friend, would know, but Umar denied it again. Simpson continued to ask the question, but Umar was insistent once more.

Simpson eventually ended the witness statement and escorted Umar out of the building. Simpson's witness statements were over for the day. He went to a monitor and saw Pettigrew was still interviewing Mary McNair.

Mary McNair had rushed into the police station, thinking she was late. As Pettigrew took her along to the interview room, she reassured Mary that she wasn't late. Like many of the interviewees, Mary initially came across as a nice person. She was friendly, even if it was a nervous friendly. Pettigrew also perceived a woman who was slightly unsure of herself.

Perhaps that was another trait to be expected in individuals who had been unemployed for some time. Like Pettigrew, Mary had a fuller figure and wore a pale blue blouse and trousers. She was very smart, and Pettigrew wondered why this clearly intelligent and well-presented woman was unemployed. As with the other trainees, in asking herself the question, Pettigrew knew there was probably a story of simple bad luck or complicated life behind this person's insecurities.

As Pettigrew sat down making small talk with Mary, she could also understand why Jess and Kelly were trying to get Mary into trouble. There was possibly some jealousy at play with the thoughtful Mary, no doubt having many of the qualities Jess and Kelly secretly envied. Pettigrew began her questions.

'So, Mary, this is a more formal witness statement than the one you gave on Monday, so we can get down on record in more detail what happened last Friday. As you may know, we're talking to everyone who was at the café that day. First, can I ask, did you know Gideon well?'

'I wouldn't say well, exactly. I spoke to him occasionally. He seemed a nice person, I think everyone kind of liked him.'

'It must have been a shock hearing about

his murder.'

'Of course it was, it still is, you don't expect something like that to happen to someone you know. I mean, murder. You won't believe how many times I've cried since.'

'During our investigation, we discovered that Gideon was probably dealing drugs, and he probably made phone calls related to that from the café, which is why he went into the disabled toilet. Were you aware of that?'

Mary shrugged. 'Possibly.'

'We're not trying to get anyone in trouble, we just want to find out the truth about Gideon.'

Mary smiled. 'Yes, I was aware of it. I think everyone at the café was. I know maybe we should have said something, but we just let him get on with it, whatever exactly he was doing.'

'On Friday afternoon, did you see anyone go into the toilet, apart from Gideon?'

Mary thought for a moment, then shook her head. 'No, no one. I have seen people do so on other occasions, but not on Friday.'

'Who went in on other occasions?'

Again, Mary seemed reluctant to expand and needed another prompt.

'Mary?'

'Danny used to go in, Umar of course, he

was like Gideon's friend, Kelly and Jess, and Andy used to go in.'

'You never went in there yourself?'

'No,' said Mary, with a deeper, serious voice, 'I would never go in there.'

'The thing is, Mary, we have a couple of people who say they saw you enter the disabled toilet on Friday afternoon.'

'Me? But I...Oh, I get it. Well, they're lying.'

'Who's lying?'

'Jess and Kelly. It's obviously them who said that. As I said, they're lying. Why would I go into the disabled toilet?'

Pettigrew had to agree with her.

Mary then shifted in her seat and gave a small cough. Was that a tell? If Mary was playing poker, was that small cough a sign she was bluffing? Pettigrew had a feeling that it might be, as she knew that small cough was with so many.

'Mary, I need you to be completely truthful with me. Gideon has been murdered, and we need to find out who did it. I'll ask you again. 'Did you go into the disabled toilet on Friday afternoon?'

Mary shook her head and looked down at the table. If she wasn't lying, she was now giving a very good impression of someone who was.

'Mary, look at me.' Mary looked up. 'The truth, did you go into the toilet on Friday afternoon?'

Mary became tearful, shook her head and then slowly nodded. She reached into her handbag and took out a hankie from a packet.

'Yes, I did,' Mary said softly.

Although thinking Mary could be lying about something, Pettigrew still didn't expect Mary to say she had gone into the toilet. 'You mean you did go into the disabled toilet on Friday afternoon?'

Mary nodded. 'Yes, I did.'

'And was Gideon there when you went in?'

Mary nodded once more.

'What time did you go in?'

'Around three, I think, maybe just after three.'

'Why?'

Mary straightened up and was suddenly very angry, her face crimson. 'Because Gideon owed me money! He borrowed money from me a couple of weeks before and never paid it back.' Mary was furious as the memory came back to her, and she was almost shaking with rage. The instant change in Mary's demeanour took Pettigrew by surprise.

'As I understand it,' pursued Pettigrew, 'Gideon usually wasn't short of money; why would he borrow money from you?'

'Exactly!' said Mary, now trying to keep her anger under control, wiping her eyes and nose with the hankie. 'One day, he said he needed some money to pay a bill. He said he had forgotten to bring money out with him from the house, and he promised to give it back to me the next day. It's because I knew he usually had money that I stupidly said yes. I don't have that much money myself, but I trusted him. Of course, the next day, he just made excuses, and now it's been over two weeks. He just kept fobbing me off. Then, on Friday, he said he was going to buy doughnuts for everyone! He handed Umar money there right in front of me—the absolute cheek of it. That's when I knew he had no intention of ever paying me back my money, so later I decided to confront him about it in the toilet. I was so, so angry. When I went in, he was on the phone. I told him I wanted my money back there and then, but, of course, he just made the same excuses as always, telling me he'd pay it back as soon as he could.'

'So…what did you do?'

'What could I do? I just left.'

'You just left? You didn't do anything?'

Mary looked directly at Pettigrew, meeting

her gaze. 'Oh, do you mean did I murder Gideon?' Mary looked away and shook her head. 'No, of course, I didn't. I admit I felt like killing him, God, yes, there's no doubt about that, but I just left, like an idiot. I still couldn't believe it when I heard he had been murdered, but I swear to God, I didn't do it.'

'How much did you lend him?'

'£50. It may not seem that much to you, but for me, that's a fortnight's groceries.'

'So you left the toilet, then what?'

'Nothing. I sat back with the others, filled out more paperwork and then left the café.'

'What time did you leave?'

'About a quarter past four.'

'Did you see Gideon leave the toilet?'

'No.'

'Did you see anyone else enter the toilet?'

'No.'

'You understand, Mary, this doesn't look good. By your own admission, you went into the toilet around the time we believe Gideon was murdered, you said yourself you were angry, presumably you argued with him. Now, before we go any further, I want you to tell me the truth: Did you murder Gideon?'

'No! God, I knew I shouldn't have told you.

Yes, I was angry, I said that, but when I left the toilet, Gideon was alive, all smug and smiling and thinking he was so clever for taking my money, but no, I didn't murder him.'

'OK. Mary, I'd like you to stay there for the time being. I need to speak with a colleague. You know you're entitled to legal representation if you would like legal advice or a lawyer present.'

'Is that necessary?'

'It's advisable. So far, you've been here to give a witness statement, but given what you have said, we're going to have to ask you some more questions, and it may be best for you to have a lawyer present.'

'Then yes, I'd like a lawyer.'

'Do you want me to assign one for you?'

'No, I have a lawyer who deals with family things, John.'

'Then you can call him. Just give me a moment—I need to speak with a colleague. Would you like a tea or coffee?'

Mary asked for tea, and Pettigrew left the interview room to speak with Simpson.

CHAPTER 21

Now What?

Pettigrew relayed to Simpson what Mary had said before she returned to the interview room. Simpson then went upstairs to see Patterson.

'Sir, there's been a development. Pettigrew was getting Mary McNair's statement, and Mary said she went into the toilet around the time that Gideon was murdered.'

'Anything else?'

'She says she went into the toilet because she was angry with Gideon and wanted to confront him. Apparently, Mary had lent Gideon some money, and he didn't pay it back.'

'I didn't think Gideon would need to borrow money from anyone; he seemed fine, financially.'

'That's why Mary was angry. The last straw was seeing Gideon buying doughnuts for everyone, when he still hadn't paid her back the money he owed her.'

'Where's Mary now?'

'Still in the interview room. She's just asked for a lawyer. Claire's on her way up.'

'No sooner had he said this than Pettigrew appeared in the doorway.

'Has Jack told you?' asked Pettigrew, sitting down.

'Yes, do you think she's guilty?' asked Patterson.

'Honestly? I'm not sure. She hasn't mentioned she was in the toilet before, perhaps for obvious reasons. She showed real flashes of anger; her temper turned just like that. It was scary how quickly her mood changed, and she did have a motive, even if it was quite a trivial one.'

'It often is with murder,' said Patterson.

'So what should we do, now?' asked Simpson.

'We wait for her lawyer and then you continue the interview, Claire, this time with Mary as a possible suspect. If she did murder Gideon, the best way, perhaps the only way, to prove it is for Mary to confess,' said Patterson.

'Unless we find the murder weapon,' said

Simpson.

'The chances are that the murder weapon is at the bottom of the Clyde by now if she had any sense,' said Patterson. 'OK. Jack, I want you to sit in on the interview alongside Claire. If there are no further developments, then we'll have to let her go for now, continue our investigation and see if anything else turns up to implicate Mary or not as the case may be.'

'There's something else,' said Simpson. 'Umar, Gideon's good friend, said he saw Gideon leave the café around half-three.'

'Really?' said Pettigrew. 'He hasn't said that before, has he?'

'No, I guess it's a day for surprises,' said Simpson.

'Do you think he's telling the truth?' asked Patterson.

'Not sure. I don't know why he would lie, but since no one else saw Gideon leave, it could be that no one else actually saw Gideon leave even though he did. According to Umar, he didn't say goodbye to anyone, but just left.'

'But if he left…' said Pettigrew.

'How did he end up being found in the toilet on Monday morning?' Simpson asked in agreement.

'OK,' said Patterson. 'Let's just take this one

step at a time. As I said, once Mary's lawyer arrives, you two interview her. I would like to hear both of your professional opinions afterwards on whether you think Mary could have been responsible for Gideon's murder and—'

The phone rang. Mary's lawyer had arrived.

'OK. You're on in five. Let's get to it.'

Pettigrew and Simpson headed to the interview room while Patterson followed to watch the interview on the monitor.

CHAPTER 22

Optics

It was the next morning, Thursday, the third of May, three days after Gideon Semanyo's body had been found, and Patterson drove into Partick police station car park with a new sense of optimism.

They had to let Mary go the night before, as she steadfastly stuck to her story that she had left the toilet with Gideon very much alive. However, they now had a prime suspect. Afterwards, when Patterson asked Simpson and Pettigrew for their professional opinions on whether they thought Mary could have murdered Gideon, neither could give a definite answer.

Nevertheless, that optimism stayed with Patterson. It was not only because of the development with Mary McNair. Some of the other witness statements Patterson reviewed raised some interesting questions. Added to his talk with Inspector Pearce the day before, he was even less inclined to think it was a far-right extremist behind the murder and more inclined to believe it was a fellow trainee. However, if it were another trainee, the question remained: which one? Was it really Mary who, in a fit of rage, stabbed Gideon over £50?

Patterson parked his car and lingered inside the vehicle, as always, enjoying an extra moment's quiet before another hectic day began. It also gave him a chance to ponder another question that yesterday's witness statements raised. If Gideon had left the café as Umar claimed, how did he end up being found in the toilet on Monday morning?

Patterson was still pondering these questions as he left his car and entered the station reception area. He noticed with surprise that the out-of-order sign wasn't hanging on the elevator door. His first assumption was that it was still broken, and someone must have removed the sign by mistake. However, when Patterson pressed the *door open* button out of sheer curiosity, the door duly slid open. It seemed they had finally fixed the elevator. Patterson walked into the small space, as if revisiting an old friend, though still sceptical that it would take him upstairs, even as the doors closed. Yet, after pressing the number 2 button, he quickly heard a whirring sound, felt movement, and thirty seconds later, the doors opened to reveal that he was on the second floor.

On entering the main investigation room, he couldn't resist saying to McKinnon with a sense of wonder, 'The elevator is working.'

McKinnon, nonplussed, replied, 'I know.'

Patterson resisted the urge to tell anyone else as he walked into his office. Twenty minutes later, he came back out to stand in front of the whiteboard and his investigation team.

'OK, everyone, it's another day and I just want to bring everyone up to date with everything that happened yesterday for those of you who don't already know.'

The investigation team gradually stopped moving so that Patterson could continue.

'Following the witness statements given by the trainees yesterday to Claire and Jack, we have one or two new possibilities regarding who murdered Gideon. The main one being that Mary McNair admitted she was in the disabled toilet just around the time we believe that Gideon was murdered. Of course, we'll be pursuing this more, but, for now, I also want to look at some of the other interesting statements made yesterday. For instance, apart from Mary's statement, Umar Olowe now says he saw Gideon leave the café, around half-three. Moses, has Gideon still not been captured on CCTV?'

'No. Gideon has not been seen anywhere outside of the café. All the CCTV footage we've reviewed—of the surrounding area, and we've reviewed a lot—doesn't contain a single image of Gideon. If he did leave the café, then it's strange that he hasn't been picked up on CCTV somewhere.'

'Which means he most probably didn't leave the café, and Umar Olowe is either genuinely mistaken or lying. OK—'

Patterson was about to say something else when a tall, smartly dressed man popped his head in the door.

'Excuse me,' the man said in a well-spoken voice. 'I'm looking for Chief Superintendent Dunard.'

'Inspector Dunard? You've got off on the wrong floor. He's on the next floor up, through the swing doors, first door on the left.'

'Excellent, thank you,' the man said, and left.

'How hard is it to get off on the right floor?' asked Patterson, not for the first time.

'The lift isn't working,' said Davies.

'Since when? I've just used it.'

'That's as maybe, but it's broken down again.'

'You're kidding? It was only operating five minutes.' Patterson shook his head before continuing with a sigh, 'OK, listen, I'll leave it there since I've a feeling I'm going to be called to see Dunard in a minute, and I forgot I have to make a phone call. Keep on with what you're doing.'

Patterson went into his office, picked up his mobile and called Billy.

'Hi Billy, just a quick call. Did you find anything out about Gideon?'

'Aye,' replied Billy, 'you were right. Gideon was selling drugs. Cocaine, ketamine, amphetamines, a bit of hash...he wasn't a big player, but a few people I talked to knew him by reputation. Apparently, he was especially popular with quite a few celebrities.'

'Celebrities? Such as?'

Billy gave the names of a local weather forecaster, a radio DJ and a stand-up comedian. Patterson had never heard of any of them.

'So Gideon was definitely dealing?'

'Oh aye, like I say, celebrities loved him. He was known for hosting parties.'

'Parties?'

'Aye, pretty wild as well apparently. Some called him P. Giddy. Most of the dealers I talked to left him to it—said he wasn't a threat.'

'These parties. Do you know where he held them?'

'Wherever Gideon lived, I think.'

'So he held the parties at his flat?'

'Apparently.'

Patterson thought back to the flat. It was spotless; you wouldn't have thought he held parties there.

'And did Gideon hold these parties regularly?'

'As far as I know.'

'OK, Billy, thanks. How's it going with your fiancé?'

'Good, thanks. We're thinking of buying a property.'

'Really? You're certainly keeping busy. I didn't think you were that flush.'

'I'm not, but Lorraine's family has a bit of money; actually, her father's loaded.'

'Get you, eh? Well, if you find out anything more, let us know. Bye, Billy.'

Patterson put the phone down only to hear it ring again. He knew who it would be, and he was right: Dunard asking to see him.

Patterson walked up the stairs, glaring at the broken lift as he passed it, knocked on Dunard's door and entered. He was hit by an overpowering smell of eau de cologne. He immediately identified the source, the well-dressed man who had earlier popped his head round the door of the investigation room.

The man was sitting in front of Dunard's desk, and he turned round to look at Patterson and smiled. Patterson could tell he was another political figure, here, no doubt to ask how the case was going—something Dunard confirmed as soon as Patterson sat down.

'Mike, this is Stephen McDonald. Stephen is the MP for Glasgow West. He's just come to see how the case is going.' Even Dunard had a kind of weariness in his voice as he announced another visitor.

McDonald smiled, but it was a politician's smile, more for show than genuine.

'I don't want to take up your time,' said McDonald. 'I know you're very busy, and I think you're doing a sterling job, by the way, but you may have seen that this case has touched a nerve with many in my constituency…'

Patterson noticed that McDonald said 'my constituency' as if he owned the land where the peasants lived.

'… I thought I'd come down and find out for myself, how you're getting on, first hand,' the MP continued.

'Of course,' said Patterson, 'well, I can tell you we're investigating a few definite lines of enquiry at the moment. We took witness statements from the trainees yesterday, and there have been one or two interesting developments.' Patterson was, as always, reluctant to share too much information. 'We're questioning one of the trainees in particular about what they told us. Of course, there is still a chance of an extremist group being behind his murder, but so far, there is no evidence to back up that possibility, apart from a couple of letters we received. It's just been confirmed to me that Gideon had been involved in dealing drugs, so that too could also be another reason why he was murdered.'

'Excellent. It seems you have everything in hand,' McDonald said. 'What's your own personal assessment at this time, Inspector?'

Patterson was a little taken aback by having a politician actually praise him, and it took him a moment to gather his thoughts.

'…I'm not entirely sure,' said Patterson honestly. Although he still didn't entirely trust this man, he couldn't resist the opportunity to turn over some ideas in his mind and to speak those ideas out loud. 'As I said, we've found nothing to back up the extremist angle apart from the initial threatening letters. Our counter-terrorism liaison has found no evidence of a link between—'

'But surely, ' McDonald interrupted, 'If the group had received threats...'

Patterson should have known it was too good to last.

'Yes, I'm well aware of that, but as I say, so far there is no additional evidence to suggest a far-right group is linked to Gideon's murder.'

McDonald nodded and looked at Dunard before turning back to Patterson.

'OK, listen, I respect you're the Inspector and I'll take your word for it. However, there's something else I would like to bring up, and forgive me if it sounds impolite, but I'd rather be blunt with you.'

Patterson took off his glasses and pinched the top of his nose. He really wasn't in the mood for another pointless conversation with a politician. He had woken up with a wonderful sense of optimism that morning, and he was determined to hang on to it for as long as possible.

'Of course, be as blunt as you like,' said Dunard, graciously.

McDonald turned towards Dunard. 'Frankly, I wonder if Inspector Patterson is the best man to lead this investigation.'

'OK,' cut in Patterson, 'would it be impolite to ask why you don't think I am the best man to lead this investigation, or is that a silly question?'

'I'd hate for you to take this the wrong way, I understand you're an excellent officer and I'm in no way trying to undermine your credentials, god forbid, but the fact remains your demographics aren't entirely suitable.'

'My demographics? Oh, I see, you're suggesting I'm not the best person to lead this investigation because I'm a middle-aged white man, is that it? Believe it or not, I think I've already had this conversation with someone else in your line of work.'

McDonald smiled as if he were talking to a child and instantly ignored what the child said.

'Inspector, face the facts, you're in charge of the criminal investigation of a young black man who may have been the victim of a racist murder. As I've said, it's absolutely no reflection on your skills as a police officer, but frankly, my community sees someone, older, white, and they believe, rightly or wrongly, the investigation will not be handled properly.'

'OK, I'll not take offence at what you've just said, although many would, I'll just say my skin colour or my age doesn't affect how I do my job and never has done.'

'And I repeat, I'm absolutely sure that's the case,' said McDonald, 'but I was talking about the optics.'

'That's curious. I'm sure I've also heard

someone else use that phrase,' said Patterson, looking at Dunard. 'Maybe I dreamt it. Anyway, call me old-fashioned, but I'm a great believer in judging people by their actions, not how they look. For instance, and do forgive me for being blunt, you come across as a privately educated middle-aged white man yourself who has probably never had a proper job in his entire life.'

'I'm a member of parliament.'

'Exactly, and isn't that a whiff of cigar smoke I smell coming off your expensive-looking clothes? Penetrating through your overpowering, no doubt expensive eau de cologne? However, I'm sure you're good at your job—if it can be called a job—and I suppose whether you are good at your job or not has nothing to do with the colour of your skin, your expensive clothes or your expensive cigars, your eau de cologne and quite frankly I'm getting a little pissed off with politicians coming down here criticising my skin colour or my age and telling me how I should be doing my job!'

Patterson wasn't one for raising his voice, but when he did so, it was always with feeling.

'I don't see how liking cigars has got to do with anything?' the MP said quietly in a curiously hurt tone of voice.

'Again, I rest my case.' Patterson hated losing his temper because losing his temper always made him want to lose his temper even more. He knew he had to calm down, so he took a deep breath.

McDonald looked confused, but continued.

'Unfortunately, if you were in my game—'

'Your game?'

'Politics,—you'd understand that how things appear can be very important even if we would all like to live in a world where that isn't the case. The point I'm making is you appear to have nothing in common with the murder victim or the community he belonged to. A number of black community leaders have come to me with their concerns, and it's my job to listen to these concerns.'

'Mr McDonald, I can only tell you what I know. I may not be a young black man, but, if I say so myself, I'm good at what I do, and that, most of the time, is catching murderers.'

'That still doesn't change the optics.'

Patterson took another deep breath and gratefully heard Dunard interject.

'Mr McDonald,' said Dunard. 'I've every confidence in my detective inspector. There's no one else I'd rather have on this investigation than him, and I think you'll agree with me that the best way to calm this whole situation down is to find the murderer as quickly as possible. For that, we need the best detective on the case and in my opinion, DCI Patterson is the best detective I have.'

'Regardless of the optics,' mumbled Patterson.

The MP tugged at the hem of his coat. 'Yes, well, I suppose you have a point in that regard, but you said yourself you do need to find the culprit ASAP.'

'Yes, thanks for that reminder,' said Patterson. 'I'll try to speed up finding the killer for you.'

McDonald smiled again, but each smile was more strained than the previous one.

'Anyway, I've said my piece. Just find this murderer as soon as possible, will you?'

'And I'd appreciate it if you didn't give demands,' said Patterson. 'I'm sure you mean no harm by it, but you must understand it's bad optics.'

Patterson abruptly stood up, afraid he would do something he would regret. 'Now, if you'll excuse me, I've a murderer to catch.'

'Where are you off to?' asked Dunard, who, like Stephen McDonald, was surprised by Patterson getting up to leave.

'Right now, I'm off to Gideon's flat and then who knows what this middle-aged white man will do.'

With that, Patterson left the room.

CHAPTER 23

Misinformation

Patterson tried to ignore the anger he felt after meeting Stephen McDonald, yet this was outwith his control. First, his investigation room had been criticised for being white, and now he himself was being judged, again, on his skin colour. When did that become an issue? Patterson needed to get out of the station.

'Brian, want to come to Gideon's flat with me?'

'Sure, why not?' McKinnon replied, grabbing his jacket.

So Patterson headed down to the evidence room to get Gideon's keys and then headed to the car park with McKinnon by his side to drive the short distance to Gideon's flat.

'Is there any particular reason we're going there?' asked McKinnon.

'No...except that I spoke to a contact who

confirmed that Gideon was not only selling drugs but that he sometimes held parties at his flat. Only, last time I was there, I didn't get the impression parties were held there—it seemed far too clean—but maybe I missed something... You know, I've just been criticised for being white.'

'For being white?'

'The local MP, Stephen something-or-other, said that, in his words, it's bad optics for me to be in charge of Gideon's murder investigation because I'm a middle-aged white man investigating the murder of a black man.'

'That's plain daft.'

'I know, but he still managed to annoy me. You know, I bet he's putting pressure on Dunard right now to have me replaced. There's already been another politician at the station trying to do the same thing. The thing is, at this moment in time, I'm not sure I would object to being bumped.'

'Just get on with your job, sir. You know, a journalist approached me this morning while I was out and asked me questions about the case. Kept going on about extremists. I referred her to the media department. They really are making a big hullabaloo about it. I know there are possibly racial elements, but they're making out that the Ku Klux Klan is roaming the streets.'

'Tell me about it. I guess the best thing we can do is find the murderer as soon as we can.'

'Aye, as always,' said McKinnon, looking out of the side window.

'How's Georgina, by the way?' asked Patterson. Patterson was fond of McKinnon's wife.

'Georgina? Fine, same as usual, just getting on with everything. I don't know how I'd cope without her sometimes. She's been such a support, especially these last few months.'

'Well, just appreciate every day you have with her. I guess you were lucky enough to meet the right woman.'

'I guess I was.'

Patterson turned right into Crow Road.

'I saw you with Inspector Pearce earlier,' said McKinnon. 'What do you make of her?'

'She seems all right. She's good at her job, at least I think she is.'

'And she hasn't found any evidence linking any far-right group to Gideon's murder?'

'None. She's still checking, but it's quite possible those letters may be entirely unconnected to Gideon's murder.'

'Well, if she's right, at least that cuts down the possibilities behind Gideon's murder, though I'm not sure the press will be too pleased.'

'Aye,' said Patterson, turning the car into Gideon's street. 'Which is another reason why I want to see Gideon's flat again. This drug angle may well be significant, as I've always thought.'

They exited the car, and Patterson let himself into the stairwell with the fob.

'I saw Gideon's car, by the way, nice.'

'Aye,' said Patterson, 'although it didn't cough up anything significant evidence wise.'

'You haven't been here before, have you?' Patterson asked McKinnon as he opened the front door to Gideon's flat.

'No, can't say I have.'

They both walked in through the front door, and McKinnon was immediately impressed.

'Wow, nice place. I wouldn't mind having a place like this myself if I were single.'

'Yes, but I doubt even that for yourself, you'd struggle to keep it this clean.'

They walked through to the living room.

'See,' said Patterson, 'that's what I don't understand. The place is pristine, and my contact said Gideon used to hold wild parties here. So how come it's so clean?'

'So, what are you thinking?'

'I'm not sure. Have a look around and see

if you find anything. I know it's already been searched, but maybe they missed something.'

Has this place been dusted for prints?' asked McKinnon.

'Aye,' said Patterson, 'there were quite a few, and those we did find didn't bring up anyone significant, along with a significant number of unidentified prints.'

Patterson and McKinnon walked around, looking in drawers and cabinets, under the bed and in the bathroom cabinet. There was nothing of real interest. Patterson opened a cupboard in the hallway. It had a couple of mops, brushes, and lots of cleaning products, as well as similar items for polishing and freshening the house.

'Maybe, this explains how it's so clean,' said McKinnon as he came over and looked in the cupboard. 'Gideon might just have been a good housekeeper.'

'Possibly,' said Patterson. 'OK, come on, let's get back to the station.'

Walking back down the stairs, a neighbour came out of a flat on the second floor.

He was a slim, well-dressed man in his late thirties.

'Oh, hello,' he said, taken by surprise at seeing the two officers coming down the stairs. 'Are you the police?'

'Is it that obvious?' said McKinnon.

'Yes,' the man said, smiling. 'What with all that's gone on with the murder of Gideon.' He locked his front door. 'Have you found who did it yet?'

'We're still making enquiries,' said Patterson. 'Did you know Gideon well?'

'I can't say well, I talked to him now and then, only on passing, though. He seemed pleasant enough. Still terrible to think what happened.'

The three men slowly walked down the stairs together, talking as they went.

'He was here about six months, is that right?' asked McKinnon

'About that, I think, yes. He was such a good neighbour. Never any trouble.'

'What about the parties? You must be glad there is less noise now?' asked Patterson.

'Parties? I don't believe Gideon had parties, at least I didn't hear anything. He had the odd visitor or two, but I don't know anything about parties.'

'I must have been given the wrong information then,' said Patterson. 'I was told Gideon liked to have a party or two.'

The man shook his head. 'Not that I'm

aware of.'

The three of them stopped on the bottom landing.

'And there hasn't been any trouble with Gideon?' asked McKinnon.

Again, the man shook his head. 'No, he was the ideal neighbour. Quiet, never any trouble,' the man said. 'Listen, I'm sorry, I have to get going. Good luck with catching whoever did it.' The man rushed out through the main door as McKinnon and Patterson paused on the ground floor.

'Well, it seems I was indeed given the wrong information. It sounds like Gideon was a perfectly good neighbour who didn't like to party,' said Patterson.

Patterson and McKinnon walked out of the close and, as they reached the pavement, a woman holding a notepad rushed up to them. A small man was beside her, taking photographs.

'DCI Patterson? Rachel Murray, *Daily Chronicle*, do you have any updates on the murder of Gideon Semanyo?'

Patterson shook his head. 'No, I'm afraid not. If you get in touch with the media department, they'll tell you all you need to know.'

'Have you not made any progress in finding the far-right extremists reputedly behind the murder of Gideon Semanyo?'

Patterson brushed past her. 'I believe Chief Inspector Dunard will be holding a press conference later.'

Patterson walked around to the driver's side of the car, and McKinnon, hearing the car doors click open, quickly bent down and got in the passenger seat.

'What do you have to say to the African community who say they're living in fear?' Patterson didn't answer, which prompted another question. 'Have you nothing to say to those concerned that the police aren't treating this murder seriously due to the victim's ethnicity?'

'We treat every investigation with the same thoroughness,' said Patterson as he got into the car beside McKinnon and locked the doors. The reporter continued to ask muffled questions outside.

Driving away, Patterson turned to McKinnon. 'Was that the same reporter who cornered you this morning?'

'No, a different one. I wonder how they knew to find us there?'

'Luck, I suppose, unless they followed us from the station. We'll need to be more vigilant in future.'

'Aye,' agreed McKinnon as the two officers

headed back to Partick station.

CHAPTER 24

What are the Chances?

Back at the station, Patterson walked up the stairs and knocked on Dunard's door. Without waiting for a reply, he entered.

Dunard looked up. 'Mike, any news?'

'Nothing major. I've just been to Gideon's flat again. I was told parties were held there and, presumably, that was where a lot of drug dealing took place. However, as I thought before, if he did hold parties at his flat, they must have been very low-key affairs.'

'Why do you say that?' asked Dunard.

'For one thing, the place was immaculate,' said Patterson as he sat down. 'You would expect to see cigarette burns on the carpet or drink stains here and there, or other little signs. However, there was none of that, and when I was going out, I bumped into a neighbour who said he was unaware of any parties being held there.

As I say, it could be that the parties were low-key, but anyway...'

'After you left, Stephen McDonald again asked for you to be replaced.'

'I thought he might, and what did you say?'

'What do you think? I told him where to go. I said there was absolutely no question of that happening.'

Patterson silently questioned if this was the case, but gave Dunard the benefit of the doubt.

'What I don't understand,' said Dunard, 'is if Gideon was making money from his drug dealing, why would he go on this training program?' asked Dunard.

'It's good cover. Although his asylum claim was settled, he would still want to keep his nose clean, no pun intended. Training to be a catering assistant on a program run by the DSS, signing on, while still being able to do his dealing on the side, was ideal for him.'

'And you still think dealing drugs could be a factor in why he was murdered?'

'It's a distinct possibility. Yes, I know we now have Mary's confession that she was in the toilet around the time Gideon was murdered. However, putting that aside for the moment, drugs are definitely another possible motive for murder. Although apparently, according to my source, the volume of drugs Gideon was selling was not substantial enough to bother any bigger players.'

'So what's your next move?'

'Not sure to be honest. We're still gathering as much information as possible about the other trainees, including Mary, in case we've missed anything. Along with the drugs angle, a trainee being responsible is still the most likely scenario for Gideon's murder, in my view. As I say, though, proving that is another matter.'

'Well, I hope you find something soon. The press are constantly on my back. Believe it or not, I'm now having to deny that we're not treating this case seriously.'

'I know. As I was leaving Gideon's flat with McKinnon earlier, a journalist accused me of the same thing.'

'How's Moses fitting in, by the way?'

'Fine, he seems a very capable young man, that's what I wanted to talk to you about. I was surprised by him being transferred to my team.'

'Why?'

'Hasn't it always been the unwritten rule that if someone is being considered for my team, you run it by me first? Isn't that how we always do it?'

'It was just the way it worked out, this time. I have a good friend in the Met who contacted me. He said he had an excellent officer who wanted to transfer to Glasgow ASAP and wondered if I'd be interested. I did some quick checks, and Moses was indeed highly regarded. So, I said yes.'

'He contacted you? Your friend in the Met? You didn't contact him?'

'No.'

'Nevertheless, you've always run a candidate by me first in the past. After all, it is my team he's being transferred to. I thought I always got final say.'

'I know, but it just so happened there wasn't time.'

'Why the rush?'

'Moses wanted a transfer to Glasgow, but there were a few other divisions he could have gone to. Word gets around quickly. You know how it is.'

'Really?'

'OK. Out with it, Mike. Just what are you getting at?'

'What I'm getting at is it seems a bit of a coincidence that one day we had Councillor McKenzie in here complaining about my investigation team being all white, and then, lo and behold, a few days later, I arrive to find a new member has been added to my team, fast-tracked apparently, who just happens to be black.'

'I consider it fortunate. You said yourself, Moses appears to be an excellent officer. I don't see what the issue is.'

'The issue is you still didn't run it by me first. I should always have the final say, no matter how big the rush.'

'OK, so I took an executive decision. We had the opportunity to gain a very good officer for our team, so I took it. I am the Chief Superintendent, in case you've forgotten.'

'That's not the point.'

'What is the point?'

Patterson sighed.

'Come on, out with it,' Dunard encouraged.

'Frankly, I don't like the idea of an officer being assigned to my team, possibly based on the colour of their skin.'

'Oh come on, Mike, don't be ridiculous. I told you the circumstances; it's just coincidence.'

'Coincidence? Listen, if we start recruiting officers based on their physical appearance rather than ability, then we will soon have a much weaker team.'

'That's not going to happen.'

'Isn't it?' said Patterson, standing up. 'I certainly hope not. With all due respect, next time, if you find an officer who wants to be transferred to my team, you run it by me first. Otherwise, you'll have to find a new DCI of whatever colour you prefer to replace me with.'

Patterson left the office before Dunard had a chance to reply.

CHAPTER 25

Bridge Over the River Kelvin

In addition to formal statements being taken from the trainees, statements were also obtained from the liaison officer, Siobhan Sutherland, the caretaker, Jim McLintock, and the kitchen manager, Eddie Collins; however, no new revelations were made. One person left to be interviewed was Alistair Carmichael, the team leader.

As he couldn't attend during the week, arrangements were made for him to come in on Saturday afternoon. Patterson said he would do the interview as it would give Simpson and Pettigrew Saturday afternoon off. Although Alistair had left the café at midday the previous Friday, Patterson had a number of questions regarding the café itself which he wanted to ask Alistair.

In the meantime, Patterson spent Saturday morning catching up on household chores, paying bills, and attending to other general home duties he had neglected. He inadvisedly went online and saw the same-themed stories about the Bunhouse Murder and who might be responsible. The Ku Klux Klan had gone slightly down the pecking list of likely culprits, but other armed lynch mobs had similarly risen up the rankings. Patterson was surprised it was still a newsworthy story, though it seemed politicians were still poking the fire.

An anti-racism march had been organised by Gillian McKenzie that Saturday, starting at Kelvin Walkway and ending at George Square. There were still questions being asked in the media about Partick police station and Police Scotland in general, and how endemic institutional racism was in the force. Dunard had done his best to protect Patterson, but he was still being cited in various articles as an example of an outdated policeman in an outdated police force that wasn't up to handling modern-day issues.

Patterson knew he had to just ride it out. Yet, he couldn't help occasionally looking out of the window to see if any journalists were outside his house. So far, there hadn't been, and he could only hope that would continue.

Patterson thought again about how it appeared that the press almost wished there was a far-right connection to Gideon's murder, hoping that some extremist organisation would claim responsibility and justify their all-in headlines. Upon reflecting on extremism, Patterson's thoughts turned to Annabelle Pearce.

Maybe he had been too hard on Pearce when he first met her. She was all right, really, seemed like a nice person, give or take. He would go as far as to say he kind of liked her, even if he didn't know why. Still, she did seem OK—nice even. He wondered if she would be in the station that afternoon.

Patterson decided to make the most of his morning off and have a nap. Waking up forty minutes later, he got off the settee and set off for the station just after midday. Arriving, he popped along to Pearce's office to say hello, but was disappointed to see she wasn't there. He realised she must have the weekend off. Just before 2 pm, Patterson came down from his office, met with team leader Alistair Carmichael, and led him to Interview Room One.

As they walked along, Patterson studied the man who was in charge of the trainees. He was quite commanding in his manner. He was slim, walked with a straight back, and had a keen sense of style. He looked fit, like an ex-marine who still took care of himself.

Once they had settled, Patterson began.

'As I mentioned before, Alistair, this is a formal statement following up on what you said on Monday. I know you left the café at midday last Friday, but there are a few aspects of the investigation that I'm not quite sure about, and I would like to clarify them. You, as the team leader, may be better equipped than most to help me clear up some matters.'

'Of course, if there is any way I can help, I'll be glad to do so.' Alistair seemed genuinely willing to help.

'First of all, we believe Gideon was buying and selling drugs outside of the café. In fact, our sources confirm that this was the case. That said, we also suspect that this drug dealing overlapped with Gideon's time at the café, specifically, that may be why he often went into the disabled toilet, to make phone calls and the like. I'm particularly interested in this because I believe his drug dealing could be linked to his murder. I assure you that we're not trying to get anyone into trouble; we just want to know what was going on in case it could help us find Gideon's murderer. Were you aware of Gideon dealing drugs?'

Alistair shifted in his seat and then leaned forward, resting his arms on the table.

'Gideon was a good guy.'

'That's not what I asked you.'

'Yeah, I knew. Everyone knew. I warned him about it countless times. I said to him, "If I catch you making phone calls dealing drugs again, you're off this program."

'You actually heard him on the phone doing drug deals?'

'Oh aye, he was always arranging meets and setting up deals. He even met people in the function room. I wasn't having any of it. I told him that if he didn't pack it in, I would tell the DSS and get him thrown off the course.'

'What did he say to that?'

'He always promised he would stop, but then I would find him sneaking off into the toilet to make his phone calls again. Did my head in, to be honest.'

'You say he even met people in the function room to deal drugs?'

'Yeah, you can access the function room from the street.'

'But as I understand it, you need to push in a code beside the door so that the alarm doesn't go off.'

'I know. Gideon knew the code.'

'Gideon knew the code? How?'

'Search me, but he did. I caught him in the act a couple of times. One time, he was handing over a small package in exchange for money to this sleazy-looking git, and another time, I walked in and he was tapping in the code to cancel the alarm. Some guy was waiting outside. I swear I kept warning Gideon about it, and frankly, I mean, I know it sounds bad in a way, but if he wasn't murdered, then I would have definitely got him thrown off the course. Definitely. He was a good kid, but trouble, my God, he was trouble.'

'Alistair, it sounds like you should have told someone about this a long time ago.'

'I know, I know, but…'

'But what?'

Like I say, I was doing everything I could not to get the wee guy in trouble; he was a good kid.'

'To be honest, Alistair, the more I hear about Gideon, I'm not sure I would describe him as a good kid. I would go with your other description, trouble.'

Patterson thought for a moment about what he'd just been told.

'When was the last time you walked in on Gideon dealing drugs in the function room?'

'About a couple of weeks ago?'

'Tell me exactly.'

'Not that much to tell. Like I say, I walked in just as Gideon was handing over a small grey packet with one hand, and this guy was putting a load of notes in Gideon's other hand. I couldn't have timed my entrance better. In flagrante delicto, as they say in Japan. Gideon quickly ushered the guy out the door and came over to me, saying it was just a friend. Gideon could be a right charmer when he wanted to be. Still, I said to him, 'OK, that's it, Gideon. If I catch you in here one more time, you're out the door,' and I would have done it too, honest to God.'

'What did this guy look like, the guy who came into the function room?'

'Just like your typical druggie. Acne, greasy black hair. Skinny as hell. A definite user.'

'And you hadn't seen him before?'

'Nah, each time I saw Gideon with someone—'

'Each time? How many times were there?'

Alistair shrugged and looked down at the table. 'A few...listen, do you really want me to go to my superiors and say a black kid in my training program was dealing drugs? Gideon would just deny it and I'd be out on my arse as soon as I opened my mouth.'

'Not necessarily.'

'Aye, necessarily. You know fine well that was what would happen. I'd be branded a racist and never be able to work again. That's the way it is. Still, even so, I swear I was going to say something, but well, obviously, events took a different turn.'

Patterson sighed. This was a new development that could have a strong bearing on the case. Gideon knew the alarm code for the door and let druggies into the function room. Could it have been one of them who strolled across to the toilet and murdered Gideon? A deal gone bad? But then, how did he get the knife from the kitchen? It seemed the more Patterson tried to whittle down the number of potential murderers in this case, the larger the number grew.

'I thought some other trainees went into the function room from time to time,' asked Patterson.

'Aye, on breaks n' that. Gideon always timed it so he met someone when it was empty. The other trainees would usually be in the kitchen.'

As Alistair wasn't at the café on Friday afternoon, there wasn't anything Patterson needed to ask specifically about that time, but he was still curious about the café.

'When I last spoke to you, Alistair, you gave me the impression that everyone was happy to be on this training program. Is that really the case?'

'I'd say so; they all know how lucky they are to be on this scheme. They're learning something which will stand them in good stead for the future, more or less.'

'See, that's what I'm talking about. When I first heard about this café and the training program, I was under the impression that the trainees would be doing the refurbishing. Yet, it turns out the refurbishment is being done by tradespeople, and the trainees are learning how to make sandwiches and coffee.'

'Nothing wrong with that. There's always a demand for people making sandwiches and coffee.'

'Of course, but that's not my point. It's kind of misleading, is it not? As you say, there's nothing wrong with making sandwiches or coffee, but it's that, for instance, the news reports I watched, this refurbishment gave the impression it was being carried out by the trainees.'

'Well, see, that was the original idea, but there was a change of plan. The plan was, at first, for the trainees to refurbish the café and learn skills like you said—carpet fitting, painting and decorating, plastering, and what have you—but there just wasn't time. See, this course was supposed to have started last November, but it was delayed. If the trainees had started doing the refurbishment in March, trying to learn skills at the same time, then it would never have been finished in time for the July opening, so they scrapped that idea and brought in professionals to do the work every Tuesday and Wednesday when the trainees were at college.'

'And meanwhile, the trainees get shoved on to how to make sandwiches and coffee?'

'Nothing wrong with that,' said Alistair indignantly once more.

'Anyway,' said Patterson, 'as I was saying, you told me everyone was happy to be on this training program, but I've heard a few of them say they are only here because if they didn't come, they would lose their dole money.'

'Ah, so you've been talking to Andy?'

'Andy McLean? Why do you say that?'

'Because Andy is always complaining. Always. Saying he's only here cos he had to be.'

'Isn't that the truth, though?'

'Maybe.'

'Andy said a lot of the trainees were also unhappy, not just him, so much so that you had to give them a pep talk to try to keep them onside.'

'Maybe.'

'Maybe?'

'OK, maybe at the beginning there was some discontent. Actually, there was a lot of discontent, aye, and maybe I did have to give them a little pep talk.'

'What was the discontent about?'

'Some were no' happy because they were working for the DSS, and yes, maybe some were unhappy because they felt they were being forced to do this training scheme. Plus...'

'Plus what?'

'Well, like you said, some were promised they would be learning proper trades like painting and decorating and things, not making sandwiches and coffee.'

'And were they promised that?'

'Maybe.'

'So why tell me differently? Why would you say that everyone was happy with the training program?'

'Cos that's the official line. The head honchos said to me "If anyone asks, just say everyone is delighted to be here."'

'But the reality is much different?'

'It's better now. Like I said, I gave a wee speech to try and raise their spirits.'

'And that changed everyone's mind, did it? Just like that?'

'Maybe.'

'So what was the wee speech you gave?'

'I just tried to get them onside, know? I mean, I was in the same boat as them, just about. See...listen, bear with me here, but do ye know that film The Bridge on the River Kwai?'

Patterson wondered where Alistair was going with this, but decided to let it ride.

'Aye,' said Patterson. 'One of my favourite films, as it happens.'

'Me too. Well, I asked Andy what his problem was, and he said he didn't want to work for the enemy. I asked him what he was on about working for the enemy, and he said the DSS are the enemy, because, by extension, they're part of the government. He said working at the café was nothing but a glorified PR exercise for the DSS and the government.'

'He's got a point, hasn't he?'

'Of course, he's got a point, but like I said, it's my job to keep the trainees onside, so anyway, I started going over what Andy was saying about working for the enemy, and it got me thinking.'

'About The Bridge on the River Kwai?'

'About The Bridge on the River Kwai.'

Patterson took a sip of his coffee, trying to control his urge to tell Alistair to get to the point since he knew it would be better if Alistair got there in his own time.

'Go on.'

'Well, you know how the Alec Guinness character, forget his name—'

'Colonel Nicholson.'

'Aye, him. Colonel Nicholson. You know how Colonel Nicholson says that what we'll do is work with the Japanese, rather than against them. We'll build them the best bridge they've ever seen. Show them the best of British, and do you know why?'

'Why?' asked Patterson, trying to remember what the original question was.

'We'll do our best work because we're doing this for us, not them. We're not working for the DSS, the government, or anyone else but ourselves. People will come to this café for years to come and say that a group of unemployed people from Partick Jobcentre did that training program here.'

'To make sandwiches and coffee? Sorry, you've lost me. I don't get what this has to do with The Bridge on the River Kwai.'

'Because the DSS are the Japanese. We're the captive soldiers, and I'm the one who says to them, You're doing this for yourselves, not the Japanese; I mean the DSS. Now do you understand?'

'Almost, so you're saying the DSS are the Japanese, this café is the Bridge on the River

Kwai, and…you're Alec Guinness?'

'Precisely. I said, You're doing this for your own self-worth, for your own self-esteem, to show the world just what you are capable of; is that not worth working for?'

'OK, I get it. Did it work?'

'Not really, but ye get what I was trying to say, though, don't ye. I like to think it helped a little bit for a few days at least, but if I'm being honest, that apathy slowly crept back in again. With people like Andy McLean about, it's always going to be an uphill battle to get them onside.'

Patterson thought for a moment. 'Well, it's certainly an interesting analogy–A sort of Bridge on the River Kelvin.'

'Ha,' said Alistair, delighted. 'Exactly. I never thought of that. Bridge on the River Kelvin, that's exactly what I'm saying.'

Patterson smiled as he thought some more.

'You do know, at the end of the film, The Bridge on the River Kwai, the bridge gets blown up.'

'Aye, of course I know. How?'

'I was just thinking if you should really be happy with that analogy?'

'Why shouldn't I be?'

'Well, apart from the bridge getting blown up, if you're Alec Guinness, doesn't he also die at the end?'

The team leader thought for a moment before deciding to laugh, but it was a short laugh as if he wasn't sure what he was laughing at.

Patterson smiled. 'Anyway, I think that's all we need. I'll escort you outside.'

Alistair Carmichael followed Patterson and exited the building, still lost in thought.

CHAPTER 26

Tea and Biscuits

The next day, Patterson arrived at the station still slightly confused by what Alistair Carmichael had told him the previous day. However, he had determined to watch The Bridge on the River Kwai again sometime soon.

Walking into the station foyer, he couldn't believe the lift still hadn't been fixed. He hadn't even seen the lift engineers for a couple of days. It was as if they had given up. He would need to speak to Dunard about it.

A couple of hours after he had walked upstairs and been in his office, Pearce entered.

'Annabelle, I didn't think you'd be in today.'

'Oh, why's that?'

'I didn't see you yesterday. I assumed you were off the whole weekend.'

'No, unfortunately not, I'm in all day today, still checking up on things.'

'Ah, well... so anything to report?'

'No, I'm afraid not, though I think I can say almost certainly now that those letters didn't come from any extremist organisation I know. Plus, the more I ask questions of my contacts, the more I also believe the far-right almost certainly has nothing to do with the murder of Gideon.'

'Really? Well, that's something,' said Patterson. 'As you know, I was always more inclined to think it was one of the other trainees we should be looking at. The problem is that, in effect, everyone is a suspect. At least all the trainees who were at the café that Friday afternoon.'

'I know, though I can also tell you that nothing has come up in our files to suggest that any of the trainees are linked to the far-right.'

'Have you had a chance to look at the witness statements?'

'Almost all. It seems that Mary is now in the frame more than anyone else.'

'Yes,' said Patterson, 'though I interviewed Alistair Carmichael yesterday, and he said Gideon let some people, possibly drug users, into the function room.'

'You're kidding?'

'I'm afraid not, and Gideon knew the code to cancel the door alarm.'

'So...if Gideon did leave the café on Friday

and just wasn't seen—'

'Actually, another trainee, Umar, said he saw Gideon leave the café.'

'In that case, even more so, if Gideon did leave the café, is it feasible he could have re-entered the café during the weekend?'

'Possibly, but he would still have to have had keys for the door.'

'If he knew the code,' said Pearce, 'then I wouldn't put it past him to have keys as well. He seems a bit of a slippery character, does Gideon.'

'That's putting it mildly,' said Patterson. 'Anyway, I'm going to see a couple of the trainees at their homes today. Looking over the statements, I'd like to ask them a few additional questions.'

'Oh, who's that?'

'Andy McLean and Umar Olowe. Alistair Carmichael, who, as I was saying, I interviewed yesterday, said Andy McLean was very disgruntled with the training program. I just want to check if that's really the case, and if it is, I wonder if Andy being disgruntled could be a factor in all this somehow.'

'How?'

'Not sure, just a feeling.'

'And Umar?'

'Like I say, Umar is insistent that he saw Gideon leave the café. However, he's the only one who says so, and we have no CCTV of Gideon outside the café after Friday. I just want to gauge for myself if Umar is genuinely mistaken or if he's lying, and if so, why?'

'Would you mind if I tagged along?'

'No, I'd be delighted. Are you ready to go now?'

'Two seconds, just let me grab my things and I'll meet you downstairs.'

Patterson waited in his car as he watched Pearce come out of the station entrance. As he watched her approach the car, he had to admit she looked after herself. On first meeting her, he had thought she was in her late thirties, but was surprised to learn she was in her mid-forties. She smiled at Patterson as she saw him sitting in his car, and he smiled back, gave a little wave and then felt daft for giving a little wave.

Andy McLean lived in a semi-detached, pebble-dashed ground-floor flat just off Dumbarton Road in Yoker. It was a pleasant street with well-kept gardens and an air of respectability. An elderly man was washing his car, lifting a large sponge from a bucket and covering the bodywork with loving, soapy caresses. Knocking on Alistair's front door, Patterson noticed gnomes in the garden, still intact, still there, another tick in the street respectability box.

As with Umar Olowe, Patterson had contacted Andy earlier to say he would be arriving that day. Andy McLean opened the door and greeted the two officers with a broad smile as if they were family members arriving for Sunday lunch.

'Come in, come in,' Andy said. 'I thought you'd never get here,' he beckoned them inside, and they entered, finding themselves in a carpeted hallway that had a bookcase, flowers and an air of niceness about it. 'First door on the left,' Andy said, and the two officers successfully followed the directions, walking past a bright, clean kitchen.

They now found themselves in a living room also full of niceness. The TV was on mute, but playing a war film, as Patterson and Pearce sat down on the light green, flower-patterned settee.

'Now, what would you like, tea, coffee, a soft drink perhaps?' Andy asked, clasping his hands together as if to say, 'Let's get this party started.'

'I'll have a tea if you're offering,' said Patterson, and Pearce said she'd have the same.

'One sugar and milk,' she added.

'The same,' said Patterson, and the two

officers glanced at each other as if they had just discovered they shared the same birthday.

'Great, two teas coming up,' said Andy, and he disappeared out of the door to be followed by the sound of kitchen cupboard doors opening and closing and the clinking of cups.

'This is nice,' said Patterson, looking around. He noticed a framed photo of a middle-aged woman taking pride of place on the side-board and thought of his own framed photo of Stephanie on his sideboard. He had read that Andy's wife had died of cancer a few years back. How many wives' or husbands' photos stood on their remaining partners' sideboards? Patterson wondered.

Pearce got up and walked to one of the bookcases. Patterson watched as she lightly fingered the spines of various books, now and then venturing to take one out to look at further.

Patterson turned his attention to the film, which showed soldiers pouring out of a landing craft with varying degrees of fortune. Patterson recognised the film as one that seemed to be on every Sunday afternoon.

Andy came back in with a large tray, and he gingerly placed it on the glass coffee table in front of the settee. On the tray next to the cups was a large yellow teapot, three bone China cups, and a saucer splayed with various biscuits.

'I could get used to this,' said Patterson, smiling.

'I prefer my tea out of a pot,' said Andy, 'it gives a much better flavour.'

Patterson was about to reply that he did too when Pearce interrupted.

'You like reading, Andy,' she asked.

'Aye, don't do much else nowadays if I'm honest. Most of the books I keep down here are factual. I keep my fiction books in my bedroom and the hallway.'

'What do you like to read?' Pearce asked.

'Military books, mostly, espionage, medieval history is a favourite, that sort of thing.'

'What about yersel', Inspector, are ye a reading man?'

'Yes, I am actually, I like medieval history, myself, fact and fiction. Have you read Ivanhoe?'

'Have I just. One of my favourites.'

'It's quite an eclectic mix you have here,' said Pearce, looking at the books. 'You like trains?'

'Trains?'

Pearce showed him the book she was looking through—*Twenty Great Railway Stations of Britain*.

'Oh aye, a wee bit, come and get your tea, Inspector.' Pearce came and sat down.

'Aye,' Andy continued, 'I wouldnae say I'm a trainspotter or anything like that, but I guess I like trains. A few years back, I got to ride on the Flying Scotsman —what an experience that was. Now, if there's a train gala going on somewhere, I more than likely will head to it. Anyway, how are you getting on with finding out who murdered poor Gideon?'

'Enquiries are still ongoing,' said Patterson. 'There are a few discrepancies we're trying to iron out.'

'Oh aye?'

'For one thing, there are conflicting reports about whether Gideon left the café or not. You said in your statement you didn't see him leave.'

'Naw, ah didn't see him leave. I'm not saying he didnae leave, maybe I just didnae see him leave.'

'Tell me a little about yourself, Andy,' said Pearce. She nodded towards a photo on the wall of an army emblem. 'Were you in the military?'

'Aye, Royal Engineers, we were based in Paisley, but we went all over. Northern Ireland, Cyprus and the like. I loved it—those were the best years of my life. Then I came out and got a job at Yarrows, the shipbuilders down the road, and I was laid off in 1999. I've been doing various jobs since then, nothing special; you name it, I've done it. I'm not proud—I'll do any job—but even so, I still cannae find anything at the moment. Been unemployed for nearly a year now. When they said about this training scheme, I thought, aye, why not, better than sitting round the house all day.'

'You enjoying it, then?' asked Patterson.

'It's fine for what it is. I like meeting people, and most of the trainees are all right.'

'I was talking to Alistair, you know, your team leader, and he's under the impression you hate the place.'

Andy laughed. 'Aye, well, I don't mind admitting I like to wind Alistair up now and then; he's so pompous at times, coming out with all these big speeches, as if he's Winston Churchill, when he's more like Captain Mainwaring. Ach, I know he's just doing his job.' Andy poured the tea and then offered the plate of biscuits. Both officers accepted.

'What did you think of Gideon?' asked Patterson.

'He was fine...'

'Truthfully,' added Patterson.

'Truthfully? OK, I thought he was a bit of a

tit. Didn't like him.'

'Your witness statement said you knew he dealt drugs?'

'Aye, that's one of the reasons that put me off him. I don't want anything to do with people like that. I was going to say something to someone about him, but...you know.'

'He took drugs himself,' said Patterson.

'Oh aye, I know. You could see it in his eyes. Half the time, he was as high as a kite.'

'You said you didn't see anyone go into the disabled toilet on Friday?'

'Naw, I didn't see anyone go in, that's no to say someone didn't go in.'

'What do you think of Mary?'

'Mary? Who's Mary?'

'Mary, she's about 28, dark hair, quiet.'

'Oh, the quiet lass? She never says a word. I like her, though. What are you asking about her for?'

'No reason,' said Patterson, who didn't want to give the reason. Most of all, Patterson was still curious about why Alistair had said Andy hated being on the training program. Patterson wasn't convinced it was all an act to wind Alistair up.

'So, you actually like training at the café

then?'

'Aye, I do actually, I'll be sorry when it's over.'

'I heard, though, when you first started, you were promised you'd be learning different skills from catering.'

'Aye, that's true. I was told I'd be learning carpet fitting. Ach, no matter, at my age it doesnae really make any difference.'

Patterson nodded. Andy didn't seem that bothered about being promised he'd learn other skills. Alistair must have just been convinced by Andy's act.

They chatted some more and decided it was time to leave. Patterson hadn't really learned anything new, apart from the fact that Andy seemed to be a nice guy.

They stood in the hallway, and Pearce was drawn once again to a bookcase of Andy's.

As she bent down and looked over the titles, she said, 'Are these your fiction books, then?'

'Aye, I read anything, fact, fiction, you name it.'

'Oh, you have Lord of the Rings.'

'Aye,' said Andy. 'I love Tolkien.'

'Me too,' said Patterson, 'The Hobbit and

The Silmarillion, great books.'

'They certainly are,' said Andy.

Pearce straightened up and smiled.

'Right,' said Patterson, 'thanks for your time, Andy.'

'You make a great cup of tea,' added Pearce.

'Anytime, it was nice to have a bit of company.'

'You're back at the café with the other trainees a week on Monday, is that right?'

'Aye,' said Andy. 'Sad to say, but I can't wait.'

'OK, well, thanks again,' said Patterson.

'Bye, Andy,' said Pearce as both officers exited the house.

CHAPTER 27

Patterson and Pearce

Patterson walked back to his car with Pearce by his side.

'Seems a nice man,' said Patterson as he unlocked the car and Pearce got inside. Pearce was strangely quiet.

'What?' asked Patterson. 'What are you thinking?'

'Nothing...it's just that...I dunno, there was just something not right.'

Patterson hesitated to switch on the car engine.

'Not right? Not right about what?'

'Not sure. Just something.'

Patterson wondered what she was on about as he eventually switched on the engine and drove away.

'What? Was there something wrong with

your tea?' Patterson asked as little splashes of rain hit the windscreen. He glanced at Pearce. 'You're not thinking Andy could have anything to do with the murder of Gideon, are you?'

'Don't you? You said earlier that everyone who was in that café on Friday afternoon is a suspect.'

'Yes, but—'

'But what? That means Andy is a suspect just like everyone else. I just felt he was lying about something.'

'Lying about what? Annabelle, I know what I said, and you're right, everyone's a suspect, and I had my suspicions about him before, but now...I just don't believe Andy McLean is responsible for Gideon's murder.'

'Why?'

'Why what?'

The rain started to fall to a degree that Patterson had to switch on the windscreen wipers.

'What's changed your mind? Because Andy makes a nice cup of tea? Because he seems like a nice guy?'

'No, of course not. Listen, Annabelle, I've been in this business for a long time, and you develop a sense for these things. Andy just doesn't come across as a murderer.'

'Oh come on, you're not seriously going by that, Mike, are you? In my experience, and you must know this yourself, bad people usually have a great knack for hiding they're bad people. I know I may not have been in this business as long as you have, but I also have a feel for who's guilty and who's not.'

'OK. So what could possibly have given you the idea that Andy McLean is Gideon's murderer?'

Patterson put the car into gear as the rain fell even heavier, and the windscreen wipers worked even harder as Patterson turned back onto Dumbarton Road.

Pearce shrugged. 'I don't know. Just little things.'

'Little things?'

'Little things,' repeated Pearce.

'Such as?'

'For one thing, he's ex-military.'

'Oh, of course. Ex-military.' Patterson shook his head, smiling. 'That's a fairly broad church, Annabelle. Forgive me for saying, but I would need more than that to make an arrest.'

'Then there were his books.'

'What about his books?'

'His interest in trains.'

Patterson turned to Pearce again as they

drove slowly along the road. The road was quite busy for a Sunday afternoon.

'Please tell me you're not serious.'

'As I said, Mike, I may not have been in this business as long as you have, as you put it, but in my time I've found these little things can be signs.'

Both officers were now speaking louder to each other.

'What, so someone has a book on railway stations and that makes him an extremist? You know, I'm beginning to worry about our security services.'

'As you said, you just get a feel for these things.'

'I've got that book,' said Patterson.

'What book?'

'Twenty Great Railway Stations of Britain, it's actually very good.'

'You've got that book?'

'I've got that book. Why wouldn't I have that book? I was working on a case a couple of years ago involving the Glasgow subway. I began researching old trains in the area, and I found it to be very interesting. I've had an interest in trains ever since.' He looked at Pearce. 'You can turn me in now if you want. It's a fair cop.'

'That's different.'

'How is it different? The point is, you're saying Andy is a suspect because he owns a certain book about railway stations.' Despite himself, Patterson couldn't help raising his voice even more. 'Tell me, were there any other little signs that made you think Andy could have something to hide?' Patterson couldn't help keep the sarcasm out of his voice.

'He had British flags in his kitchen.'

'Er, I think that's called bunting, Annabelle, bunting. Which I suspect means he is not so much an extremist but a fan of the Great British Bake Off, or, I suspect, his late wife was.'

'The Great British Bake Off?'

'You've not heard of the Great British Bake Off? It's a cooking programme. ...You know we should be having this conversation the other way around.'

The rain stopped as quickly as it had begun, and Patterson switched off the windscreen wipers.

'Mike,' said Annabelle in a quieter, controlled voice, 'of course, I'm not saying Andy is a suspect just because he has read a certain book or has British flags up in the kitchen, but these small indications can often, in retrospect, and in my experience, be significant when you add them up. Andy is ex-military, he's a widower, he has traditional hobbies like trains, and he's obviously proud enough of his country to hang British flags up.'

'Bunting. It was bunting, Annabelle. OK, you've got me. Andy is obviously a raging extremist. Of course he is. I'm surprised I didn't see it before. We should go back later and catch him in the act of watching Antiques Roadshow.'

Patterson looked across at Pearce, who glared back at him, and for a reason neither could explain, both started laughing.

'Do you really like Lord of the Rings?' asked Pearce.

'I do, and I'm warning you now, if you start saying Lord of the Rings is extremist, you'll be walking back to the station. I assume you're not a fan?'

'Never read it. I liked the films, though.'

'Ah ha, it's all coming out now. Oh, here it is,' said Patterson, as he saw the street on which Umar lived.

Umar lived in a five-storey block of flats just off Dumbarton Road in Whiteinch. As Patterson pulled up, he saw a group of men with a Middle Eastern appearance standing outside the tower block. Other men with scattered appearances were also scattered around the street.

'This looks nice,' said Pearce in a slightly sarcastic tone Patterson would be proud of.

As the two officers exited the car, they were the centre of attention for everyone around the tower block and in the street. Patterson could feel the animosity towards them, and although he was used to it, he wondered if Pearce was.

Pearce, though, seemed unperturbed, and as Patterson walked forward and pressed the intercom buzzer for number seventeen, Patterson could now tell the unspoken intimidation was nothing more than bravado.

A loud voice came over the intercom. 'Hello?'

'It's inspectors Patterson and Pearce.' The door buzzed open.

'Patterson and Pearce,' said Pearce, 'we sound like a cop show.'

'Maybe we are,' said Patterson as he pulled open the door for his colleague. He still wondered how serious she was about Andy McLean. Did she really think he could be a suspect because of a book he read?

Inside the foyer of the tower block, it wasn't as bad as some others Patterson had visited. For one thing, the lift worked, and after the short journey to the third floor, Patterson and Pearce exited onto the landing.

'This brings back memories,' said Patterson.

'What does?'

'The lift working,' said Patterson.

On the third floor, the block of flats didn't seem as nice; the claustrophobic landing had a fair amount of litter and some curious, unhygienic smells. Cries and shouts were heard from both above and below.

Patterson chapped the door as he watched Pearce firmly holding on to her handbag.

Umar slightly opened the door, looking both officers over before opening the door fully. Inside the flat was pleasant enough, neither immaculately tidy nor messy. Umar directed them into the living room.

There was a large TV which was switched off, and a games console lay on the floor. However, the small flat was pleasant enough, though there was a distinct fusty smell which could have easily been dispelled by opening a window during the last couple of months.

Patterson and Pearce sat down on the settee. Patterson could see straight away that Umar seemed nervous.

'There's nothing to worry about, Umar. This is Inspector Pearce, by the way. She's a trainee, I'm just showing her the ropes.'

Pearce turned to Umar. 'He's joking, Umar. I'm helping with the enquiry.' She looked back at Patterson as she walked to the window.

That's a lovely view you have,' said Pearce.

Umar didn't respond and instead gave Patterson a quizzical look, probably because it wasn't a lovely view, as it mostly looked over the passing dual carriageway. In fact, Umar hadn't spoken a word since the two officers arrived. He seemed to be nervously waiting for Pearce to sit down, which she duly did next to Patterson.

I know you've already given a witness statement to my colleagues,' Patterson began, 'I just want to check up on a couple of things. I believe you were good friends with Gideon.'

'The best. He was like a brother to me.' Umar's accent was strong and noticeably Nigerian.

'Did you meet through the training program?' asked Pearce.

'Kind of. I had seen him before at the job centre, but not to talk to. We got to know each other on this training program.'

Patterson was told that Umar was a bit slow, but his speech seemed fine.

'Umar, the main reason we're here,' said Patterson, 'is that you said in your witness statement that you saw Gideon leave the café. Is that still the case?'

Yes, I saw Gideon leave the café around half three.'

'And you're absolutely sure about that?' asked Pearce.

'Yes, I already told the other officer.'

'I know you told the other officer, but now you have to tell us. Did you definitely see Gideon leave the café at half three?' Pearce asked again.

There was an aggressiveness in Pearce's tone which Patterson thought could do more harm than good; nevertheless, he let her take the lead, which she seemed to do regardless of him.

'You see,' continued Pearce, 'Gideon's autopsy has confirmed he was murdered between three and five pm. Then there's the small fact that Gideon was found in the disabled toilet on Monday morning. What you say about Gideon leaving the café completely contradicts that. How do you account for that?'

Patterson could see that Pearce's questions were making Umar even more nervous, and he wanted to put Umar more at ease.

'Umar,' said Patterson, 'I assure you we're not trying to trap you in any way. We just —'

'Umar,' Pearce interrupted. 'On Friday afternoon, when you were with all the other trainees, did you sit with Gideon during the afternoon?'

Patterson still wasn't sure that Pearce's manner would encourage Umar to open up or have the opposite effect. He was also aware that Patterson and Pearce were turning into a good cop, bad cop situation, with Patterson being the good cop.

'Yes, I sit with him, although I went to the bakery to get doughnuts because Gideon bought them for everyone.'

'Why didn't Gideon go?' asked Pearce.

Umar shrugged, 'He just didn't, he asked me.'

'Oh, so Gideon asks, and you jumped,' asked Pearce, mockingly. 'Why didn't you tell him to get them himself?' Pearce's harsh tone of voice seemed to be getting harsher.

'I don't—don't know,' Umar stuttered.

'You don't know? It seems to me—'

It was Patterson's turn to interrupt. He didn't know if Pearce had realised the good cop bad cop scenario and was now overplaying her part. 'Umar, I assure you there is nothing to worry about—'If my colleague could just calm down for a moment—'

'Calm down? Inspector Patterson, the man is clearly lying or, at the very least, confused. All I want is to—'

Patterson still couldn't tell if she was acting or not. He decided she wasn't acting.

'As I said, if you could just calm down for a moment!' Pearce clearly needed to learn to control her emotions; she was doing more harm than good. Thankfully, Pearce seemed to take the advice.

'Umar,' said Pearce in a softer voice. 'I'm sorry, my colleague is right. Do you mind if I use your toilet?'

Both Umar and Patterson looked at her with suspicion.

'Yes, it's—'

'Don't tell me, I'll find it.' Pearce rose before Umar could say anything more and walked into the hallway.

Umar stared after her and heard one door open and then another. He quickly got off the settee and went into the hallway.

Patterson listened as he heard Umar say. 'That's the toilet, there.'

'Of course, it is,' said Pearce. Patterson could see Umar continue to watch as Pearce entered the toilet and closed the door. Umar stayed in the doorway waiting for Pearce to come back out, which she eventually did. Both Pearce and Umar sat back down at the same time.

'Sorry about that,' said Pearce, 'my bladder

isn't what it used to be.'

Umar and Patterson again looked at her with suspicion.

'I'm sorry, Umar,' said Pearce, 'I realise you have lost your good friend. It's just that my colleague and I really want to find out who murdered Gideon.'

'I don't know who murdered him,' said Umar.

'Of course, you don't,' said Pearce in a neutral voice.

'Umar,' said Patterson, 'Do you know why Gideon went into the disabled toilet?'

Umar shook his head.

'We believe he used to make phone calls there to do with drug dealing. You were his good friend. You must have been aware of that.'

Umar paused for a moment and decided to tell the truth. 'Yes, I know that.'

'We also know that Gideon met some clients in the function room, were you aware of that as well?'

Umar nodded. 'I know.'

'You should have told someone,' said Pearce, who had apparently decided to abandon her soft tone once again. 'Dealing drugs is illegal in this country. You also must be aware of that.

Why didn't you say anything to someone?'

Umar seemed very nervous.

'I don't want to get Gideon in trouble.'

'Oh, so—'

Patterson interrupted her raised voice once more and glared at her to try and say she wasn't helping the situation by being so aggressive.

'Umar,' said Patterson, calmly, 'If I can get back to you saying you saw Gideon leave. You stated that you saw him leave the café and start walking up Bunhouse Road. Is that right?'

'I saw him leave and walk up Bunhouse Road, yes.'

'The thing is, if he walked to the top of Bunhouse Road, we would have caught him on a camera on Argyle Street or Dumbarton Road. He isn't seen on CCTV anywhere. Plus, no one else in the café saw him leave. You're the only one. Are you absolutely certain you saw Gideon leave?'

Umar paused for a moment before saying. 'I am sure I saw him leave....Maybe I was mistaken.'

'Umar, I don't want you to say you were mistaken if you really did see him leave. I just want the truth. Nothing more. I assure you, you can say you did see him leave, or perhaps you were mistaken. We just want to know the truth.

You're now saying you could have been mistaken? You may not have seen him leave?'

'I don't know. You're confusing me.'

Patterson realised Umar had a point; he was beginning to confuse himself.

'OK, listen, I'll ask you one last time, and that will be the end of it,' said Patterson, pleased that Pearce was keeping quiet. 'Did you or did you not see Gideon leave the café?'

Umar paused for a long time. 'Maybe...I was mistaken.'

'So you didn't see him leave?'

'Then why did you say you did!' said Pearce again in a raised voice.

'I—thought—I did but, I was wrong,' said Umar quietly.

'OK. That's fine, Umar. We'll leave it there,' Patterson said, smiling. Patterson stood up quickly, followed by Pearce.

'Will you be going back to the training program at the café, when is it, a week tomorrow?'

'A week tomorrow, Monday, yes. Yes, of course, I go back, I love the cafe, everyone is so friendly. I can't wait,' Umar said with genuine excitement.

'That's good to hear,' Patterson said. 'Anyway, thanks for your time, Umar.'

'Yes, thanks for your time,' Pearce echoed, smiling warmly. Maybe she was acting after all. Patterson and Pearce left the flat.

CHAPTER 28

Lunch

Outside the flats, various men were still standing around, and once again they glared at Patterson and Pearce with animosity. To her credit, Pearce didn't seem bothered; perhaps, like Patterson, she knew it was all for show.

Once seated in the car, Pearce turned to Patterson.

'Why don't we go and grab a bite to eat? I'm starving.'

'I really should be getting back to the station, Annabelle.'

'Oh, go on, be a devil. You must be hungry yourself; the station canteen is all well and good, but let's treat ourselves to food that's actually edible.'

'You're really not impressed with Partick station, are you?'

'Apart from the coffee and the food and the lift not working, it's OK, I suppose,' said Pearce, smiling. 'Come on, I know a good café not far; it's just along Argyle Street. I'll treat you.'

'There's no need. I...' Patterson was unsure what to say. For some reason, he still couldn't figure Pearce out, but Pearce insisted.

'Go on, you old fuddy duddy. We can talk about the case. Call it a working lunch.'

This swayed Patterson's decision; it would actually be good to talk over the case.

'OK, what café are you talking about?' Patterson asked.

'It's just across from the Art Galleries.'

'I know it.' Patterson put the car into gear and headed toward it.

Soon, they arrived at the café, and it was busy as would be expected on a Sunday afternoon. Luckily, a couple were just leaving as they arrived, and they sat down at a table in the corner. Patterson ordered a sandwich, and as she shook her head at his conservative choice, Pearce ordered an all-day breakfast.

'You weren't kidding when you said you were starving, were you?' said Patterson.

'Famished,' said Pearce, and she confirmed this when the food arrived and she immediately attacked the food on the plate like she hadn't eaten in a month.

Patterson found that Pearce always took him by surprise. He didn't know if this was a good or bad thing. At first, she seemed very professional, and then he thought about how she had judged Andy McLean based on the books he was reading and the bunting in his kitchen. Then he regarded her as quite restrained, and she proceeded to interrogate Umar as if she were trying to get a confession out of a hardened criminal. Patterson then saw her as very lady-like, and here she was sitting across from him, attacking her all-day breakfast as if she were a starving trucker. Patterson found her a little unnerving, yet... anyway, as Pearce said, they could use this lunch to go over some thoughts on the case.

'So Annabelle, tell me, do you think Umar saw Gideon leave the café or not?'

'Not. I don't know what the reason is, but he's lying.'

'You think? Why, though? Why would he lie? To what end?'

'Because he was the one who murdered Gideon.' Pearce seemed pleased with Patterson's surprised reaction. 'I'm joking. I don't know. Maybe he knows who murdered Gideon and is covering for him or her. I honestly don't know,' said Pearce as she ruthlessly cut another sausage in half as if it had personally offended her and stuffed it in her mouth. 'We know the extremist angle is less likely, but the murderer could still be an individual with a racist or far-right motive, and that could still be a trainee.'

'But you said you didn't find any trainee with far-right associations.'

'That could just mean that one of the trainees with far-right leanings hasn't come to our attention yet.'

'You mean like someone who has an interest in trains and has bunting in their kitchen?'

'Perhaps,' said Pearce, as she devoured the last piece of bacon and Patterson politely nibbled at his sandwich. 'So, tell me, Inspector Patterson. What trainee has caught your attention?'

'Well, of course, there's Mary McNair. I think her saying that she went into the toilet was a spur-of-the-moment admission. If she had kept quiet, no one would have been any the wiser. The problem is proving her guilt. As I've said before, we either need to find the murder weapon or hope she somehow makes a confession. Then again, with Alistair Carmichael now saying Gideon let drug users into the function room, who's to say one of them didn't follow Gideon into the disabled toilet? I still feel Gideon's drug-dealing could be significant in some way.'

'I fear, Inspector Patterson, we're beginning to go round in circles,' said Pearce as she devoured a fried egg she had appeared to have kept till last as a treat.

'That's what I'm worrying about,' said Patterson.

Pearce pushed her plate aside, having eaten absolutely everything, and now sipped at her tea. Patterson found Pearce looking at him, resting her chin on her hands.

'What?' asked Patterson.

'Nothing. Listen, tell me to get lost if I'm being too personal, but one of the officers told me you lost your wife a couple of years ago. That must have been hard; I'm sorry.'

This change of subject took Patterson by surprise, but he took it in his stride. 'Yes, it was. Still is, in a way, but things are slowly getting better. It's true what they say about time being a great healer, in most respects.'

'Have you any children?' asked Pearce.

'Two kids, Calum and Ashleigh. What about yourself?'

'Divorced, thankfully. No kids, thankfully. It wasn't that bad a marriage, but we just drifted apart. Me into my work, him into the arms of a woman young enough to be his daughter. I'm single, always daydreaming Mr Right will waltz into my life someday, that I'll find the one, but as Feargal says, a good heart is hard to find.'

Patterson almost got the reference and silently nodded to make out he did.

'Well, I guess we had better get back to the station,' said Patterson.

'How long were you married?' asked Pearce, not moving.

'Twenty-two years. I'll get this, I'll put it on —'

'Twenty-two years? That's quite an achievement.'

'It is... Stephanie was a special woman...' Patterson stood up. 'As I say, I'll put this on expenses.'

Pearce smiled and wiped her mouth with a hankie 'I enjoyed that.'

'So I noticed,' said Patterson, smiling as he went up to the counter to pay for the meal, not sure whether he'd bother claiming it on expenses. After paying the bill, Patterson and Pearce left the café.

CHAPTER 29

All Right Really

Patterson drove back to the station with Pearce, and as she returned to her office, he spent the afternoon reviewing the witness statements once more. He couldn't help but feel that not just one person was lying, but everyone was. He didn't know why.

What Pearce said to him also hit a nerve. It was indeed as if the investigation was going round in circles. Yet, now there was one development that had his attention more than any other. Not that Mary had been in the toilet around the time Gideon was murdered. Rather, he strongly suspected that Umar was lying about seeing Gideon leave the café. Even if Umar now said that maybe he was mistaken, why did he lie in the first place? Why did he say he saw Gideon leave the café if he didn't? There must have been a reason.

With this question still foremost in his

mind, Patterson headed home from the station. He made himself a good meal—that sandwich he had for lunch really wasn't enough—and sat down on the settee. He switched on the television and watched a documentary about the Knights Templar and the Holy Grail. It seemed the far-right was everywhere.

This prompted him to think once more about the investigation; in truth, any investigation he was on was never far from his mind. He knew he had reached that point where if there weren't a breakthrough soon, the investigation would grind to a slow, slithering halt.

Maybe he was overthinking things. Maybe he had to go back to basics. Perhaps the far-right was to blame? Was his reluctance to accept this possibility due to his antipathy for politicians and the media?

In the morning, he needed to sit down with Pettigrew, Simpson, and McKinnon and review everything they had learned so far. This had often worked in the past to regain momentum in an investigation, and maybe it would work again. There was one other factor he had neglected to consider properly. If there were extremists behind the murder of Gideon, then who's to say they wouldn't murder again? If the politicians and the media were correct, then that was a distinct possibility.

Patterson really needed to find out who murdered Gideon Semanyo and fast.

His thoughts turned back to the events of that day and the time he had spent with Pearce. Patterson and Pearce. He smiled at Annabelle's little joke. Cop show indeed. He didn't realise she had a sense of humour. Always full of surprises was Pearce. Yeah, she wasn't that bad.

Although she had brushed it off lightly, Patterson sensed Annabelle's marriage and its ending had been more traumatic than she was letting on. Pearce. Annabelle Pearce. He quite enjoyed being with her. Yeah, maybe he had been too hard on her. He actually quite liked her. No, he did like her. OK, maybe he didn't agree with her work methods, trains and bunting, I mean, really, but anyway. Patterson and Pearce. He smiled at her little joke once again. He even had to admit that Patterson and Pearce might be a cop show he would watch.

CHAPTER 30

Morning briefing

The next morning, Patterson arrived at Partick station and parked the car, ready to start another week. As he walked towards the station entrance, he noticed Pearce sitting in her car. When she saw Patterson, she smiled broadly, got out and walked across to him.

'Morning, Annabelle: lost in thought? I sometimes wait in my car for a few moments to get my thoughts together.'

'Yes, just thinking. Good night's sleep?'

'Fine, you?'

'Good.'

They walked across to the station entrance together, and Patterson could see through the glass doors that the lift was still out of order.

'You know, I think they've given up on that lift.'

'Ah, well, I suppose it's no great inconvenience to take the stairs.'

'You think?' said Patterson, quietly.

They walked up the stairs and entered the main investigation room together.

Simpson was standing with Pettigrew by the coffee machine and turned to her, saying quietly, 'Aye, aye, look who it is.'

Pettigrew turned around. 'Who?'

'Patterson and Pearce,' said Simpson.

'They sound like a cop show,' said Pettigrew.

'They're getting a bit pally, are they not?' said Simpson.

'Good,' said Pettigrew, 'I hope they get even more pally. Our inspector could do with a bit of extra company in his life.'

Pearce came over to say hello to the two officers.

'Coffee?' asked Simpson, who was pouring himself a cup.

'Um, no thanks, just had one,' said Pearce.

'Good weekend?' asked Pettigrew.

'Yes, it was actually: I spent yesterday with DCI Patterson.'

Simpson and Pettigrew glanced at each

other.

'Yes,' continued Pearce, 'he was interviewing Andy McLean and Umar Olowe, so I tagged along.'

'Did you learn anything new?' asked Pettigrew.

'Not particularly. Umar started to waver on whether he had actually seen Gideon leave the café. I believe DCI Patterson will be asking for your wisdom later. He seems a bit unsure where the investigation should go next.'

'Well, that's what we're here for, our wisdom,' said Simpson, smiling.

After putting his things in his office, Patterson came back out and looked across at Simpson, Pettigrew and then McKinnon. 'If you three could come to my office, I'd like a word with you.'

'Told you,' said Pearce, smiling.

A few minutes later, all three officers were sitting in Patterson's office with Patterson behind his desk.

'OK,' began Patterson, 'Since it's the start of another week, I want some ideas about where we go from here. Frankly, I'm at a loss about any new avenues we should be exploring. We have Mary McNair to pursue, of course, and we now know Gideon met drug contacts in the function room. I was just wondering if any of you have other ideas worth investigating. Something we may have missed. Anything else you can think of which would give me some hope.'

'I may have something,' said Pettigrew. 'Although it's a bit of a long shot.'

'Long shots are perfectly fine by me,' said Patterson.

'Russell O'Neill,' said Pettigrew.

'What about him?' asked Patterson.

'When I took his witness statement, I was just talking in general, you know, asking about how he got on with the other trainees, and we started talking about Jess and Kelly. He said he liked Kelly, but Jess just ignored him.'

'And?' asked Simpson.

'I got the distinct impression Russell really liked Kelly and even Jess, despite what he said. In fact, I'm willing to put money on him having a crush on one or both.'

'Any particular reason for thinking that?' asked Patterson.

'When I asked him if he liked Jess, meaning did he get on with her, he said, No, she wasn't his type. I just found it a curious thing to say, like he was thinking of her sexually, and I just meant as a colleague. Plus, I think the opposite was true; I think one or both were very much his type.'

'So what would be the significance of that?' asked McKinnon.

'I was just thinking if Russell did have a crush on Jess, or Kelly, and then found out one or both was having sex with Gideon, then Gideon wouldn't exactly be Mr Popular with Russell.'

'You think he would go as far as murdering Gideon, because of that?' asked Patterson.

'Russell is a quiet guy,' said Pettigrew. 'I could imagine rage quietly building up in him. I know it's a long shot, but anyway, I thought it was worth mentioning.'

'And you're right to mention it,' said Patterson.

'What did Russell say about what happened on Friday afternoon?' asked McKinnon.

'Same as the others. Nothing unusual happened; he filled out forms and went home around four fifteen, I think.'

'OK, well, it's something to consider,' said Patterson. 'I think we need to re-concentrate our efforts on finding out all we can about every trainee. I know we've done background checks, but I want further extensive checks done in case we've missed something. I want confirmation that every trainee left that café when they said they did. I'll put more people on CCTV duty. For the trainees who have come from overseas, get in touch with the Home Office again, double-check all the information we have on them, and they're telling us everything. This week, I want us to study every detail of every trainee—whether it's Mary, Russell, or whoever—and we'll bring them in again for further questioning if necessary. Split the trainees among the three of you and see what additional information you can find. OK, that's all for now; let's get on with it.'

Pettigrew, Simpson and McKinnon left the office, but Patterson still wasn't optimistic they would find something to re-energise the investigation.

CHAPTER 31

A Day of Surprises

As Patterson feared, the next few days were uneventful for the investigation. Real progress seemed a distant memory. The lives of each trainee had been analysed, dissected, and pored over in an attempt to find some new thread to follow, but it was all to no avail, even if some enquiries were still ongoing.

One of those lines of enquiry was the attempt to identify someone on CCTV visiting the café's function room to do a drug deal with Gideon. However, this was almost impossible since the nearest CCTV camera was on Argyle Street and there was no description of who actually visited the function room apart from the vague description Alistair Carmichael gave of one of the visitors—as such, identifying someone mostly came down to studying possible suspects by judgment alone, someone who resembled a druggie, and so far, that had drawn a complete blank.

It was another sign that Patterson was getting desperate, as the media was still saying that the police simply weren't that bothered in catching the culprit due to Gideon's ethnicity. As ludicrous as this was, many media outlets still ran with this take because it created a better, more controversial narrative.

As much as he tried to ignore it, Patterson couldn't help but feel the pressure mount. In the meantime, he also had to find morsels of information to feed the press via Dunard's now regular press conferences.

So it was that a frustrated and slightly dejected Patterson entered the investigation room on Thursday morning. Later, he asked Pettigrew to come into his office.

'Everything all right, sir?' asked Pettigrew as she sat down in his office. She could see that Patterson was worried, and she didn't like it on either a professional or a personal level.

'Fine,' said Patterson distractedly, 'in fact, tell Simpson and McKinnon to get in here as well, would you?'

'They're both out at the moment. I don't know where Simpson is, but McKinnon's with Dunard. It's his final day of being an acting DS.'

'Oh, of course it is,' said Patterson. 'I forgot all about that. So after today, our DC McKinnon will officially be a DS McKinnon, at least that's some good news.'

'I take it that means there's also some not-so-good news?' Pettigrew asked.

'The lack of progress in our investigation is the bad news. I'll be honest, Claire, I'm stumped about how to move the investigation forward. Every avenue is proving to be a dead end.'

'Oh, I wouldn't say that.'

Patterson and Pettigrew both looked up to see a smiling Simpson in the doorway. Simpson came in and sat down, holding a sheet of paper.

Patterson and Pettigrew looked on as Simpson explained the reason for his statement and smile.

'I've just been meeting a friend of mine who works in the Home Office. Haven't seen him in ages, but nevertheless, he has been doing some additional checking for me, and it turns out one of the trainees is not who he says he is.'

Simpson looked down at the sheet of paper.

'Mohammed Sayyid from Afghanistan is actually Youssef Al-Jabri from Syria. He was granted asylum two years ago as Mohammed Sayyid, and although his real identity eventually became apparent, he was still processed under the name Mohammed Sayyid.'

'OK. As interesting as that is, Jack, I'm not

sure it automatically qualifies him as a murder suspect.'

'Perhaps not,' Simpson said, 'but the reason he changed his real name is that Youssef Al-Jabri was convicted of murder twenty-five years ago.'

'In Syria?' asked Pettigrew.

'In Italy. Youssef claimed asylum in Italy, and while he was waiting for his claim to be processed, he got twenty years for murdering a shopkeeper during an argument, and listen to this, he killed the shopkeeper with a single stab wound.' Simpson announced this last fact with an air of triumph.

'But you said he was granted asylum here?'

'Yes, once he had served his sentence in Italy, they threw him out, yet instead of going back to Syria, he came over here five years ago and successfully argued that because he is a convicted murderer, he would get mistreated if he went back to Syria. The judge agreed, and his asylum claim was settled three years ago. He moved up to Glasgow from Birmingham two years ago.'

'OK,' said Pettigrew, 'that is interesting. Well done, Jack.'

'There's something else. According to my mate, Youssef has also been convicted of drug dealing in Birmingham. He got six months. Of course, it doesn't mean Youssef murdered Gideon, but it's all a bit of a coincidence, don't you think? Not only has he been convicted of murdering someone with a single stab wound, but he has also been convicted of drug dealing. I think we're getting close to a motive, namely that Gideon and Youssef could have argued over drugs for some reason.'

'Let's not get ahead of ourselves,' said Patterson, still erring on the side of caution. 'Do we know anything else about Youssef? Who took his witness statement?'

'I did,' said Pettigrew. 'To be honest, he seemed perfectly fine—at least, he didn't say or do anything that gave rise to any suspicions.'

'Well, he wouldn't, would he?' said Simpson. 'So what do we do now?'

'We bring Youssef in for further questioning. Do you want to do the honours, Jack?'

'I'd be delighted,' said Simpson. 'Want to come with me, Claire?'

'I'd be delighted,' said Pettigrew.

'Hang on,' said Patterson, 'I need to arrange some backup. If Youssef is a convicted murderer, he could be dangerous. Give me a moment.' Patterson picked up the phone.

Patterson had no sooner arranged everything than Simpson and Pettigrew left the station to bring Youssef Al-Jabri in for questioning.

Patterson couldn't help but be pleased. He had needed some sort of breakthrough, and this could be it. As he said himself, this information didn't mean Al-Jabri murdered Gideon, but he knew coincidences were always promising.

A moment later, McKinnon came in.

'Brian,' said Patterson, 'have you heard?'

'Yes, Jack told me. Good news.'

'It is, indeed. Oh, and apologies, I completely forgot about today. Is that you officially a Detective Sergeant then?'

McKinnon shut the door and said, 'Not quite.'

Patterson was confused by both the words McKinnon spoke and his muted demeanour. McKinnon sat down in front of Patterson's desk.

'I didn't get the promotion.'

Patterson looked at McKinnon, waiting for the punchline, but there wasn't one.

CHAPTER 32

Another Coincidence

'You didn't get the promotion?' Patterson continued to look at McKinnon, still expecting him to burst out laughing and say he was only joking, but he didn't. 'How's that, you didn't get the promotion?' Patterson repeated. 'It was done and dusted. You passed the exams. You've done your trial period. Plus, you were the only candidate. How could you not get it?'

'Apparently, there was a last-minute change of plans. As you know, there was only enough money in the budget for one person to be promoted.'

'Exactly, and you were the only candidate.'

'Not exactly. Someone else applied, and Dunard has just told me that person was promoted instead.'

'Someone else? No one else in my team applied for the position.'

'Yes, they did; DC Price, or I should say DS Price.'

'Moses? Moses had applied for the DS position—how? He hasn't passed his exams or done his probation period.'

'Yes, he has. Down south. He was due to be promoted to Detective Sergeant, just before he came up here. So, they promoted him with our force instead. As the Chief Inspector said, it was just coincidence.'

'Just coincidence?' Patterson sighed, took off his glasses and massaged his eyes. Putting his glasses back on, he said, 'I don't know what to say, Brian; I honestly knew nothing about it.'

'I know you didn't, but don't worry about it: I'm sure there'll be another opportunity—'

'That's not the point. You were due that promotion.' Patterson stood up, roughly pushing his chair back against the wall. His cheeks were flushed, and McKinnon wondered when was the last time he had seen Patterson so angry.

'I'm going to see Dunard about this.'

'Sir, please don't make a fuss, it's fine really.'

'It's not fine! Don't worry, Brian. I'll get it sorted. You just get on with what you have to do, and I'll see you later.'

Patterson left the investigation room to

see Dunard. He walked upstairs and knocked on Dunard's door, but didn't wait for a reply before entering.

Dunard sat behind his desk with his palm up as if taking an oath.

'Before you say anything, Mike, I'm just as disappointed as you are. I knew nothing about it until a few hours ago.'

'Reverse it,' said Patterson, not taking a seat. 'Brian is due this promotion now.'

'It was just the way it worked out. If I had the funds to promote two officers, I would have been glad to do so. You know how much I like McKinnon.'

'So, why was Price promoted ahead of him? Why couldn't Price be the one to wait? He's only been here five minutes.'

'He's done everything McKinnon has done, except down south. Like I said, it was just the way it worked out. I honestly didn't know about Price's impending promotion to DS. I had a chat with other senior officers and they felt, on balance, that Price would be more suitable for the promotion at this time.'

'More suitable? An officer just up from London is more suitable than an officer who has worked here for over seven years?'

'As a matter of fact, yes. They thought a

new officer would give a fresh perspective, and as I have already said, Price is very highly thought of.'

'So is McKinnon. Listen, I want that decision reversed now. End of.'

'I'm sorry, but it's already done and dusted. If it weren't, I'd gladly acquiesce. There'll be another opportunity for McKinnon to be promoted at some point. It's just a matter of waiting until there is more money in the budget to pay for another DS.'

'Why do I get the feeling everything has been going on behind my back? This smacks of … politics.'

'Politics?'

'I mean … listen, if I find out McKinnon has been…well, if I find out he has been discriminated against because of…some other reason, then I won't stand for it. In fact, I would like to inform you now of my impending resignation. I'll hand in my formal resignation in the next few days.'

'Mike, stop overreacting and think for a—'

'I'm done thinking. I mean it. Either you get that decision reversed or you'll be looking for another DCI.'

With that, Patterson stormed out of the office.

CHAPTER 33

Youssef Al-Jabri

Youssef Al-Jabri was a small, slightly chubby man in his mid-forties. He had a round, friendly face, topped by short, straight salt-and-pepper hair, the type of man who would play the good-hearted neighbour in a sitcom. He entered the interview room smiling, but it wasn't a mocking smile, more one that was a permanent expression of amiability.

His Asian lawyer arrived soon after and sat down next to his client. Everything about his lawyer was shiny. He wore a shiny three-piece suit, had shiny hair, a shiny face, and was coiffured to within an inch of his life. He was clearly expensive, experienced, and used to winning whatever he had to win. His expression towards Simpson was one of fatigue, as if Simpson were yet another fly he had to swat.

Youssef wore a pink-and-white striped shirt, faded jeans, and trainers. He wore a large, expensive watch that was almost as shiny as his lawyer. His natural smile was misleading, though, since he wasn't happy about being brought back to Partick station.

Simpson sat down opposite Youssef with an air of expectation. He had been pleased that it was his contact who had led to discovering the real identity of this man, yet now he had to follow it up by somehow obtaining a confession from Youssef. However, it quickly became apparent this would be a tough ask.

For one thing, the answers Youssef gave were exactly the same as the ones he had given in his witness statement. Namely, Youssef had filled out paperwork on Friday afternoon, nothing unusual had happened, and then he had left the café around half four and gone home. He had seen Gideon around earlier, but hadn't seen him enter the toilet or leave the café.

Youssef said he didn't particularly like Gideon, just like he didn't particularly like any of the other trainees, but no, he didn't murder Gideon.

'Why had you kept your true identity secret?'

'Why do you think?' Youssef answered, still with that permanent smile. 'I am starting a new life in Scotland. I am not proud of my past, but why should I be burdened by mistakes I have made? I am now Mohammed Sayyid. For me,

Youssef Al-Jabri no longer exists.

'Did you murder Gideon Semanyo?'

'No, I did not murder Gideon Semanyo,' said Youssef in that same calm, quiet and controlled voice.

Simpson probed and scrutinised each answer Youssef gave, but Youssef remained consistent, and each answer still corresponded to his previous witness statement. By early evening, Simpson, now with Pettigrew by his side, was making no progress at all. His lawyer didn't intervene simply because he didn't have to. Youssef was easily batting away every question on his own.

His lawyer did eventually say in a tired voice, 'DS Simpson, it is clear you have absolutely no evidence or reason to hold my client. I suggest we end this now, unless you want a claim of harassment brought against you and your station.'

Simpson knew there was no doubt the lawyer would follow through with his threat if given the chance.

Not sure what to do, Simpson went and spoke with Patterson. They agreed they had no choice but to let Youssef go pending further enquiries.

CHAPTER 34

Chocolate Hobnobs

When Simpson triumphantly revealed Mohammed Sayyid's true identity as Youssef Al-Jabri, complete with convictions for murder and drug dealing, it had naturally felt like a breakthrough. However, that optimism now seemed like a lifetime away with the prospect of proving that Youssef had murdered Gideon very slim. As with Mary, the most probable way of doing it was finding the murder weapon or having one of them confess, and that was unlikely.

So it was that Patterson arrived home frustrated and angry. Frustrated at the situation with Al-Jabri and angry at the situation with McKinnon. McKinnon deserved that promotion, and despite what he said, McKinnon himself knew he deserved that promotion.

On the way home, Patterson stopped off at the chippy for a fish supper. Now, in the kitchen, as he emptied the contents of his paper-wrapped meal onto his plate, he remembered he had promised to give his resignation letter to Dunard in the following days. Patterson didn't regret saying that; he felt he had no choice. One of his officers, someone who meant a lot to Patterson, had been screwed over. He couldn't stand by and let that happen. He had to resign. Patterson opened his can of Irn-Bru and took a swig before taking the drink and meal through to the living room.

Sitting on the settee, he was about to switch on the TV when the doorbell rang. With a sigh, he rose and opened the door. It was Pettigrew.

'Claire. Is everything all right?'

'Fine, I just thought I'd drop by.'

'Come in: I'm just having my dinner; do you want anything yourself?' Patterson asked as she entered the hallway.

'No, but I'll take a cup of tea if you're offering.'

Patterson made his way towards the kitchen, but Pettigrew stopped him, seeing the plate of fish and chips on the living room coffee table. 'I'll get it: I think I know where everything is; you go and have your tea—it'll be getting cold.'

Patterson did as he was told, keeping the living room door open so he could see through to the kitchen.

'Are there any developments with Al-Jabri?' asked Patterson in a loud voice.

'Nope, Jack's determined to find a chink in his armour, he's going over the interview once again, but as you know, it will be difficult to prove Al-Jabri murdered Gideon.'

'Aye, did you hear about Brian?.

'I did,' replied Pettigrew as she filled the kettle. 'How the hell did that happen?'

'Coincidence, apparently,' said Patterson, as he broke off another piece of fish.

'Coincidence?' asked Pettigrew, looking through the doorway at him, understandably confused.

'Long story,' said Patterson. 'Don't worry, I'll make sure Brian gets his promotion. I told Dunard I was resigning.'

'You what?' Pettigrew came through to the living room. 'You're not going to, are you?'

'I have to…Ach, I don't know,' said Patterson. 'At the very least, I need an assurance that Brian will definitely get his promotion.'

'Don't do anything rash. I know you're upset about Brian, but think for a moment—that's what you're always telling me.'

Pettigrew walked back through to the kitchen as the kettle clicked off.

'There are some biscuits in the cupboard, top right,' said Patterson.

Pettigrew opened up the cupboard and took a couple of the biscuits out of the packet. 'Ooh, chocolate Hobnobs. Someone has been treating themselves.'

Patterson wiped his hands on a tea towel. 'Aye, I like to think I deserve it sometimes,' he said as Pettigrew came through and sat on the armchair. Soon, Patterson had finished his dinner, taking his empty plate and Irn-Bru can through to the kitchen and returning to sit on the settee with his own cup of tea.

'So, you just thought you'd drop by?' asked Patterson.

'Aye, well, like I say, I heard about Brian and everything. I knew how much you wanted him to get that promotion, plus this whole Bunhouse investigation is turning out to be a real pain. It's like the more we investigate, the messier it gets.'

'Tell me about it. So Claire, given everything you know so far, if you had to say who was Gideon's murderer, who would you put your money on? Youssef? Mary? Russell? The Ku Klux Klan?'

'So, we're down to playing games now, are we? OK, I'll play. First of all, I would say the murderer is...one of the other trainees.'

'Agreed, but who?'

Pettigrew took a sip of her tea and thought for a moment. 'I think we have to find the motive. I know that's usually the case, but even more so here. I understand in some ways, this seems an unplanned killing, but I can't help thinking Gideon was murdered for a specific reason.'

'So what was the reason?'

'Absolutely no idea.'

'So much for playing games,' said Patterson as he decided to go back to the kitchen and get himself a couple of chocolate Hobnobs.

Coming back through, he asked, 'Do you think there is anyone we've overlooked? A trainee, I mean. '

'If we go down that route, I think almost all the trainees could have had a reason for murdering Gideon.'

'Really?'

'Trust me. I've studied each of the trainees, and I found a possible reason for each one to have murdered Gideon.'

'That's quite depressing,' said Patterson quietly. 'Give me an example.'

'OK, like, I told you about Russell, but I don't think I've mentioned this: I was thinking Gideon could have tried it on with one of the women and got stabbed for his trouble.'

'You mean Jess, or Kelly?'

'I know he already had sex with Jess, but that doesn't mean she wouldn't have said no the next time he tried it on, and it's the same with Kelly. One of them goes to the kitchen in a rage, grabs a knife and stabs him. He could have even tried it on with Mary. '

'I'm not sure Mary is his type.'

'With someone like Gideon, anyone is his type, and then there is someone else who may have slipped under the radar.'

'Who?'

'Tegan.'

'The Welsh girl? Her who sounds—'

'—yes, her. If she had gone into that toilet for whatever reason, I would say there is a good chance that Gideon would have tried it on with her. Oh, and then there's Brenda Finnie. I get the distinct impression she likes a drink. If she went in that toilet with a drink in her…'

'OK, I get the picture. You see, that's the problem: the more I look into this case, the more suspects emerge. I fear we may never find out who murdered Gideon, and the press will have my guts for garters.'

'Guts for garters? Not heard that phrase

in a while. Anyway, I wouldn't worry too much about them; the press will write whatever they want to write, regardless of what you do. Press standards ain't what they used to be...You know, I never seem to get the chance to ask: how have you been keeping, anyway?'

'Me?' Patterson shrugged and looked over at the photograph of Stephanie on the sideboard. 'Fine, just taking each day as it comes. It still seems like yesterday, though, since...'

Pettigrew noticed Patterson looking at the photograph.

'...it does,' agreed Pettigrew. 'I miss her.'

'Aye ... How's Mark?' asked Patterson about Pettigrew's husband..

'Fine, we're thinking of moving somewhere further out of the city centre. '

'Oh, aye? You'll need to bring him over for dinner sometime.'

'Definitely, once this case is over. If it's ever over.'

'It will be,' said Patterson, trying to convince himself.

'How are you getting on with Pearce?'

'Pearce?' Patterson shrugged. 'Fine, I guess; she seems good at her job. Why?'

'Nothing...You know she would be good

for you, I mean, if you got to know her better.'

'Got to know her better? What brought this on?'

'Nothing. Just thinking. You should ask her out?'

'Ask her out? What is this, high school?'

'You should. It would do you good. Give you some company. I heard she's single.'

Patterson looked over at the photograph of Stephanie again and said quietly, 'I'm not.' He stood up. 'Another tea?'

'Aye, why not,' said Pettigrew, 'and I'll take another of those chocolate Hobnobs if you're offering.

'You're worse than me,' Patterson said, smiling as he walked back through to the kitchen.

CHAPTER 35

Bali

It had been a tough day for McKinnon. Despite the apparent breakthrough with Youssef Al-Jabri and despite what McKinnon had said to Patterson, McKinnon was devastated not to get the promotion. Yes, he knew he would, hopefully, still get the promotion at some point, but he had thought it was just a formality that he would get it now. He didn't just feel let down; he felt betrayed —not by Moses, but by his superiors. He even questioned whether he wanted to stay in the force.

Yet, it was more than that; he couldn't help feeling embarrassed, ashamed even. Of course, the promotion, or lack of it, was through no fault of his own, yet it was as if he had failed in some way. He couldn't help but feel that he had let people down: Patterson, his colleagues, his family.

Now, with the kids upstairs in the bedroom, and as he sat at the dinner table with his wife, Georgina, he didn't feel hungry. As a professional police officer, he knew he still had to do his job, and right now that job was to help try to find the murderer of Gideon Semanyo. Yet…maybe he would make this his last case. Perhaps it really was time to leave the police force.

However, if this were his last case, he would like it to have a successful conclusion. As with his fellow officers, his suspicions for Gideon's murderer centred around one of the other trainees. Was it really Al-Jabri? Or Mary? McKinnon suspected there might be a love triangle going on. He was intrigued by Pettigrew's idea. That Russell O'Neill could have had something to do with it, at least, there was some kind of romantic connection. Russell O'Neill could very well have become jealous of Gideon; jealousy was always a strong motive for murder.

'You're quiet,' said Georgina.

McKinnon looked up, 'Eh? Oh, just thinking about the case. You know, it seems more likely another trainee did it, but it's hard to prove, and that's not even knowing which one it could be.'

McKinnon's wife was a petite, blonde woman with a kind face that reflected her gentle nature. Her loving eyes shone whenever she talked to her husband, or even just looked at McKinnon, since she absolutely doted on him, as he did on her. At the moment, though, Georgina worried about her husband; she could always sense when he was troubled, and she could sense that now. So despite her horror of violence and not liking to talk about McKinnon's work, she knew it would be good to be a sounding board for her husband.

'So you still think it was a fellow trainee who murdered that asylum seeker? But the news is saying it's the far right, fascists or something. Isn't that the case?'

McKinnon shook his head. 'It's unlikely. At least, we've found no evidence that's the case.' McKinnon suddenly wanted to change the subject. 'How was your day?'

'Fine,' said his wife, 'I saw Grace.'

'Yeah, how is she?'

'Just the usual. She's on another diet.'

'Another one? What is it this time?'

'She only eats green food.'

'Seriously?'

Georgina nodded, smiling, and they both started laughing.

'Green food, that must be her daftest diet yet.'

They ate some more in silence before Georgina asked, 'Did you see Mike?'

'Yeah, of course,' McKinnon said, concentrating on his dinner once more.

'What did he say?'

'You know...' McKinnon shrugged.

'I bet he was delighted.'

'Yeah, he was.'

'So what did he say?'

Brian shrugged again. 'Just that he was really pleased.'

'He must have said more than that. I know how much he wanted you to get that promotion.'

'Yeah, he...gave me a hug.'

'A hug?' Georgina laughed. 'My God, I knew he'd be pleased, but not that pleased. You know, we should invite him over for dinner sometime. In fact, how about tomorrow? Thank him for all he's done; besides, it's been ages since he's been.'

'Yeah, definitely. I'm not sure about tomorrow, though. It's busy with this case and everything. We'll do it sometime. We've just got a lot on.' Brian looked down at his plate, lost in thought.

'Brian, are you sure you're all right? You seem—'

'I'm fine, like I said, it's just this case. It's difficult. We've got the media on our backs every day.'

Georgina still sensed something was wrong. 'I wouldn't let it get to you. Now that they've got the best detective sergeant in the country on the case, you're sure to find out who did it.'

'...This is a nice dinner,' said McKinnon.

'Is it? It's just the same as usual, and besides, if it's so nice, why aren't you eating it?'

'Just not hungry.' McKinnon pushed the plate away.

Georgina looked at her husband.

'I was thinking, Brian, that maybe when you next have a holiday, we could go away somewhere nice, I mean somewhere special, somewhere we haven't been before.'

'Like where?'

'Like Bali.'

'Bali? Whatever made you think of Bali?'

'Well, Grace said—'

'Grace! I might have known.'

'No, listen, Grace had a brochure and it looks really lovely. Besides, now we've got extra money coming in, we—'

'Listen, Georgina, will you just...!' Brian raised his voice and then put his head in his hands. 'Sorry, I didn't mean to shout. I guess this case is getting to me more than I thought.'

He reached out and took Georgina's hand. 'Bali sounds great. We'll see. You know, I think I'm going to have an early night: it's been a long day.'

'Aye,' said Georgina, still surprised at her husband raising his voice, a rare event indeed.

McKinnon rose from the table. 'Do you want a hand with the washing up?'

'No, you're fine, you get yourself off to bed: I'll do it.'

McKinnon nodded. 'I'll just say night to the kids.' Georgina stood up, and he went and hugged her. 'I do love you, you know.'

'I know, Brian. And I love you too.'

'I know.'

They kissed, but Georgina still couldn't help but be troubled by her husband's demeanour.

McKinnon left the room and went upstairs to bed.

CHAPTER 36

Dinner

The next day, Patterson sat in his office, looking over the transcript of Youssef Al-Jabri's interview. He couldn't find any discrepancies in it, and it also matched his previous statements. Youssef said that on Friday, he had left the café at four-thirty, and CCTV footage showed him walking along Dumbarton Road about fifteen minutes later. From what could be surmised on CCTV, Youssef didn't seem troubled in any way. Yes, Youssef had convictions for murder and drug dealing, but there was no evidence to suggest he had murdered Gideon.

As Patterson thought about this, McKinnon came into the office.

'Brian,' said Patterson.' How are you getting on?'

'Fine,' replied McKinnon. Ever since McKinnon had missed out on the promotion, Patterson had been treating him in an overly gentle manner, which McKinnon still wasn't comfortable with.

'I was just wondering,' continued McKinnon, ' if you'd like to come to dinner with Georgina and me tomorrow night?'

'Tomorrow? Em, yes, I'd be delighted. What time?'

'Seven thirty?'

'Great, I'll look forward to it.'

'Great,' echoed McKinnon.

Although McKinnon usually liked to have dinner with his boss at his house, McKinnon was quietly hoping his boss would refuse the invitation this time. It was only because Georgina had insisted that McKinnon make the invitation that he had felt compelled to invite Patterson. Patterson, for his part, really wasn't in the mood to have dinner with McKinnon and his wife, as much as he usually enjoyed their company and the lovely meals Georgina would cook, but he felt obliged to accept the invitation, given what had happened to McKinnon.

As such, both men smiled awkwardly at each other as McKinnon left the office.

So it was that the next night, Patterson found himself parking in front of McKinnon's home for dinner.

McKinnon lived in a semi-detached house on the western outskirts of the city. It stood on a single road, with a line of houses on one side and open fields on the other. Once he had parked his car, Patterson walked to the front door, approached via a downward-sloping driveway occupied by a couple of cars. He slid back the latch on a wooden fence and knocked on the white wood-and-glass front door. He could hear bird song as he waited, partly coming from the large garden at the back and the fields opposite. Cool, fresh air also reminded him that he was some distance from central Glasgow.

Footsteps were heard, followed by a smiling McKinnon answering the door in an open-necked teal shirt and grey trousers. Patterson was glad to see him look so calm and relaxed.

'Sir, right on time as usual. Mon in.'

Patterson entered a hallway, and he handed McKinnon a bottle of wine. Patterson was just about to say something, but before he could, McKinnon said in a hushed voice, 'Oh, hey, there's something I forgot to tell you.' He led a curious Patterson into a side atrium looking out onto the back garden.

'Listen, I was going to mention it earlier, but the thing is I haven't actually got round to telling Georgina I didn't get the promotion yet, so if you could just kid on I did, I'd really appreciate it.'

'Haven't told her? But—'

Before Patterson could finish his sentence, McKinnon had walked quickly back through to the hallway and shouted, 'Hey Georgina, Mike's here.'

Georgina arrived smiling and politely kissed Mike on the cheek.

'Michael, it's great to see you again: it's been so long.'

'It has, hasn't it: you're looking well.'

'Thanks. Everything's been a bit hectic as usual. The kids are staying overnight with my sister. Come through to the living room.'

Patterson smiled at Georgina before glaring at McKinnon as he walked through to the living room.

'It must be about three months since you've been here,' said Georgina.

'At least,' Patterson said as he sat down on the settee, and they continued small talk.

'We just thought,' Georgina continued, 'we'd invite you for dinner to thank you for Brian's promotion and all you've done for him recently.'

'Oh, it's nothing,' said Patterson, 'it's Brian who deserves all the credit.'

Patterson looked over at McKinnon, who was watching the TV, which wasn't on.

'I'll just see how dinner is getting on,' McKinnon said, jumping up from the sofa and going through to the kitchen.

Patterson and Georgina continued to chat before Georgina went to help Brian serve the meal. A few minutes later, she came back through to announce that dinner was ready. Patterson got up to sit at the kitchen table with McKinnon and Georgina on either side of the table.

As always, it was a lovely meal. Patterson thought the last time he had such a nice meal was when he last visited McKinnon and Georgina. The dessert was also delicious, and Patterson was thoroughly enjoying it as he turned to Georgina.

'Oh, by the way, Georgina,' said Patterson, 'Brian didn't get the promotion.'

Georgina's smile became a confused expression as Brian turned white.

'But I don't understand...' said Georgina. 'Brian told me he got the promotion.'

'So I gather. I'm assuming that Brian didn't want to tell you the truth because he felt so bad about not getting the promotion. See, if he told me earlier, I'd have told him he has nothing to worry about because he has a wife who loves him very much, and she's also intelligent enough to know that if he didn't get the promotion, it would have had nothing to do with anything he did or didn't do.'

'I still—don't—understand,' said Georgina, confused as McKinnon sat with his mouth open, not saying anything. 'Brian, is this true?'

McKinnon slowly closed his mouth and silently nodded before bowing his head.

In a soft voice, he said, 'I just didn't...know how to tell you. I knew you'd be upset, I—'

'Upset? I'm more upset you didn't trust me enough to tell me...But I still don't understand: I thought it was all set. Why didn't it happen?'

'Coincidence,' said Patterson, finishing his dessert and wiping his mouth. 'It's a long story. That was an absolutely lovely meal, by the way.'

Brian looked down at the table, unable to meet his wife's gaze, as Georgina looked back at him.

'Oh come here, you silly bugger,' Georgina said as she rose from her chair, went across to McKinnon and put her arms around him. 'You should have told me. It doesn't matter.'

'What about Bali?'

'Who cares about Bali? It's not important.'

'I know, it's just...'

'It had absolutely nothing to do with Brian,' said Patterson. 'It's politics. Besides, Brian will get his promotion sometime. I've told Dunard it's got to happen sooner rather than later.'

Georgina sat back down, and Patterson explained the whole situation. Georgina wasn't happy with what had happened and thought Brian had been treated terribly, but by the end of the night, they were all laughing about how McKinnon had kept the non-promotion a secret.

'You know,' said Georgina. 'I'll be glad when this case is over. I was talking to Brian again about it earlier. Are you any nearer catching who did it?'

'I'm afraid to say I don't believe so,' replied Patterson. 'There's one or two leads, but if I'm honest, it's clutching at straws. Having said that, we have a trainee from Syria who has a murder conviction, but nothing, so far at least, indicating he murdered Gideon. The training program restarts at the café tomorrow, so I'm going to the café to give them a kind of pep talk. I'm sure a few of the trainees are still traumatised by what's happened.'

'I can imagine,' said Georgina.

Later, McKinnon and Georgina sat on the settee holding hands. It was nice that Patterson could see they were both so in love, even after so many years of marriage.

They talked some more, and soon it was time for Patterson to leave. He had really enjoyed himself and had a good night. With McKinnon and Georgina standing in the doorway still holding each other close, Patterson said his goodbyes and headed home.

CHAPTER 37

A New Start

As Patterson parked his car outside the Bunhouse Café on Monday morning, he was once again struck by how shabby the place looked. For a refurbishment, the café barely looked any different since that first morning Patterson saw it, and it wasn't long before the grand opening on July 1st.

Patterson had notified Siobhan that he would be arriving that morning. Walking inside, the trainees were patiently sitting at tables and booths around the main café.

Patterson walked up to a booth where Siobhan Sutherland, Alistair Carmichael and the chef de cuisine, Eddie, were sitting together with DC Linda Dawson.

Dawson had been instructed to stay at the cafe during the first couple of days the trainees returned to reassure them with her presence. Her presence wasn't just for appearance, though;

it was also to ensure that nothing happened to the other trainees returning to the café. Although on balance it was unlikely, whoever murdered Gideon could still be a threat to the other trainees.

'Morning,' said Patterson, 'I take it you've all got acquainted and Linda has told you why she's here.'

'I've told them,' said Dawson, 'but I haven't spoken to the trainees yet.'

'You can do so after I've had a word. As I said over the phone, it's just a precaution to reassure everyone on their first couple of days back.'

'Of course, we understand,' said Siobhan.

'Any news about the investigation?' asked Alistair.

'No, not at the moment. There are one or two new leads we're following.'

Alistair nodded, clearly unconvinced.

'Right, well, I won't stay long,' said Patterson. 'I'll just have a word with the trainees, and then you can talk to them, Linda. 'Has everyone arrived?' Patterson asked Siobhan.

'All except Umar,' answered Siobhan. 'He should be here any minute.'

Patterson looked at his watch. 'OK, I'm

afraid, I'll have to start without him, I'm pushed for time. You can fill him in, Linda, when he arrives.' Dawson nodded.

Patterson went and stood before the trainees. He unexpectedly felt another sliver of anxiety again, but nothing that seemed an imminent threat.

'Hello, everyone. I just wanted to have a quick word with you all before you restart your training again. I know it has been a difficult time after what happened to Gideon, and I know all our thoughts are with him this morning. However, I just want to reassure you all that my initial enquiries do not indicate that there is any threat to yourselves...'

Patterson looked at the trainees. Youssef Al-Jabri, still known as Mohammed Sayyid, was sitting smiling and innocent next to James Halliday and Ahmed Farooq. Was Youssef a threat? Then there were Jess and Kelly sitting together, both looking hungover, as did Brenda Finnie. Andy McLean sat with Danny Wilson while Mary McNair sat with Julie Campbell...Russell O'Neil sat by himself, and then there was...as Patterson looked over them all, he realised Pettigrew was right, almost anyone in this group could have murdered Gideon. He shook himself out of that thought and continued.

'...However, it is better to be safe than

sorry, and I always like to err on the side of caution. As such, I would advise everyone to be just a little more vigilant when going about your daily business. For instance, if any of you see anyone hanging around outside, or just think something is not quite right, tell DC Dawson, that's what she's here for. Likewise, if anything happens when you're away from the café and you notice anything odd, no matter how trivial, please get in touch with Partick police station. You can ask for me, DCI Patterson, or just mention it's to do with the Bunhouse, and they'll know what you're talking about. In the meantime, DC Dawson, Linda, will be here today and tomorrow to make sure you are all looked after, but in any case, I'm sure everything will be fine.' Patterson said this as much to reassure himself as the trainees.

Indeed, some trainees still looked worried, and Patterson wondered whether his talk and DC Dawson's presence could do more harm than good. Nevertheless, he ploughed on.

'As I said, obviously, all our thoughts are with Gideon this morning...anyway, I'll leave you in DC Dawson's capable hands and let her introduce herself in a moment. OK, I hope you all have a great first day back. '

Patterson walked back to the booth with DC Dawson, Siobhan, Eddie and Alistair.

'You know what to do, Linda. I have to get back to the station. If you need any help, get in touch.'

'Will do, sir.'

'I see Umar's still not arrived,' Patterson said to Siobhan.

'No, but he does have a tendency to be late.'

Patterson thought for a moment. Umar was probably fine, but it was better to be safe than sorry. He looked at Siobhan.

'Do you have Umar's mobile number? It's best to give him a call just to make sure he's on his way.'

'Yes, I'll call him.' Siobhan opened a folder and looked at a list, then pressed some numbers into the mobile and held it to her ear.'

After a minute, she held the phone away from her ear and shook her head. 'It's just ringing out.'

Patterson thought for a moment and looked towards the door and the street outside.

'OK, maybe I'll pass by his flat to see if he's there.'

'Do you know where he lives?' asked Siobhan.

'Yes, I was there the other day. Keep trying his mobile and if he arrives in the meantime, give us a call.'

'I hope nothing has happened to him,' said Eddie.

'I'm sure he'll be fine,' said Patterson, and he tried to smile reassuringly but failed. 'OK, I'm away, I'll call to let you know what's happening.' Patterson took out a business card and wrote his mobile number on the back. 'Likewise, phone me immediately if Umar turns up or gets in touch.'

'Of course,' said Siobhan as Patterson threaded his way through the trainees to the café exit and headed to his car.

CHAPTER 38

Umar's Flat

It was a short drive to where Umar lived. As Patterson arrived outside his block of flats, no men were standing outside, and the street seemed quiet. Patterson rang the buzzer for Umar's flat, but there was no reply. He rang again, but still there was no answer. Patterson pressed the buzzer for the concierge, introduced himself, and was let in.

On the third floor, Patterson exited the lift and knocked on Umar's door. He didn't expect an answer, and there was no surprise. He hit the door louder with the palm of his hand, then shouted through the letterbox, 'Umar! It's me, Inspector Patterson.' Still nothing.

A tall, haggard-looking black man in his twenties came out of next door. He wore a ragged tartan dressing gown, open to reveal a grey T-shirt and matching Calvin Klein boxer shorts.

He didn't say anything but just stared at

Patterson accusingly as if Patterson had woken him up.

'You don't happen to know where Umar is, do you?'

The man slowly shook his head and, without saying anything more, continued to stare at Patterson. Patterson went back downstairs and pressed the intercom button for the concierge.

'A crackled voice answered, 'Hello?'

'Hi, it's DCI Mike Patterson again. I need to get into flat number seventeen. Umar Olowe. I'm concerned about his welfare. Could you let me into his flat, please?'

There was a silence before another crackled reply, 'Hang on.'

A short time later, a small, middle-aged security guard with a very youthful spiky black haircut and a grey moustache entered the lobby. On his thick woollen navy-blue jumper was an insignia for the housing association.

He nodded a hello before asking, 'Can I see your ID?'

Patterson showed him his warrant card.

'Who is it you want to see, again?'

'Number seventeen. Umar Olowe.'

The man looked at the keys in his hand, picked one out, and held it between thumb and forefinger before walking to the lift to open the door for Patterson and himself.

'What's Umar done then?'

'Nothing, as far as I'm aware,' said Patterson. 'I'm just concerned for his welfare. He didn't turn up for work this morning.'

The man smiled and slightly jerked his head back. 'Probably still in his kip.'

The lift finished its quick ascent to the third floor, and the caretaker put the key in the door of number seventeen. The door opened, and Patterson told the security guard to wait on the landing while he went inside.

The state of the flat couldn't have been more different from the last time Patterson had visited. Before, the flat was relatively tidy. Now, clothes were strewn all over the floor. Patterson first went into the living room. It was a complete mess, with empty takeaway cartons, other food wrappings, and general rubbish strewn all over. There was a very strong, dank smell, along with other aromas Patterson couldn't—and didn't want to—identify.

Patterson walked through to the kitchen, which was cluttered with filthy dishes, pots, and pans piled up in and around the sink and on the sideboards. The bathroom had towels on the floor, and the toilet bowl needed to be flushed. The smell was almost overwhelming, making

Patterson feel nauseous even after he put his hand over his mouth. The bedroom door was closed. Patterson gently pushed the door open and walked inside. Like the other rooms, it was a complete mess, with a very dirty duvet lying on the floor, revealing a bed sheet covered in numerous stains. Patterson went back to the living room, wandered up to the window, and opened it.

Looking out, Patterson wondered what could have happened to Umar. Not so much because of the mess, but because his sixth sense told him something wasn't right. So much so, Patterson began to fear the worst. He phoned Siobhan at the café, but she said Umar still hadn't arrived. He called Pettigrew.

'Claire, I'm at Umar Olowe's flat. I'm worried something could have happened to him; he didn't turn up at the café this morning. I want Jack, Moses and you over here ASAP. Get Brian to compile a list of Umar's known contacts and any place he could be.'

Waiting for his colleagues to arrive, Patterson went outside to talk to the security guard.

'Is he no' in there, then?' the security guard asked.

'No, listen, I'll need to look at the CCTV for the last couple of days. I noticed a camera outside the main entrance. Can you arrange that?'

'Aye, sure.'

'A couple of my colleagues will be arriving shortly. Where's your office?'

'Across the way.'

'Has there been any report of trouble, a disturbance or anything?'

'Naw, nothing as far as I'm aware. It's been quite quiet, actually.'

'OK, how long will it take for you to get the CCTV?'

'Should only be a few hours, if that.'

'OK, when you have it, come back here and give it to one of my officers.'

'Will do.' The concierge descended in the lift and soon Price, Simpson and Pettigrew arrived.

'What's happened?' asked Pettigrew.

'Umar didn't show up at the café this morning. It may be nothing, but I remember Umar saying how much he was looking forward to going back. I just want to make sure nothing has happened to him. Hopefully, he'll turn up at the café. In the meantime, Jack, I want Moses and you to go around the doors and see if the neighbours can tell us anything. The concierge has said there hasn't been any trouble, but find out all you can, especially if anyone has seen Umar.'

'Has there been a disturbance in here?' asked Simpson, looking around the dishevelled flat.

'No, I just think Umar isn't the tidiest of people, unless he's having visitors.'

'It stinks,' said Price.

'I know,' said Patterson, 'I opened a window, for all the good it will do.'

Simpson and Price left to knock on the neighbours' doors, and Patterson turned to Pettigrew. 'What do you think?'

'As you say, with a bit of luck, he'll probably turn up at the café later. He could have been staying somewhere, at a friend's, maybe, and got held up. Have you had a look around?'

'Just a quick scan. Apart from the mess, I haven't seen anything that suggests a disturbance. It's impossible to tell when his bed was last slept in. I've asked security to get me the CCTV for the last couple of days.'

'You think that's necessary?'

'If something has happened to Umar, the sooner we find out, the better. Let's have another look around to see if there is any clue to what's happened to him.'

Pettigrew and Patterson looked around the flat, but they found nothing significant.

Eventually, Simpson and Price came back, but they had drawn a blank from the neighbours. Sooner than expected, the security man returned with the CCTV tapes and handed them to Patterson, who then passed them to Price. 'Sorry, Moses, but you're our designated CCTV guy at the moment. Get back to the station and see if you can find Umar on them, particularly when he last left the block of flats.'

Moses left, and Patterson called for a uniformed officer to keep guard at the flat entrance. Then all the officers returned to the station. Patterson phoned the café again, but Umar still hadn't appeared.

Patterson sat down at his desk. As each hour passed, he naturally became more concerned that something had indeed happened to Umar. Had Patterson underestimated the threat to the café trainees? Of all the trainees to go missing, was it just a coincidence that it was another young black man who had gone missing? Patterson's main concern was Umar's welfare, but he couldn't help thinking that if something bad had happened to Umar, not only would the press have a field day, but Patterson's career would be over.

With these worries occupying Patterson's mind, Price walked into his office.

'Sir, I think I've found some CCTV footage

of Umar.'

Patterson got up and walked with Price back to his work desk, where they were joined by Pettigrew, Simpson and McKinnon, who realised Price had found something.

'This is from 5:15 pm last night, Sunday,' said Price.

The footage showed Umar emerging from the building entrance with a large red holdall slung over his shoulder. The holdall looked pretty full. Umar walked quickly, though you couldn't tell from the CCTV what his facial expression was like.

'What about the lift? Doesn't it have CCTV?'

'Usually, yes, but the CCTV isn't working at the moment.'

'Of course,' said Patterson as the officers continued to look at the images on the screen. As Umar walked towards the main road, he went out of camera range.

'There are no more images of him?' asked Patterson.

'No, that's it from these cameras,' answered Price.

'Find out if there are any more CCTV cameras on the main road,' said Patterson. 'We need to find out where he went.'

'It's a good sign, he took a holdall with him, isn't it?' asked Simpson.

'Possibly,' replied Patterson, 'I still want to know for certain he's all right.'

Over the coming hours, additional CCTV footage was obtained surrounding the flats, from Dumbarton Road to Yoker and Byres Road. Umar was nowhere to be seen.

Pettigrew, McKinnon and Simpson now sat in Patterson's office.

'He must have gone somewhere,' said Simpson, 'he can't have just vanished.'

'He could have got on a bus into town,' said McKinnon

'We would have still picked him up at the bus stop,' said Pettigrew.

'Still, contact the bus companies, Brian: see if they have any footage from buses along Dumbarton Road between five and six. McKinnon left the office.

'As you said, Claire, at least we know he was carrying a holdall, which suggests he was planning on going somewhere and didn't come to harm.'

'But why?' asked Simpson. 'You said that Umar was looking forward to going back on the training program. Why would he leave the day before he was due to go back?'

‘There could be a few reasons,’ said Patterson. ‘Maybe he was scared...’

‘Scared of what? ’asked Simpson.

Patterson didn’t have an answer for that, but Pettigrew did have another question.

‘Do you think he’s dangerous?’

‘What do you mean?’ asked Patterson.

‘Well, it could be classed as suspicious, running away, if that’s what he has done.’

Patterson shrugged. ‘You mean he could have run away because he’s guilty of Gideon’s murder? I’m really not sure that’s the case, Claire, but I get what you’re saying. We just need to find him, regardless of why he has gone away. Anyway, I'd better give an update to the rest of the team about what’s happening.’

‘There’s something else I think you should be aware of,’ said Pettigrew.

‘Enlighten me,’ said Patterson with a sense of dread.

‘There’s a bad feeling within the team towards Moses. Some of them blame him for Brian not getting his promotion.’

‘But Moses didn’t know anything about the situation.’

‘We know that, but some others in the team still blame him.’

Patterson sighed. 'OK, I really can't be doing with this at the moment, but you're right to let me know.' He stood up. 'Come on, I'd better update the team.'

Patterson left his office and stood in front of the whiteboard, while Pettigrew and Simpson sat down at their desks. Pearce came in, having heard Patterson was making an announcement.

'OK, everyone, in case you haven't heard, there has been a development in the case. Umar Olowe didn't turn up for the restart of the training program at the café and is, at this moment, missing.'

Some team members hadn't heard this, and they looked at each other in surprise.

'Now, we have CCTV of Umar leaving his flat yesterday, late afternoon, around 5:15 pm. The good news is he was carrying a large holdall slung over his shoulder, indicating he was planning on going somewhere. He has some contacts down south, and Brian has found a couple of addresses of people he knows in Glasgow, which are currently being checked.'

'How does this affect the investigation?' said Pearce.

'It doesn't. That is, until Umar is found, I want you all to carry on with your current tasks as normal, regardless of what's happening with Umar. Naturally, our number one concern is Umar's welfare. Above all, we want him found safe and well. It could be that, for whatever reason, he may have got scared about returning to the café. We understand that Umar and Gideon were very good friends. His death was probably a traumatic experience for Umar more than anyone. However, we can't rule out that something has happened to Umar. At this stage, we just don't know.'

The team began resuming their duties.

'Hang on, there's something else I want to address,' said Patterson. We all know that Brian didn't get his promotion as we all thought he would. It also turned out that Moses was promoted because he had successfully completed all the relevant stages of promotion down south. The fact is, Brian not getting his promotion had absolutely nothing to do with Moses himself. Moses knew nothing about it and is just as innocent in this as Brian. So, if I find anyone treating Moses with any less respect than he deserves, I don't care who you are or how long you've been here, you're out the door. I mean it, and that's my last word on the matter. You have been warned. OK, everyone, get on with what you have to do.'

Simpson went back to his office, still hoping he would receive a phone call at any minute to say Umar had been found.

CHAPTER 39

Visitors

The reassuring phone call never came, and Patterson sat in his office, wondering what his next move should be. Yet, he knew it was mostly a matter of waiting until Umar turned up somewhere and, in the meantime, getting on with the investigation, just as he had instructed the rest of his team to do.

Patterson heard someone knocking on the open office door, looked up and saw Zach Andrews standing in the doorway. Patterson's heart sank. 'Mr Andrews, I really don't have time to talk right now. If you wouldn't mind—'

'I've just heard,' Andrews said, sitting down and ignoring what Patterson said.

'How did you hear?'

'Siobhan told me. I was at the café to wish the trainees well on their return. 'Is there any update on Umar?'

Patterson sighed. 'No, we've alerted the relevant agencies. Umar was seen leaving his flat yesterday afternoon, but hasn't been seen since. Listen, Mr Andrews, I don't want to be rude, but as I said, I do have a lot to be getting on with in trying to find Umar...'

'Of course, and I won't take up more of your time than necessary,' said Andrews, taking up more of Patterson's time than necessary. 'But you do realise the significance of this,' he continued in a serious tone of voice.

'Actually, no, it hadn't occurred to me,' Patterson replied, knowing his sarcasm would go right over Andrews' moustachioed, wide collar and kipper tie head.

'If it turns out, god forbid, something bad has happened to Umar, then your career is over.'

'Andrews, if you've just come here to be a pain, then congratulations: job done; now, if you would kindly get the fuck out of my office, it would be much appreciated.' Patterson said it loudly enough for the rest of the office to hear. Most had never heard Patterson swear before.

'I'm just saying you were warned about this. I told you from the beginning that far-right extremists were behind the murder of Gideon, but you just wouldn't listen. Now, it's possible another black asylum seeker has come to harm. I realise that means nothing to you, but this will cause absolute panic within the immigrant community.'

Patterson stood up, walked around his desk and stood over Andrews.

'Please get out of my office now. If you have any queries, then direct them to Chief Inspector Dunard. I'm unavailable.'

Andrews stood up. 'You're not helping yourself, inspector. I only hope for your sake that Umar is found safe and well.'

Andrews left the office, chaperoned by Patterson, who led him out of the investigation room's main door, leading to the corridor.

As he opened the door, Patterson saw Stephen McDonald coming up the stairs. Patterson took off his glasses and pinched the top of his nose as Zach Andrews went down the stairs and Stephen McDonald approached Patterson.

'Can I have a word, Inspector?' McDonald said in a serious voice.

'No. I'm afraid I'm busy—with a sigh, Patterson relented—'What is it you want?'

'I'd prefer to talk in your office.'

'Why not? Come on through, won't you?'

McDonald and Patterson walked through and sat on either side of Patterson's desk.

'I've just heard,' said McDonald.

'What a surprise,' said Patterson, 'I assure you we're doing everything we can to locate Umar. He was last seen leaving his flat with a holdall, so chances are he's gone somewhere rather than come to harm, but I assure you that as soon as I have news, I'll let you know, OK?'

'So you don't think he could have come to harm?'

'Unfortunately, that is still a possibility. However, our main concern at the moment is just finding Umar. As I say, as soon as there is any news, someone will be in touch: now if you don't mind...'

'You see, I'm worried about my constituents. Do you not think it would be best to put out a warning that someone could be targeting the refugee community? This could just be the beginning.'

'If we find evidence of an ongoing threat, we'll certainly issue a warning. Frankly, we've not long discovered that Umar has disappeared. Now, please, if you'd let me get on with my job...'

'Of course, I just thought I'd come and voice my concerns. Please keep me informed with everything going on.'

'I'll do that. Bye, Mr McDonald.'

'Bye, Inspector,'

McDonald left the office, and Patterson felt

his heart beat a little faster and his breathing suddenly shallowed. His anxiety was growing, and he knew there was nothing he could do to stop it. He got up, shut the door, and then sat back down again, trying to calm himself.

The phone rang. Patterson didn't want to answer it, but realised it could be news about Umar.

'Hello?'

'Inspector Patterson? This is Lorna Beattie from the Daily Chronicle: I wonder—'

'I can't talk right now,' Patterson slammed the phone down. He still wondered how journalists were getting his direct number. Still, his anxiety grew inside him, and he could feel the room starting to spin. He continued to take deep breaths and held on to his desk, hoping the attack would pass without doing too much damage.

Eventually, the panic subsided, but as soon as the room came back into focus, Patterson started to think about the case again, almost triggering another attack. Patterson knew Umar had to be found alive and well; otherwise, everything would get much, much worse.

CHAPTER 40

Found

Patterson felt he had to get out of the office. Picking up his jacket, he walked into the investigation room to find Pettigrew.

'Claire? Let's go to Umar's flat to see if we can find a clue to where Umar has gone.'

Fifteen minutes later, both officers were acknowledging the police officer standing outside Umar's flat as they went inside.

They put on their nitrile gloves as they stood in the living room. Patterson wished they had brought a couple of breathing masks as well.

'What are we looking for anyway?' asked Pettigrew.

'I don't know, a bus or train ticket, a reservation, an address, something, just use your judgement.'

They started the search.

'God, this place is an absolute pit,' said Pettigrew.

'Yes, I did notice, Claire.'

Pettigrew and Patterson both looked around the living room. First of all, there were scraps of paper, takeaway menus, and many DSS leaflets, but no ticket or clue as to where Umar could have gone.

As Pettigrew went into the kitchen, Patterson went into the bedroom. There was a small picture of Jesus on the cross on one wall next to the bed, and Patterson now noticed a bible on top of a cabinet. Umar was apparently religious. Could he have gone to a church? It was a possibility.

Patterson looked through a chest of drawers and found several notebooks containing cash amounts, initials, and dates. The type of notebook a drug dealer or a money lender would have. Was Umar dealing drugs alongside Gideon?

No sooner had Patterson asked himself that question than he noticed a wardrobe was curiously pulled slightly away from the wall at an angle. Patterson looked behind it and thought he could see something, though he wasn't sure what. He moved the wardrobe further away and noticed a piece of wood propped up against the wall. He took the piece of wood away, revealing a hole in the wall. He turned the wardrobe further so it was almost side on to the wall, allowing him full access to the cavity. Taking his pen torch from his jacket pocket, he shone the light into the cavity and saw that the hole was filled with bags of powder, pills and capsules. Drugs.

'I've found something!' Patterson shouted through to Pettigrew in the kitchen.

'So have I,' Pettigrew shouted back.

'Drugs?' asked Patterson.

'Come and have a look,' Pettigrew shouted once more.

Patterson walked through to the kitchen to see Pettigrew kneeling down before the open cupboard door under the sink.

'What is it?' asked Patterson.

Pettigrew pointed to a green Asda' Bag for Life' lying under the sink. Without moving the bag, she gingerly opened it so Patterson could see inside.

Lying at the bottom of the bag was a bloodied kitchen knife with a bright green handle.

CHAPTER 41

A Doubtful Coincidence

Patterson and Pettigrew looked at each other and back at the knife.

'You haven't touched it, have you?' asked Patterson.

'Of course not. The bag was lying at the back of the cupboard just like that. I opened it up, and the knife was inside.'

'OK, we need this whole place sealed off and secured, and once it's photographed in situ, we need that knife taken to forensics ASAP.'

'You think it's the murder weapon,' asked Pettigrew.

Patterson looked at his DI. 'Well, I doubt it's coincidence, Claire. I also found bags of drugs hidden behind a cupboard in the bedroom, and there are notebooks full of cash amounts and dates, so it also looks like Umar was also dealing drugs. Come on, we need everything in this flat bagged up and gone over thoroughly. I also need time to digest what we've found here. Let's get the professional search teams in, and let's get ourselves back to the station.'

Patterson made a couple of phone calls and, once everything was arranged, walked out onto the landing. The next-door neighbour, the black man whom Patterson had seen before, was standing outside his door again.

'You find Umar, yet?' he said in a tired voice.

'No, why? Do you have any idea where he is?'

The man shook his head. 'Ain't seen him for days. Don't want to see him either.'

'Oh, why's that?' asked Patterson as Pettigrew and the uniformed policeman looked on.

'Cos, I'm enjoying my sleep. Umar is the loudest motherfucker in the building.'

'Yeah?' asked Patterson.

'Yeah. Always having parties. Two, three times a week, he's having a party. Unbelievable man. Hey, I hope he's all right, n'all but until he's found, I'm enjoying my peace and quiet.' He laughed.

Patterson nodded and turned to the uniformed police constable.

'Under no circumstances does anyone get in there that isn't authorised. There will also be a number of officers arriving shortly to search the place and take some items away.'

Pettigrew and Patterson drove back to the station, and soon Patterson was standing in front of the whiteboard and his fellow officers.

'Brian, would you go along and get Inspector Pearce here. I want her to know what's happened.'

McKinnon left and came back a minute later with Pearce, who, smiling at Patterson, sat down by the side.

'OK, Annabelle, everyone, I just want you to know there has been another important development. Earlier, Claire and I were at Umar's flat, and Claire found a knife which strongly resembles the one we believe was used to murder Gideon. It's currently on its way to forensics, and it's been marked as a priority, so hopefully, we should get confirmation, or not, about whether it is the knife used to murder Gideon. For now, I think we can assume it is the knife we've been looking for. That means our search for Umar is even more urgent since we're now not just searching for a missing person; we're searching for a murder suspect. If we put out any appeals to find Umar, we must emphasise that Umar must not be approached.'

'So Umar murdered Gideon?' asked Davies.

'We still don't know that for certain, Leanne. Suffice to say, finding the knife in Umar's flat certainly makes him the prime suspect.'

'But why would he keep the knife? Why not just throw it away?' asked Simpson.

'A souvenir?' asked Price.

'Bit of a dangerous souvenir to keep,' said McKinnon.

'We know Umar was a bit slow,' said Pettigrew. 'By all accounts, he had a low IQ. Keeping the murder weapon wouldn't be that surprising for someone with Umar's intellect or lack of.'

'I should also say,' said Patterson, 'we found a substantial amount of drugs at Umar's flat, which means it's quite possible he was dealing drugs alongside or with Gideon. If we're looking for a motive, perhaps some dispute over drugs could be at the heart of it.'

'If Umar did murder Gideon,' said Simpson, 'it now explains why he insisted he saw Gideon leave the café. He was deliberately lying—trying to muddy the waters.'

'Perhaps,' said Patterson, 'there are still a lot of questions to answer. Now, I also found notebooks with dates, records of payments, phone numbers, and the like. I'm having them brought here later, once they've been photographed at the flat. I want you, Moses, Brian and Jill to go over them once they arrive at the station. See what you can make of them and possibly find another address where Umar may be. Everyone else, carry on with what you're doing. Claire, Brian and Jack, could you come to my office for a moment? I think I need the benefit of your wisdom once again.'

Everyone restarted what they were doing, and Patterson turned to Annabelle.

'Everything all right with yourself, Annabelle?'

'Fine, although I feel like a bit of a spare cog at the moment.'

'You can help the search through Gideon's things if you like. They'll be taken to a room downstairs.'

'Fine,' said Annabelle, smiling.

Patterson headed to his office, where Pettigrew, Simpson and McKinnon were already seated.

CHAPTER 42

Unanswered Questions

As Pettigrew, Simpson, and McKinnon sat waiting patiently. Patterson entered his office and sat behind his desk.

'OK,' said Patterson once he was settled. 'I've been thinking some things over, and I'd like your opinion on some thoughts I have. I'd like to set aside finding the knife for a moment. First of all, when Claire and I were coming out of Umar's flat, his next-door neighbour appeared and indicated that Umar regularly held parties at his flat. So, Claire, I expect you were probably thinking along the same lines. What if Gideon's parties weren't held at his flat, which was immaculate, but at Umar's?'

'But why would Gideon do that?' asked McKinnon.

'There are many reasons,' said Simpson. 'Perhaps he simply wanted to keep his own place clean.'

'In more ways than one,' said Patterson. 'I think it's possible that Gideon held parties at Umar's place and passed it off as his own so that he could keep his own flat out of any danger. By that I mean, if drug dealing did go on, and say a raid took place, then it's Umar who would be in trouble, not Gideon.'

'Gideon is certainly turning out to be a little charmer,' said Pettigrew.

'OK,' said McKinnon. 'So it's possible Gideon held parties at Umar's and passed it off as his own, but weren't celebrities or the like attending these parties? What would they make of Umar's place? It's a bit of a dump, to say the least.'

'I have no doubt,' said Patterson, 'they would have loved it. At the very least, they probably saw it as a novelty. It would be, what's the word…real. Brian, I'll get a list of some of those celebrities who apparently went to Gideon's parties. I want you to contact them and try and confirm where they went for those parties. Explain that they won't get into trouble as long as they tell you the truth about where the parties were held. Even if they just say it was a tower block, we'll know we're on the right track. I'll get my contact to give me their names again, and I'll give them to you later.'

'I'm not sure it would have any relevance

to Gideon's murder,' said Simpson.

'I wouldn't be so sure,' said Patterson. 'I'm thinking that if Gideon used Umar's flat for parties, he could have also used it for his drug dealing. We know Umar is a vulnerable young man, and actually, the impression I got from interviewing him wasn't of someone who dealt drugs. By that, I mean, I don't think he had the intelligence to do deals. Those notebooks I found in the bedroom were quite detailed with figures and calculations made.'

'So you think Gideon was doing drug dealing from Umar's flat as well?' asked Pettigrew.

'I'm saying it's a possibility,' said Patterson. 'I think Gideon used Umar all the time. Used him in a number of ways.'

'I did always wonder,' said McKinnon, 'why when Gideon bought doughnuts that Friday he sent Umar instead of going himself.'

'Because,' said Patterson, 'for Gideon, it was second nature to send Umar: I suspect he got Umar to do everything for him. Probably treated him like a slave. Getting these doughnuts is a prime example of that. There was no way Gideon would go himself; he would get Umar to go. Probably didn't think twice about it.'

'Which could be a motive—' began Pettigrew.

'Yes...no, sorry, go on, Claire,' said Patterson.

'I was just going to say, which could be a motive why Umar murdered Gideon,' Pettigrew continued. 'Perhaps he simply had enough of Gideon, and maybe getting the doughnuts was the last straw.'

'Yes,' said Patterson. 'I know we're getting into the realm of outside possibilities, but that is along the lines of what I was thinking. With the finding of the knife, there is a strong possibility that Umar murdered Gideon, and we now have to look for a motive. If Gideon constantly used Umar to the point when Umar finally cracks, then that is one possibility.'

'If that was the case, you're saying,' said Simpson, 'that Umar went into the café kitchen in a rage, grabbed a knife, stormed into the toilet and stabbed Gideon? Then he left him there, hoping he wouldn't be found?'

'Again,' said Patterson, 'it's just a possible scenario, but yes. Whoever killed Gideon knew that the caretaker usually didn't check the toilets, but in any case, I think it was a spur-of-the-moment killing. Umar cracked, went into the kitchen, grabbed a knife, went into the toilet and stabbed Gideon.' He possibly wanted a smaller knife he could conceal and then kept the knife on him, probably put it in his bag or jacket, went home and kept the knife because he didn't know what to do with it.'

'I just want to be clear. We're saying that Umar definitely murdered Gideon?' asked Pettigrew.

'I think that's what we're saying,' said McKinnon.

'What we need now is to find Umar and bring him in for questioning. I suspect if he did murder Gideon, it shouldn't be too hard to get a confession, but first things first, we need to find him. In the meantime, here's what I want you all to do. Jack, the contact you have at the Home Office, the one who gave you information about Youssef—ask him about Umar and see if there is anything else he can tell us that we don't know already. Brian, as I said, I'll get in touch with my contact to get the list of celebrities who attended Gideon's parties, and hopefully, they'll confirm the parties were held at Umar's flat. Claire, there was a Bible and a picture of Jesus in Umar's bedroom. Find out if Umar went to any church and, if so, where. He could well be hiding out there. If there is a church, arrange for backup before you go. Umar could well be dangerous.'

Patterson sighed. 'The good news, people, is I feel this investigation is finally coming to an end.'

As Pettigrew, Simpson, and McKinnon

made to leave Patterson's office, there was a collective feeling of relief that Patterson could just be right.

Patterson picked up his mobile to call Billy when his landline rang.

'Hello?' Patterson said impatiently.

'Inspector Patterson, it's Lorna Beattie from the—'

'Listen, I told you already, if you want—'

'I have some information for you regarding the Gideon Semanyo case.'

'I doubt there's…' Patterson realised she could have information about where Umar was. 'Go on.'

'Well, I was wondering if we could meet somewhere.'

'What do you mean you have information?'

'I can't talk over the phone. I do think you'd be interested in what I have to say.'

'Is this about Umar?'

'Who?'

Patterson knew it could just be a ruse to meet him, but then he had heard the name Lorna Beattie somewhere before. Wasn't she a respected journalist? He decided to take a chance.

'OK, I can't meet right now, but how about tonight?'

'That's fine,' said Lorna, and they arranged a specific time before Patterson headed upstairs to inform Dunard of developments.

CHAPTER 43

Secrets

Later that day, there had still been no new developments in finding Umar in the meantime. Other Police forces in the country had also been notified about Umar, as well as UK ports, airports, and train stations. Pettigrew came back to say Umar did go to a church in Partick, usually for the midweek service. The minister thought of him as a quiet young man of good character. However, he said Umar hadn't been to the church for about two weeks. With the minister's permission, Pettigrew had made a search of the premises but was satisfied Umar wasn't there.

Patterson phoned Billy and was given the names of the celebrities who had gone to Gideon's parties. Two agreed to talk and both mentioned the tower block in Whiteinch, with one also mentioning the flat number seventeen. So, it was confirmed that Gideon did indeed hold his parties at Umar's flat.

Simpson came into Patterson's office and sat down, saying he had contacted his friend at the home office about Umar.

'Any new information?' asked Patterson.

'Actually, everything that Umar told the authorities when he arrived and what he stated during his asylum claim appears to be true. Umar is a practising Christian, and by all accounts, Christians are being persecuted in the region of Nigeria Umar is from, mostly by Islamist militia such as Boko Haram.'

'So Umar's claim was settled correctly?'

'Yes. In fact, regarding Umar's asylum claim, it was backed up by a UN observer who was on the ground. Apparently, a group of armed men rounded up all the inhabitants of the village where Umar lived, locked them in a church and proceeded to set it on fire. Those who tried to escape were shot. It was still mostly the elderly and infirm who died, those who couldn't run away beforehand, along with women and children. Those who could escape beforehand did. Presumably, Umar was one of those who managed to get away. He subsequently made it all the way to the UK and came to Glasgow in 2010. His asylum application was settled not long afterwards.

'So, unlike Gideon, Umar was telling the truth when he arrived.'

'Yes, and while we're on the subject of

Gideon, I asked my contact in the home office if he knew anything else about Gideon. He says the real reason Gideon fled Ghana and claimed asylum was not because of that non-existent war but his sexuality. Gideon said he was homosexual, bisexual to be precise.'

'Is that a problem in Ghana?'

'It's illegal. That was the basis on which he was granted leave to remain here. Whether Gideon was telling the truth or not is another matter.'

'Regardless of that, it seems Umar was telling the truth,' said Patterson, thoughtfully.

'Yes,' said Simpson. 'If I'm being honest, what Claire and I took to be a very nervous young man when we interviewed Umar could well have been a very traumatised young man. Someone quite possibly suffering from PTSD.'

'Quite possibly,' said Patterson. 'Claire found the church he attended, so we can confirm he was a Christian. Putting aside the small matter of Umar probably murdering Gideon, he has certainly been through some tough times...OK, thanks, Jack. Let's hope Umar is found soon.'

Jack agreed and left the office. Patterson spent the rest of the day catching up on paperwork, still hoping the phone call confirming that Umar had been found alive and well would come through. It didn't.

Instead, the day passed, and Patterson remembered he had agreed to meet the journalist who had phoned that morning. He thought about cancelling it, as he still didn't know quite what it was about, but he had checked Lorna Beattie's credentials again, and she had a good, professional reputation. As such, he went downstairs to his car and drove to meet her.

Lorna Beattie had suggested meeting in the city centre, and when Patterson asked where exactly, she said a pub known for its selection of malt whiskies and cask ales. As such, it was frequented by a more upmarket clientele, those willing to pay more for a quality refreshment.

When Patterson entered the pub and looked around for possible Lorna Beattie candidates, only one woman was sitting alone. Lorna Beattie was a surprisingly young woman. She had a striking appearance, more like a model having a break on a photo shoot than a journalist investigating the seedier side of life. She had long red hair, eyes a shade of olive green that matched her jumper. She wore bright red lipstick, but everything else was natural.

As Patterson approached, Lorna was studying her phone, which lay on the table in front of her. Next to her was a half-pint of lager or Patterson thought, possibly a lager shandy, going by its lighter colour.

'Lorna?' asked Patterson as he arrived at her table.

The woman looked up in surprise and then smiled. 'Oh, sorry, I was miles away. Yes, I'm Lorna. Inspector Patterson?' She held out a hand, which Patterson took, surprised by its strength. He was so prejudiced it was unbelievable.

'I'll just get myself a drink, are you okay?' Patterson said, nodding towards her drink.

'Yes,' said Lorna, it's just a lager shandy. It'll last me.'

Lager shandy. *Still got it,* thought Patterson, pleased with his deduction. He went up to the bar and got himself an orange juice. Sitting back down, he noticed her studying him. On first impressions, she came across as intelligent, professional and that he'd made the right decision on meeting her.

'So, Lorna, you said you might have some useful information for me? About the Bunhouse murder?'

'Yes, although it's more in relation to a person associated with the case. I believe you've had a chance to meet the local MP Stephen McDonald.'

'Stephen McDonald? Yes, I have had that pleasure recently.'

'What did you think of him?'

'Let's just say, it's unlikely he'll be getting my vote at the next election.'

'If that means you think he's a pompous arsehole, I'd agree with you.'

'That's another way of putting it,' said Patterson, 'but what's that to do with the murder of Gideon Semanyo?'

'The thing is, before I tell you, I need you to promise me something in return.'

'I'm afraid, I'm not at liberty to hand out public money.'

'I don't mean money, I want you to promise me first dibs if and when you catch who murdered Gideon.'

Patterson already had a fair idea of who murdered Gideon. Umar. He was just waiting for forensics to come back and confirm the knife was indeed the murder weapon, and he could take it from there. Yet, if this journalist knew something about Stephen McDonald, that could still be interesting. At the very least, he could negotiate.

'I can't promise you anything, Lorna, it's often out of my control who gets to know what and when...However, if the information you give is worth hearing, I will try to ensure you get first shout. Again, it depends on what you have to tell me. If it's simply gossip, then it's no deal.'

'I'm sure you've already done a background check on me, Inspector. I don't do gossip, and I believe that although I'm still at a quite young age, I am highly respected by my peers.'

Patterson knew she had reasons for her self-confidence.

'As I say, I'll do what I can, if possible.'

Lorna thought for a moment and agreed.

'So, what is this about Stephen McDonald you have to tell me?'

'I heard that you have been getting grief about leading the investigation.'

'Who told you that?'

'Well, it's now common knowledge. For one thing, I was at a press conference with McDonald, where he questioned whether you were the right person to be the senior investigating officer, and I also saw a similar interview with Councillor McKenzie.'

Patterson took a sip of his orange juice. 'It's fair to say there had been some pressure put on my bosses to get me removed from the investigation.'

'And just why do you think that would be?'

'From what I can gather, they believe a middle-aged white man is not a suitable DCI to be leading an investigation into the murder of a young black man.'

'Have you ever thought they might want you removed because they know you are good at your job?'

'Lorna, as much as I'm enjoying your company, I am rather pressed for time. Why would anyone want me removed from the investigation because I'm good at my job?'

'Because they know you could find out something they don't want you to know.'

Patterson looked at her as if to say his patience was wearing thin.

'Right from the off, someone has been briefing journalists against you.'

'Such as?'

'For one thing, giving your personal office number out to anyone and everyone.'

That was something Patterson had already suspected.

'Do you know who?'

'Just that it was a female.'

'Gillian McKenzie?

'Who knows. It's possible. I suspect you also have a mole within your station leaking info to Gillian McKenzie and possibly others. So what do you know about Stephen McDonald?' Lorna asked.

'I know you seem to be asking a lot of questions.'

Lorna smiled. 'Sorry, but if you could just indulge me.'

'OK, I know that McDonald has been the MP for his constituency for around twelve years. He's a journeyman, never made it to any real position of importance. Probably because, from what I can gather, he isn't that well-respected or even well-liked by his peers. He's a staunch supporter of family values and a Christian, he—'

'OK,' said Lorna, 'Let me stop you there. With Stephen McDonald, there is a big difference between his public persona and his private one.'

'Isn't that par for the course for most politicians? Lorna, just what are you getting at?'

'For some time now, there have been rumours about the right honourable Stephen McDonald. It's alleged he has a taste for rent boys.'

'I told you, I'm really not interested in gossip.'

'This is more than gossip. In fact, it's widely known that he has a taste for the sleazier side of life. I've a colleague in London who managed to get an interview with one of those rent boys McDonald frequently uses. My colleague has proof that McDonald was a regular client of this rent boy and others.'

'So why haven't I seen this proof?'

'Those with influence suppressed it. They paid off the rent boy and shipped him off to Bulgaria.'

'Bulgaria?'

'That's where he's from, and if my colleague dared publish the story, even with proof, he'd be out of a job and blacklisted in an instant.'

'OK. So Stephen McDonald uses rent boys, I don't see how that ties in with my investigation.'

'Gideon Semanyo was a rent boy.'

Patterson could now see where this was going. Normally, he would still have treated this as simply gossip, but having just learned that Gideon's real reason for leaving Ghana was his sexuality, he was prepared to listen a little more.

'Oh, we know all about Gideon Semanyo and his drug dealing,' said Lorna, as she took another sip of her drink. 'But how do you think he got the money to start his drug dealing? Gideon was one of the most prolific rent boys in Glasgow.'

'So you're suggesting that Stephen McDonald was a client of Gideon Semanyo?'

'I'm not suggesting it, I'm telling you. I'm not surprised you don't know about it because I had to do a lot of digging to find it out myself. Stephen McDonald, a devout Christian and family man, has successfully kept that side of his life very quiet. Anyway, according to my sources, McDonald was not just a client but absolutely smitten with Gideon. Couldn't keep away from him.'

'And if I'm following you right, you're saying that Stephen McDonald wants me off the case because he's afraid I will find out about his involvement with Gideon Semanyo?'

'Yes, but it's not only that. Stephen McDonald has a number of properties in London and across Scotland. There have been questions recently about how he has been able to build up such a portfolio on an MP's salary.'

'We're back to gossip again,' said Patterson.

'Perhaps, but the point is Stephen McDonald has a lot to hide and he doesn't want a highly-regarded and above all, honest copper like yourself finding out more about him via his involvement with Gideon Semanyo.'

'As you said yourself, though, it isn't just McDonald who has been asking for me to be removed, there's Gillian McKenzie as well. Has she got anything to hide?' Patterson asked in the hope that the answer would be yes.

'Actually, I don't think McKenzie has so much to hide; rather, she does actually believe a middle-aged white man shouldn't be leading a case such as this.'

'Pity,' said Patterson. He thought some more. 'What do you know about Zach Andrews?'

'Zach Andrews? Apart from him being a bit of a dick and best mates with Stephen McDonald, not much, why?'

'Zach Andrews has also been trying to get me off the case. You don't think he's also been involved with rent boys or Gideon Semanyo, do you?'

'Wouldn't surprise me,' said Lorna, 'but, no, I haven't heard anything.'

'Hang on, did you say Zach Andrews and Stephen McDonald are best mates?'

'Aye, why?'

'Nothing...Listen, thanks for the information, it could come in handy, but for now, I have to go...'

'Remember about your promise.'

Patterson thought for a moment. Could he trust her? 'Listen, Lorna, I may have some important news regarding who murdered Gideon a lot sooner than you think. We're following a definite line of enquiry and have a prime suspect. I can't tell you any more than that at the moment, but once I can tell you, I'll let you know. Is the phone number you gave me still correct?'

'Aye,' said Lorna, who stood up as well.

'Do you want me to give you a lift anywhere?' asked Patterson.

'No,' said Lorna,' I can get a taxi and claim it on expenses.'

Patterson smiled and walked with her outside. 'OK, Lorna, take care, I'll be in touch if and when.'

Lorna nodded and started walking towards the taxi rank as Patterson walked in the opposite direction towards his car. Lorna had given him a lot to think about; although it may not have much bearing on the case, it was satisfying to now understand why he was being put under so much pressure to be removed from it. Patterson drove home, wondering if Umar had been found yet.

CHAPTER 44

David Gillespie

The next day, shortly after sitting down in his office, Patterson made a call to a colleague, David Gillespie, at the Serious Crime Squad. Gillespie specialised in fraud investigations.

'David,' Patterson said as the phone was answered. 'How are you? It's Mike Patterson from Partick. You may know I'm investigating the murder at the Bunhouse Café.'

'How could I not know? I hope you're enjoying all the publicity you're getting.'

'Oh yes, I'm absolutely delighted with it.' Patterson heard Gillespie chuckling. 'Anyway, I'm wondering if, on the off chance, you would have an ongoing investigation into someone connected to the café.'

'I may indeed. However, I'd rather not talk over the phone. Actually, I'm in the West End later this morning. I could pop in if you like.'

'Fine, I'm in all morning. I'll see you later, then.'

Later that morning, as promised, David Gillespie appeared in the doorway of Patterson's office.

In his mid-thirties, Gillespie was a happy-go-lucky sort of person—always smiling—and although a cliché, he really did brighten up a room just by entering it. So he brightened up Patterson's office by coming in and shaking Patterson warmly by the hand.

'Busy?' asked Patterson.

'Snowed under,' replied David. 'We're taking on extra staff to deal with it. It seems fraud has never been such a popular pastime. So, what is it you wanted to meet about?'

'I was given a tip,' began Patterson, 'that you could be looking into the financial affairs of someone associated with this Bunhouse murder—Stephen McDonald.'

'Your tip-off was correct. We had information that he was underpaying taxes on properties he was buying. The investigation is in its early stages, but there are already enough red flags to merit a much more thorough investigation, which is what we're undertaking at the moment. The thing is, McDonald loves his offshore accounts, which in itself is a red flag, so it's a bit of an elaborate trail we're following. We'll get there in the end, though, we always do. Why the interest in McDonald apart from his connection to the Bunhouse?'

'Oh, like I said, I was given a tip-off, but he's also been giving me grief, trying to have me thrown off the investigation. I also heard he may have been up to some seedier stuff, nothing illegal, alas, but well, I'm just curious about him.'

'I know all about the seedier side of Mr McDonald's life. As for his financial affairs, don't be surprised if you hear officially that he's under investigation.'

'I'll keep an eye out for that. Actually, there's someone else I'm interested in, Zach Andrews? You wouldn't have an investigation going on with him, by any chance?'

'Zach Andrews...No, I can't say we have. Though I'm sure I've seen that name somewhere recently. He's an MP, isn't he?' Gillespie brought out a notebook and jotted down the name.

'An MSP, yes.'

'That's right. Yes, it's funny you should mention that name. I'm definite I've seen it crop up a couple of times while investigating Mr McDonald. Zach Andrews...hmm, I'll get back to you on that. OK. Anything else?'

'There is, actually. I should have just given you a list. Her name's Gillian McKenzie. It's in case her name crops up during your investigation.'

Gillespie shook his head. 'Can't say the name rings a bell. Who is she?'

'She's a city councillor. She's also been involved with the café and has been making a nuisance of herself.'

'Ah, I know who you mean. She was one of those on TV slagging you off.'

'That's the one,' said Patterson. 'Like I say, I'm just mentioning McKenzie in case her name crops up in your investigation.'

Gillespie jotted McKenzie's name down as well, then put the notebook back in his pocket.

'OK, I'll look into that for you. How are you keeping anyway?'

'Fine. Keeping busy, like yourself, and how have you been doing?'

'Good, my son, Mark, just graduated from university—criminal psychology.'

'Excellent. There's always a need for criminal psychologists.'

'There is, unfortunately,' said Gillespie, standing up. 'And how is your murder investigation coming along, by the way?'

'We have a clear suspect now, Umar Olowe, a Nigerian national. We found a knife we believe is the murder weapon in his flat. I'm just waiting for forensics to come back with confirmation, though they seem to be taking their time. In the meantime, Umar appears to have gone on the run. Once we catch him, though, and hopefully get a confession, it should be case solved.'

'Nice one,' said Gillespie, 'OK, it was good to see you again, Mike. I'll give you an update if and when. Bye.'

'I'd appreciate that, David. See you soon.'

With that, Gillespie left the office.

CHAPTER 45

Found

After Gillespie had left, Patterson thought over what he had revealed about Stephen McDonald. He was already under investigation. Patterson had always sensed something untrustworthy about McDonald. At the same time, he wondered if his hunch about Zach Andrews would come to anything.

Patterson reassured himself that he was right to mention Zach Andrews to Gillespie. Surely, even with the workmen there only two days a week, more progress should have been made on the cafe refurbishment. Patterson suspected that not only were they using the cheapest materials, but the workers themselves would be on the lowest wages. It might all be legit, but doubts remained in Patterson's mind. Wouldn't that be a result, thought Patterson—they'd not only catch the murderer of Gideon Semanyo, but Zach Andrews would be investigated for fraud along with Stephen McDonald.

While Patterson was lost in his thoughts, Simpson walked in.

'I just got a call from Lanarkshire division. They've found Umar.' The downbeat tone of Simpson's voice indicated it wasn't good news.

'Go on,' said Patterson.

'Umar was found in Braemar Woods, near East Kilbride. He hanged himself.'

Patterson took off his glasses and dropped them onto his desk. He suddenly felt very deflated.

'OK…' Patterson said quietly, putting his glasses back on and standing up. 'Anything else?'

Simpson shook his head. 'That's all I know at the moment. An officer called it in, and I just happened to take the call. It was a DI Lawler. There was no ID on the body, but he knew we were trying to find Umar and recognised him from the description we put out.'

'Well, I guess we'd better get down there,' said Patterson slowly and with Pettigrew in tow, all three headed to Braemar Woods.

It took just under an hour to get there. At first, the only indication of activity was a single police car and an ambulance at the beginning of a dirt track leading into a wooded area. An officer stood guard at the entrance to the dirt road.

Patterson lowered the car window as he

drove up.

'DCI Patterson, Partick CID. Can I get down this way?'

'We'd rather you park up here,' the young officer replied, 'and proceed on foot. DI Lawler's car has already gone down, so once you see his car, I believe you turn right and walk straight ahead.'

Patterson nodded, parked up and got out of the car with his fellow officers. They walked on, and when Patterson saw another car parked on a grass verge, he looked to the right and spotted a roughly trampled path leading further into woodland. With Pettigrew and Simpson behind him, he crossed rough terrain, covered in bracken, broken branches and the odd tree stump for about ten minutes. Patterson wasn't entirely sure he was going the right way until he thankfully heard voices from the direction he was walking, and found himself entering a small clearing.

Three uniformed police officers and two plainclothes officers were standing next to a body on the ground covered with a dark blue tarpaulin.

Spotting Patterson arrive, one of the plainclothes officers came over.

'DCI Patterson? DI Lawler.'

Patterson nodded and introduced his fellow officers.

'It's quite a trek, isn't it?' DI Lawler said.

'It is. Who found him?'

'An entomologist he—'

Patterson looked confused.

'Someone who studies insects,' Pettigrew helpfully explained.

'Precisely,' Lawler continued. 'You know more than I did. It was an entomologist who sometimes comes this way. He knows this clearing as a place he can stop and have a rest. He said he came here about eleven fifteen this morning and saw Umar hanging from that tree there. The entomologist had a knife and managed to cut him down, but Umar was clearly already dead. The pathologist estimated that he had been hanging here for possibly a couple of days. Do you want to check if it's Umar?'

Patterson nodded, walked towards the body and lifted the tarpaulin.

The man looked peaceful, as if asleep. Only the pallor of his skin was a sign that he was deceased.

'Yes, that's Umar,' Patterson confirmed.

Lawler brought out a small, clear plastic pouch containing a piece of paper. 'There was a note—a suicide note—found in his pocket.' With his gloves on, Lawler took out the note, unfolded it and showed it to Patterson.

The handwriting was a scrawl, but still legible. Patterson read out the note aloud for the benefit of Simpson and Pettigrew.

I'm sorry. I murdered Gideon. I'm so sorry. Please forgive me. Tell everyone I am sorry. I just can't live any more.

Lawler folded up the scrap of paper and put it back in the pouch.

'Was there a bag—a red holdall—found anywhere?' asked Simpson.

'A holdall?' Lawler shook his head. 'We had a preliminary search around the area, but nothing has been found. We probably need to do a more thorough search later.'

'How do you think he got here?' Pettigrew asked, directing her question to Patterson, but DI Lawler answered.

'There are plenty of buses from Glasgow that pass these woods. It could even be that he got on a bus, saw the woods and got off at the stop just up the road.'

'Was a bus ticket found on him?' asked Pettigrew.

'No, nothing was in his pockets apart from some money—about thirty pounds—and some loose change. Oh, I nearly forgot,' Lawler added, walking over to another clear plastic bag and coming back. 'This was what he hanged himself with.' He held up a bag which contained a thin, coiled rope. 'It looks like a hemp rope. Looks pretty new as well.'

'So how did he hang himself, exactly?' asked Simpson.

'It was quite simple,' said Lawler. 'You see the wooden log under the tree? There are marks on the ground that indicate Umar dragged it underneath that thick branch there. All he needed to do was throw the rope a couple of times around the branch, put the noose around his neck, and then step off the log. Bob's your Uncle. There was enough leeway between the ground and his feet for him to be asphyxiated.'

'OK,' said Patterson quietly. 'Thanks.' He looked across at Umar's body one last time and then walked away with Pettigrew and Simpson towards his car.

'Well, I guess that's that,' said Simpson.

'I guess it is,' said Pettigrew.

'Aye,' said Patterson.

CHAPTER 46

It Is What It Is

It was a sombre Patterson who stood in front of his investigation team later that day. The suicide of Umar felt like a defeat. A murderer had escaped justice. To rub salt into the wounds, forensics finally returned the test results on the knife, and they were conclusive. The knife was the one with which Gideon was stabbed. The only prints on the knife were those of Umar, with a couple of prints on the blade where Gideon had tried to grab the knife. In addition, Umar's prints were both underneath and on top of the blood on the knife, meaning he handled the knife just before and after Gideon was stabbed.

So now there were only loose ends to tie up in the murder at the Bunhouse café. The first thing Patterson had to do was address his team.

'OK, everyone, as most of you, in fact, all of you know, Umar Olowe was found this morning in Braemar Woods. It appears he committed suicide by hanging himself. In his pocket was a suicide note which reads as follows:

I'm sorry. I murdered Gideon. I'm so sorry. Please forgive me. Tell everyone I am sorry. I just can't live any more.

'So Umar has confessed he murdered Gideon, even if it is in death. Forensics have also confirmed the knife found in Umar's flat was the one used to kill Gideon, so I guess it is some comfort that we can categorically say Umar murdered Gideon. All that remains now is to gather all the evidence together so we can present a final report to the Procurator Fiscal. For that, we still have some questions I want answered. For instance, why did Umar murder Gideon?'

'Well, as we speculated before,' said Pettigrew, 'it's likely Umar probably had enough of being Gideon's dogsbody. It's becoming clear that Gideon treated him like dirt. On Friday afternoon, Umar cracked, went into the kitchen, grabbed a knife and stabbed Gideon.'

'That certainly seems the most likely explanation,' agreed Patterson, 'although we may never know exactly why Umar murdered Gideon. We know that Gideon used Umar's flat to stash his drugs, do drug deals and hold parties there. All the while, Gideon kept his own flat spotless. We also now know that Umar was likely a deeply troubled young man who had escaped a dire situation in Nigeria. This is in no way to condone what he did, but there we are. OK, there are other questions we need to answer to do with Umar's suicide. Such as how did he get to Braemar Woods? Moses, could you check with the bus companies and get any relevant CCTV footage from around the woods? I assure you, you won't always be on CCTV duty; it's just to wrap up this investigation. The rope Umar hanged himself with looked pretty new. Where did Umar get it? Did he buy it, and if so, where? I'll give you all a list of what needs to be done later. With a bit of luck, we can tie up the loose ends and have this case completely finished by the end of the week. I'd just like to add that I know it's not the outcome we all wanted, but you all did a great job, and well, it is what it is. I suggest everyone finish up what they're doing today, go home, get some rest and come back fresh in the morning, and we can finally start to put this investigation to bed.'

With that, Patterson headed back to his office.

CHAPTER 47

A Conundrum

The next morning, Patterson was sitting in his office when he saw Zach Andrews walk into the investigation room. Arriving at Patterson's office, he lightly tapped on the open door even though he could see Patterson watching him. For a moment, Patterson wondered if Andrews had heard he had directed the fraud squad in his direction. Yet, his first words were uncharacteristically polite.

'Hello. Can I come in? I won't be long.'

Patterson beckoned him inside, and Andrews entered, closing the door behind him and sitting down.

He was wearing another outfit from his seventies wardrobe—a pale yellow, wide-collar shirt with a light blue kipper tie and flared jeans. As always, he looked an idiot. Then again, even if he hadn't been wearing these clothes, he'd still have looked an idiot.

'I've just heard about Umar,' Andrews began. 'I just wanted to pass by and say I'm sorry for ever doubting you. I know when to hold my hands up; you were right, and I was wrong. Admittedly, I still can't believe that Umar could have murdered Gideon; Umar seemed such a quiet, nice young man. Still, I suppose you can never tell with these things. Anyway, the fact is, it wasn't the far right at all. To be honest, I feel a bit of an idiot now for thinking it was, but I'm man enough to admit when I was wrong.'

While Andrews was talking, Patterson wondered how the MSP had heard so quickly about events once again. Then he remembered there was almost certainly a mole within the station. Yet, if Andrews was big enough to offer an apology, Patterson was big enough to accept it.

'Don't worry about it,' said Patterson.

'Nevertheless, it's only right I should say sorry for some of the things I said. No hard feelings, eh?'

Andrews held out his hand.

Patterson hesitated for a moment, but took the politician's hand and shook it.

Although he still felt this man, including his handlebar moustache, wasn't to be trusted, Patterson said magnanimously, 'No hard feelings.'

'So, have you found out why Umar murdered Gideon?'

'We're still not entirely sure, but we believe it may have something to do with how Gideon treated Umar. I'm in no way condoning what Umar did, but it seemed that Gideon used and you could even say abused Umar. For instance, Gideon used Umar's flat to hide his drugs and even held parties there. It's very possible Umar was feeling the pressure and eventually cracked.'

'Well,' said Andrews, 'the fact remains, it had nothing to do with the far right, and I was wrong. That's all I wanted to say. I'm sure you're still busy tidying things up, so I'll leave you to it. If I can say once again, Inspector, well done, despite my interference, you did a fine job.'

Patterson nodded and awkwardly shook Andrews's hand again. No, as much as he tried to deny it, Patterson still didn't like Zach Andrews one little bit. He hoped they would never have reason to meet again. Patterson was thankful to see Andrews leave the investigation room, hopefully for the last time.

Patterson picked up the phone and called the DSS liaison officer, Siobhan Sutherland, to say he wanted to see her. She said she was at the café that afternoon, and if he wanted to pop down, he could do so before three. Patterson said he would be there within the hour.

As he left the investigation room, he passed Moses, who seemed thoughtful, looking into mid-air.

'Everything all right, Moses?' said Patterson. 'You look a little lost.'

Moses looked at Patterson as if coming out of a daze. 'Eh, oh, it's nothing, just that…I just need to check something, that's all.'

Patterson nodded and headed to the evidence room to pick up Umar's suicide note.

Patterson arrived at the café and was surprised to see it looked a lot tidier than it had before. It looked just about ready to receive customers, even if it still wasn't somewhere he would fancy going himself.

Walking inside the café, Siobhan was alone in the main café area, working on a document at her desk. Looking up and seeing Patterson, she smiled, although Patterson could tell by the nature of her smile that she anticipated the bad news he was about to tell her.

As Patterson sat down, Siobhan tidied up the papers in front of her and asked if he wanted a coffee, and he couldn't resist saying yes. She slid out of the booth and went into the kitchen, coming back with a mug which was imprinted with 'The Partick Bunhouse Café' and a small photo of the café exterior.

She placed the mug in front of Patterson and slid back into the booth.

'Hard at work, I see,' said Patterson.

'Yes,' said Siobhan. 'It's sad, really. You know, I remember when you asked that first morning why I had arrived at the café so early, and I felt slightly embarrassed because this is my life at the moment. I really should get out more.' Siobhan smiled.

'No,' said Patterson. 'I think it's admirable. The DSS is lucky to have someone so hard-working...Where is everyone, by the way?' asked Patterson.

'They're in the kitchen...learning how to make a Victoria sponge.'

'Oh, so they learn more than just how to make sandwiches?'

'Oh, yes, it's really basic catering they learn...is this about Umar?' she asked tentatively.

'Yes, I'm afraid it's bad news. Umar committed suicide.'

Siobhan's reaction was muted, as if she had indeed expected this news.

'How?'

'He hanged himself—'

This brought a more expressive reaction from Siobhan—a small intake of breath—and she visibly stiffened.

'Poor Umar. Hanged. It sounds awful. If only I had a chance to talk to him. Was it at home?'

'No, actually, he went to some woodland just outside Glasgow, a place called Braemar Woods.'

'In woodland?'

'He was found hanging from a tree. We're still investigating the exact circumstances, which is partly why I'm here. I know this is distressing, but I need your help with something. Patterson brought out the small, clear evidence bag from his pocket, which contained the piece of paper. 'He left a suicide note. I wondered if you could confirm if it's his handwriting.' Patterson unfolded the bag so that the note inside could be read and showed it to Siobhan.

'It's not the clearest writing, but you can make out what he says,' said Patterson, gently.

As she read the note, tears began to form in Siobhan's eyes.

'I don't understand. He says he murdered Gideon?'

'Yes, we now have evidence it was indeed Umar who murdered Gideon.'

'But why?'

'That, we may never know. Siobhan, I just need you to confirm if it's Umar's handwriting. I know it's probably difficult to recognise it from memory, but I thought maybe you have something you could compare it against?'

'That's not necessary.'

'You recognise his handwriting?'

'No, it's not that, you see, I have nothing to compare it against. Umar was illiterate. He couldn't write a word of English.'

'Illiterate? But he spoke English well.'

'Yes, he spoke English well—very well in fact—but practically the only word he could write was his name, and even that was an effort. I always had to help him fill out forms. He would usually be the last to leave the café on Friday because of it.'

'So, he couldn't read or write at all?'

'No. He spoke English in Nigeria, but he never learned to read or write properly. He was always willing to learn, but I think it was beyond his capabilities, bless him. She looked at the piece of paper again. 'So I don't understand this note. Umar couldn't have written it. I suppose someone must have written it for him.'

'You don't think he could have copied it, say from the internet perhaps?'

Siobhan shook her head. 'I don't see how.

As I said, even writing his own name was a struggle at times. I know this isn't well-written, but it's still far beyond the capabilities of Umar. No, I don't understand why, but I'm certain Umar couldn't have written this.'

She handed the small evidence bag back to Patterson, and he placed it back into his pocket.

'OK,' said Patterson and stayed silent as he thought this over. Siobhan also stayed quiet, not wanting to disturb Patterson's train of thought. He took a sip of his coffee and smiled. 'This is nice coffee.'

'It is. We have a very good barista.'

'Who trains them to make coffee by the way?'

'Eddie.'

'Your chef de cuisine doubles up as the coffee trainer?'

'As the barista trainer, yes.'

'Maybe we should get a coffee trainer guy for the station,' said Patterson.

Siobhan smiled. 'So do you think Umar got someone else to write the note for him? That's the only explanation I can think of...but then, why do that and not alert somebody about what Umar was planning to do?'

'I guess that's a conundrum I'm going to

have to figure out.'

'I don't envy you.'

'That's why I'm paid the big bucks.' Patterson smiled. 'OK, Siobhan. Thanks for your help. Is it OK if I leave the mug there?'

'Yes, I'll take it through later.'

'How is everything going here anyway?'

'Fine, just getting everything prepared before the opening day. They're ramping up the refurbishment so it gets finished in time.'

'So I see. I'd appreciate it if you keep what we discussed about Umar quiet for now. There will be an announcement to the press in good time.'

'Of course.'

Patterson left the café to head to the mortuary to hear what Rana had to say at Umar's autopsy.

CHAPTER 48

Autopsy

From the café, Patterson headed to the mortuary to get the results of Umar's autopsy, and he arrived to find that the autopsy had been finished for some time.

'You're losing your touch, Mike. I thought you usually got here just as I finished. I was just about to call you,' said Rana.

'I got held up in traffic,' Patterson lied. 'I'm just glad you could carry out the autopsy so soon.'

'So am I. There are some interesting results for you to ponder.'

'Such as?'

'Such as, I think you've got another murder on your hands,' Rana said.

Patterson looked at Rana but didn't say anything.

'You don't seem as surprised as I thought you'd be,' said Rana.

'Well, I've just learned Umar couldn't have written his own suicide note, so on the way over here, the possibility that Umar hadn't killed himself had crossed my mind.'

'Ah,' said Rana, 'then when you hear what I've got to say, that suicide note may make even more sense.'

A thousand questions now swirled around Patterson's mind. Did he really have another murder on his hands? He waited as Rana picked up a clipboard.

'OK,' Rana began. 'First things first. Time of death. Umar died sometime on Sunday night. Best estimate is between 8 pm and 10 pm.'

Patterson nodded. 'That would make sense. Umar was seen leaving his flat around teatime on Sunday. You really think Umar could have been murdered?'

'In my opinion, Mike, this young man never hanged himself. There are multiple indications that he was hanged by one, probably two, people, and there were no traces of drugs in Umar's body; he was completely conscious when it happened.'

'How?'

'As I say, it would probably have taken two

people to overpower Umar. Umar was a big man, and there were clear signs that he had been in a struggle. For instance, there are recent abrasions on his wrists. At first, I thought these were the possible remnants of another suicide attempt, but on closer examination, they were the result of his wrists being tied tightly together with some sort of rope, identical to the one placed around his neck. The rope cut into his skin and left similar marks just above his ankles, where the rope had rubbed the skin through his trousers. I examined the trousers, and sure enough, they too have marks consistent with the victim's legs being tied together. When he was hanged, the rope repeatedly rubbed upwards on his neck, indicating his legs were repeatedly pulled down by someone, to make sure Umar was asphyxiated.'

'And you're saying he was fully conscious when this happened?' asked Patterson.

Rana nodded. 'Fully conscious. I suspect Umar fought back more than they were prepared for. There was quite a struggle, which is why there is so much evidence he was forcibly hanged. In addition, there are tiny fibres all around his mouth. I've sent them off to forensics, but I've seen those types of fibres before on several occasions. They're almost certainly the residue of black masking tape placed over Umar's mouth. Plus, there are bruises all over his body.

Just to mention as well, it appears that Umar was crying just before he died, bawling his eyes out, poor lad. Umar struggled as best he could, but it was to no avail. That's another reason why I think there was more than one assailant, or should I say murderer, and I hope you catch them soon because this young man died a horrible death.'

'Tasmina, please don't get on at me, but are you absolutely certain Umar was forcibly hanged? You're absolutely sure he was murdered?'

'As sure as I'll ever be. Umar was murdered, yes.'

'OK, Tasmina, thanks, that certainly gives me a lot to think about. Could you get the full report to me as soon as it's available?'

'Of course, I'll do that.'

Patterson left the building, lost in thought and lost in questions. It appeared that instead of a murder investigation just coming to an end, another was just beginning. Would this investigation ever be over?

CHAPTER 49

No Hard Feelings

Outside the mortuary at the Southern General, Patterson got back in his car for the drive back to Partick. Before switching on the engine, however, he started to feel dizzy and pulled his hand back from the ignition key.

He tried not to think about everything too much, but the questions and fears kept barging their way into his brain. Someone—probably more than one person—had murdered Umar. Could it have been the far right, after all? This was a lynching. Just when he thought extremists were once and for all out of the picture, they popped back into the picture.

There Patterson was, joking about the Ku Klux Klan being in Glasgow, and now extremists were possibly the number one murder suspects in the death of a second black man. Yet, as Patterson contemplated racists being the leading contenders behind the murder of Umar, they started to fade back into the pack as other possibilities came to the fore.

Patterson had to stay calm and think logically. It could still have been a fellow trainee, or trainees, who murdered Umar. He went through the list of trainees in his mind. If it were two acting together, which two would have forcibly hanged Umar from a tree?

Patterson put his head in his hands. He was overthinking again, going round and round in circles. He needed to calm down. He could feel the sweat on his brow and lowered a window for some fresh air. Would the murder at the Partick Bunhouse Café ever be solved? Patterson continued to take deep breaths, and eventually he calmed down enough for the drive back to Partick. One question, though, remained constant on his journey back north across the river, a question he never thought he would be asking at the start of the day.

Who had murdered Umar Olowe?

Eventually, Patterson arrived back at Partick station. As soon as he entered the investigation room, he was approached by Price.

'Sir, could I have a word?'

'Of course, Moses, come into the office.'

As both men sat down, Patterson sensed that something was troubling Price, just as he had when he left the investigation room that morning.

'Is everything all right? You're not still getting hassle are you, for what happened to Brian? If someone is having a go, tell me who it is and I'll have them dealt with.'

'No, it's not that. Actually, since you mentioned it in the briefing the other day, everyone has been fine. Besides, I guess it was only natural for them to think I was to blame for Brian not getting his promotion.'

'Nevertheless,' said Patterson, 'if anyone gives you trouble again, let me know.'

'I know. Anyway, as I said, it's not that.'

'What then?'

'That man who visited you this morning?'

'What man?' asked Patterson.

'The one that dresses in the colourful clothes, he's a politician, isn't he?'

'You mean Zach Andrews? Yes, why?'

'It's just that when he left, I was at the coffee machine, just looking out the window, and I saw him drive away. He drives a yellow Volkswagen Beetle.'

'Wouldn't surprise me, what about it?'

'It's just that when I was checking the CCTV around the time of Umar leaving his flat on

Sunday, I was sure I saw a similar car pull away from the flats.'

'Oh? There are probably a few yellow Volkswagen Beetles about in Glasgow.'

'Not that many,' said Moses, 'there are sixty-seven to be exact. I checked.'

'You checked?' asked Patterson, smiling. 'I must admit I'm surprised there are that many.'

'Yes, the thing is, even if there are a few yellow Volkswagen Beetles about, there are not many that have a red stripe running along the side.'

'Zach Andrew's car has a red stripe?'

'Yes.'

'And the car you saw on CCTV had that same red stripe?'

'Yes. That's the reason I remembered— it's quite a distinctive car. So, this morning, after you left, I double-checked, and I found the CCTV footage again. I was right, a yellow Volkswagen Beetle with a red stripe drove away from the area just after Umar left the block of flats.'

'Have you got that CCTV footage now?'

'Yes, it's on my laptop.'

'Let's have a look.'

Patterson walked over with Price to his laptop, and Price brought up the relevant images.

'See, here, you can see Umar leaving the block of flats at 5:15 pm, and then he walks out of view. But here at 5:21 pm, you can see the Volkswagen Beetle pull away.'

Patterson looked at Moses and shook his head. 'Sorry, Moses, but I think you're imagining things. There's no Volkswagen Beetle I can see.'

'You can,' said Price, 'if you look closely. It's not clear on this image, but if I zoom in on the top right-hand corner, you can just about see it.'

Patterson looked at Price. 'Maybe it's my eyesight, but I still don't see anything.'

'Hang on, I'll clean it up a bit more. Here.'

As Patterson looked at the screen, the distinct outline of a car appeared, just about discernible as a yellow Volkswagen Beetle with a red stripe. It appeared to be pulling out of a side street before quickly going out of view.

'That side street,' said Moses, 'I checked, it can be reached from the flats and from the direction Umar went, but there are no CCTV cameras on the path leading to it. Only this camera outside the flats picks it up in the distance.'

Patterson thought for a moment. Was it just a coincidence that a car identical to that of Zach Andrews would be pulling out of a side street near where Umar lived, and precisely at the time Umar was last seen? The implications for Patterson were immediate, and he began to realise that something was going on that, until then, he had been completely unaware of.

'Can you tell what direction the Volkswagen was headed?'

'It's hard to say exactly, but from this angle, it looks like it's heading towards the expressway.'

'OK, get onto the traffic division. They should be able to track it. See where it goes.'

He looked at Moses. 'Well done, Moses, that was well spotted. I need to see Dunard. Keep us up to date with the tracking.'

'Will do, sir.'

Patterson smiled as he realised something else. The expressway went all the way to East Kilbride, and if he remembered right, very near Braemar Woods. He also realised he hadn't updated the team about Umar's murder. However, he wanted to tell Dunard immediately of the developments. He knew he had to move fast to get the assistance he needed. He walked out of the investigation room, past the still broken lift, and up the stairs to see Dunard.

CHAPTER 50

Developments

Patterson told Dunard everything that had happened, including what Moses had spotted on CCTV. He explained what he now wanted, and Dunard said he would make sure it happened. Patterson then went downstairs and called Pettigrew into his office. Patterson explained what he wanted her to do, and she immediately headed out of the station to carry out the task.

He then called in Simpson and McKinnon and gave them similar instructions before he entered the investigation room and told the rest of the team what was now known about the death of Umar. Namely, it wasn't suicide but murder. He assigned other officers additional tasks before heading back to his office. There, he called Gillespie at the fraud squad and was delighted to hear that his colleague had some news to report.

Patterson put the phone down and sat back in his chair. He knew that the best way to absolutely ensure a conviction was to get a confession from one or both of his suspects.

So, a plan emerged. All Patterson had to do was wait until the final pieces of evidence were gathered, and then he could proceed. Getting a confession would be accomplished in three parts, and the next day, once Patterson was informed that everything was in place, Patterson moved ahead with part one.

CHAPTER 51

A Confession in Three Parts: Part One

Patterson led Zach Andrews and his lawyer to Interview Room One. The DCI apologised for bringing Zach back to the station, but explained that there were one or two loose ends that needed to be cleared up before the investigation could officially be brought to a close.

His lawyer, a heavy-set man with a bushy beard and a too-small tweed jacket, clearly wasn't convinced.

'Was this interview so urgent that my client had to attend today? Need I remind you that Mr Andrews is a busy man with many demands on his time? He has already had to postpone some very important meetings because of this.'

Patterson said he was fully aware of how busy Mr Andrews was, but it simply couldn't be avoided.

Once they were all seated in the interview room, Patterson provided further explanation.

'The main reason I've brought you in for this interview, Zach, is that some new information has come to light regarding the murder of Gideon Semanyo and the death of Umar Olowe. As I said over the phone, I advised you to bring your lawyer for your own protection, and just to add, once again, I really do appreciate your co-operation and you taking the time out to help us.'

'As always,' said Andrews, 'if there's anything I can do to help, I'm glad to do so.'

Patterson turned to Andrew's lawyer, 'If only all politicians were as public-spirited.' His lawyer rightly suspected Patterson was being facetious.

'OK,' continued Patterson, 'first of all, an autopsy has been carried out on Umar Olowe and some doubts have emerged about how he died.'

'He committed suicide, didn't he?' said Andrews. 'Wasn't he found hanging from a tree?'

'He was, but the autopsy found some discrepancies, some unexplained injuries.'

'Really?'

'Really. For instance, Umar had some abrasions on his wrists. At first, the pathologist thought they could have been the result of an earlier suicide attempt. However, she found similar abrasions on his ankles. She now believes these marks, and others, are the result of Umar being forcibly restrained. She believes Umar's wrists and ankles were tied together, and either one or two people hanged Umar. In other words, Umar didn't commit suicide; he was murdered.'

'Murdered?' Andrews seemed shocked. 'You mean someone else hanged Umar?'

'That's the conclusion of the pathologist, yes.'

'My God,' said Andrews. 'That's terrible.'

'It is,' agreed Patterson.

'...but why would anyone do that?'

'That's what I'm trying to find out,' said Patterson. 'I believe you knew Umar yourself?'

'Me?' said Andrews. 'I wouldn't say I knew him. I think he was at the café launch day, but I don't think I even talked to him, at least, I can't remember doing so.'

'And you haven't met or known Umar since?'

'No, not at all.'

'Are you absolutely sure about that?'

'Of course.'

Andrews looked at his lawyer, and his lawyer spoke up. 'Just what are you implying?'

'Zach, we know you attended parties held at Umar's flat.'

'I attended parties at Umar's flat?' Andrews looked at his lawyer again, as though he were a comfort blanket.

The lawyer spoke again. 'Inspector, I would advise you not to make unsubstantiated allegations.'

Patterson smiled. 'OK. Before I go any further, you should know I have evidence to back up everything I say.' He brought out a series of CCTV stills from a folder and placed them in front of Andrews. 'These are images from CCTV at Umar's tower block on the various nights you attended these parties held at Umar's flat. However, as you know, those parties weren't held by Umar himself but by Gideon Semanyo, Umar's friend. By all accounts, these parties could get pretty wild—not least for the drug-taking involved—and we have testimony that you were a regular attendee at those parties.'

Andrews looked at his lawyer again before looking back at Patterson, and he seemed to decide on another approach. He visibly relaxed and shrugged.

'OK, so yes, I admit I attended some parties held at Umar's flat, so what?'

'Just to be clear, a moment ago you said you didn't know Umar, but you now admit attending parties at his flat?'

'Some of the people who attend those parties are not exactly upstanding individuals. I'm sure you understand I wouldn't want my reputation unnecessarily sullied by association. Nevertheless, I don't think these parties were as wild as you're making them out to be.'

'Yet, you were still prepared to keep the fact that you knew Umar and Gideon a secret while I was conducting an investigation into their murders?'

'Maybe I should have said something, but as I said, these types of things can be weaponised by the press.'

His lawyer spoke up again. 'What you present as evidence is only hearsay from certain individuals, many of whom probably have an agenda to damage the reputation of Mr Andrews. The CCTV doesn't prove anything except Mr Andrews visited the tower block.'

'I just want to establish that Mr Andrews knew Umar, contrary to what he has previously stated.'

'Actually,' said Andrews, 'I still wouldn't say I knew Umar well; often, he wasn't at those parties. As you said, it was Gideon who was the host.'

'So where was Umar when the parties were

held?'

'Sometimes he was in his bedroom, usually with the door shut; sometimes he was out. Umar was not the most sociable of types. In all honesty, Umar was...a bit simple.'

'Simple? Out of curiosity, what were your impressions of Gideon?'

'Gideon was a very impressive young man. Absolutely lovely, and such fun. I liked him a lot; everyone did. You do realise he came to this country with absolutely nothing, seeking refuge from a horrific war, and in a short space of time and in a completely new environment, he proved himself to be a very astute businessman.'

'By dealing drugs.'

'I realise for yourself, Gideon was not the... type of person you would ever think favourably of, but whether you like it or not, Gideon was an outstanding young man.'

Patterson began a more direct approach. 'Where were you last Sunday night between 5 pm and 10 pm?'

Andrews looked to the side. 'I'm not sure... I don't think I can remember.'

'Think.'

'Think? Actually...yes, last Sunday I was at home all day responding to correspondence from my constituents.'

'Try again, Zach,' said Patterson. He brought out more CCTV images, which showed Andrew's car driving along Dumbarton Road towards Umar's flat just before 5 pm. He also brought out the enlarged CCTV image of Andrew's car pulling out of the side street at 5:21 pm, as well as an image of Umar leaving the tower block at 5:15 pm. 'Your car was seen outside Umar's flat around the time Umar disappeared. I realise that you like to be conspicuous, but it may not have been the wisest move to buy such a distinctive car, and I believe you even added that red stripe yourself. Very clever. A bright yellow Volkswagen with a distinctive red stripe may tie in with your colourful image, but it isn't so helpful when you're up to no good. So what were you doing parking in a side street next to Umar's home last Sunday teatime?'

'You don't have to answer that, Zach,' said his lawyer.

Andrews shifted in his seat. 'No, it's fine, I remember, actually, you're right, I completely forgot I went for a drive last Sunday. I often drive along Dumbarton Road and park up that side street...just for a bit of peace and quiet. I genuinely had no idea what Umar was doing at that time.'

'So, it's purely a coincidence you were there when Umar left his flat?'

'Exactly. Purely a coincidence.'

'Inspector,' his lawyer interjected again, 'just what is the point of all this?'

'The point is, we have evidence that Stephen McDonald drove and met you in that side street, where you then picked up Umar, and the three of you drove to Braemar Woods. It was there that you and Stephen McDonald murdered Umar by hanging him from a tree. Afterwards, you drove back to that side street—Patterson brought out another CCTV still of Andrew's car driving back into the side street—dropped Stephen McDonald off, who drove home, which you then did yourself.'

Andrews laughed. 'That's ridiculous. Just because I parked up in a side street near Umar's address a couple of times, you're saying I murdered Umar? And I supposedly did this, along with, who did you say, Stephen McDonald? I don't even know Stephen McDonald.'

'But you do. Zach, as I said, I have evidence to support everything I say. Your friendship with McDonald is well-known. We have proof he has been a visitor to your house and you to his, where you have no doubt met his long-suffering wife. However, you did inadvertently help me in one respect to that. The other day, when you were leaving the investigation room and Stephen McDonald was coming up the stairs, you walked right past each other without saying a word. I didn't think anything of it at the time; it was only afterwards, on learning about your friendship, that I found it curious. I realised you didn't acknowledge each other because you didn't want me to see that you knew one another, and then I thought, why would that be? What are they trying to hide? You know, if you had just said hello to each other, or even simply nodded, it would have been completely normal. The fact that you didn't acknowledge each other at all was not normal. You overplayed your hand, Zach.'

'The lawyer spoke once more. 'So, you have evidence that my client knows Stephen McDonald. Congratulations. Besides that, it appears all you have is a couple of images of a car driving in and out of a side street near where Umar lived. Now, if you don't have anything more than that, I suggest we end this interview now.'

'We also have your phone records,' said Patterson.

'My phone records?'

'Your phone data, to be exact. As your lawyer will tell you, we can remotely access someone's phone data if we have sufficient reason to believe a crime has been committed. In your own case, when I went to my superior, Chief Superintendent Dunard, he agreed that we had more than enough justification to be authorised to access your mobile phone data. It's why we know that after parking on that side street, you then drove to Braemar Woods. Oh, yes, I know you switched off your phone when you arrived at the dirt road leading into the woodland, but switching off your mobile phone at the entrance to Braemar Woods is even more suspicious than if you hadn't. In any case, we have CCTV footage of your car driving down the expressway all the way to the woods.'

Andrews looked at his lawyer for some intervention, but his lawyer remained stony-faced.

'Besides,' Andrews asked, unwisely, 'What possible reason would I have for murdering Umar?'

'That,' said Patterson, 'is something we both know. It all began when someone in your political party unwisely gave you access to the fund designated for the café's refurbishment. Something my friend at the fraud squad was able to confirm. Unfortunately, along with Stephen McDonald, you thought you deserved some of that money for yourself. That was what started all this, and ended with two young men being murdered. We know everything, Zach. The best thing you can do is confess everything yourself right now.'

'Oh, of course,' said Andrews. 'I'm going to

confess to a crime I haven't committed.'

'I'll tell you what. I'm going to give you an opportunity to speak to your lawyer. If he really wants to help you, he will advise you to tell us all you know now. You see, through that wall there, is Interview Room Two and in Interview Room Two is Stephen McDonald. I suspect Mr McDonald will have no hesitation in explaining why you murdered Umar. The sooner you give your side of the story, Zach, the better.' Patterson stood up. 'I'll be back later. In the meantime, consult with your lawyer to determine your best course of action. It could be the difference between spending a long time in prison and spending the rest of your life in prison. Oh, if you want a tea or coffee, just ask the officer by the door, and I'll see you later.'

With that, Patterson left the interview room.

CHAPTER 52

A Confession in Three Parts: Part Two

Patterson walked into Interview Room Two to see an irate Stephen McDonald, sitting next to his equally irate lawyer. The two men looked at each other before glaring at Patterson as he casually walked towards the empty chair on one side of the desk.

Gladly sensing the hostile atmosphere, Patterson said, 'Sorry to keep you waiting.'

McDonald's lawyer was immaculately dressed in a three-piece suit, complete with an over-the-top buttonhole flower, as if he had just come from a wedding. He was also dressed in a predictable, well-mannered voice that had a slight highland tilt to it.

'You do realise,' the lawyer began, 'that Mr McDonald has been waiting here for over twenty-five minutes?'

'Twenty-five minutes? I'm sorry, but I got held up, you know how it is.'

McDonald broke into a smile. 'Don't worry about it.' Despite his clear irritation, McDonald obviously thought it best to try and keep Patterson onside.

Patterson then explained the formalities of the interview before starting.

'OK, Mr McDonald, the reason I brought you in for an interview is because there have been some new developments regarding the investigation into the murder of Gideon Semanyo and the death of Umar Olowe. I wanted to ask you some questions in light of these developments.' Patterson waited for McDonald's lawyer to say something just for the sake of saying something, but was pleasantly surprised when he didn't.

'I'll begin by explaining the reason I was held up,' continued Patterson, 'I was held up because I was interviewing a good friend of yours, Zach Andrews, the MSP for this area.'

'I'm not sure I'd go as far as calling Zach Andrews a good friend.'

'Oh, but he is. We know he is. Granted, I thought when you completely ignored each other at the station the other day, you didn't know each other. However, I've since learned you ignoring each other was purely for my benefit.

Anyway, that's by and by, Mr Andrews has just admitted he went to parties held by Gideon Semanyo at Umar Olowe's flat.'

'And?' asked McDonald,

'I'm mentioning it to show that there are numerous connections between four people in this affair, Umar Olowe, Gideon Semanyo, Zach Andrews and yourself.'

'If you're suggesting I attended parties held at this Umar's flat, I haven't,' said McDonald.

'Oh, I know you haven't.'

'Then what are you on about?'

'I know you never went to parties held at Umar Olowe's flat, far too downmarket for the likes of yourself. However, we do have evidence that you have visited Gideon's flat in Laurel Street countless times.'

McDonald hesitated. 'So?'

'It turns out you began your acquaintance with Gideon by being a paying client of Gideon's...services. Gideon was known as one of the hardest-working sex workers, or rent boys if you prefer, in the city. In fact, by all accounts, you weren't just a paying client of his, you became absolutely smitten by young Gideon.'

'Inspector—' the lawyer began.

'Yes, I know. I know, it's only hearsay. The

fact remains, we know you went to see Gideon numerous times at his flat. You really couldn't keep away from him, could you? A colleague of mine asked around Gideon's neighbours, and two of them said you were a constant visitor. I can only assume your wife must have long ago accepted the situation. Anyway, predictably, you fell into that age-old trap of thinking Gideon wasn't just with you for the money but had developed the same feelings for you as you had for him. Sadly, you were wrong. In fact, let me tell you what I believe happened, and you can stop me at any point if I get something wrong.'

'Inspector,—' his lawyer began again.

'No,' said McDonald, interrupting, 'I'm curious as to what Inspector Patterson has to say.'

'Thank you,' said Patterson. 'As I was saying, I believe your... relationship got to a point when you thought you could completely trust Gideon. So, one day, you foolishly told Gideon what was actually going on at the café, about how Zach Andrews, who had access to the café's funds, and yourself were syphoning off money meant for the café's refurbishment. In return for your own slice of cash, you assisted Zach with an elaborate maze of offshore bank accounts, which you said would hide the whereabouts of the money. The fraud squad, by the way, now know all about it. Anyway, you really thought Gideon would be impressed when you told him what you were doing, didn't you? It must have been quite a shock when, instead of Gideon being impressed and saying how clever a boy you were, he immediately decided to blackmail you. Namely, that if you didn't give him money, he would go to the papers and expose Andrews and yourself.'

McDonald visibly shuddered, and Patterson knew that the memory of Gideon's betrayal still caused the MP intense emotional pain. 'So then you found yourself in a right pickle, didn't you? You now had Gideon threatening to expose you siphoning off money, knowing Gideon would gladly follow through with his threat because, for Gideon, it was a win-win situation. He knew that either he would get money from you or else he would get money from the newspapers. It made no difference to the ever entrepreneurial Gideon. At the same time, you knew Gideon would never stop demanding money. So, what could you do? You talk it over with Andrews and realise the only solution was to somehow get rid of Gideon, so Andrews and yourself, take the bold decision to murder him.'

'I think that's enough, Inspector,' said his lawyer. 'Now, you're in the realm of pure make-believe.'

'I notice Mr McDonald isn't denying it,' said Patterson.

'Continue,' said McDonald, quietly with head bowed, and Patterson did.

'So, you know you have to murder Gideon, but how? Talking with Andrews, one of you says, You know, why don't we get Umar to murder Gideon? You knew it was feasible. Umar is a very vulnerable, mentally traumatised young man, absolutely terrified of being deported back to Nigeria. You knew that was all the leverage you needed with poor Umar. With Andrews and you, making out, you had far more influence than you did; you got Umar to believe that if he didn't do as you asked, you would have him deported back to Nigeria. So, in absolute fear of being deported, that Friday afternoon, Umar does as you demand and murders Gideon. Am I right so far, Stephen?'

McDonald didn't answer, but it was clear he was on the brink of breaking down, his hands shaking.

'Stephen,' said Patterson, 'I can tell you're getting emotional, so do you know what I'm going to do? I'm going to pause this interview for a moment to give you a chance to talk to your lawyer. What age are you, by the way?' Patterson looked at a sheet before him. 'Fifty-three? If you're found guilty, you'll likely be spending the rest of your life in prison. You do have one final option open to you. If you make a full confession now, the judge may look kindly upon it, although I cannot promise anything. As I was saying earlier, the reason I was held up was because through that wall there is Interview Room One, and in Interview Room One, I was interviewing Zach Andrews. Zach is on the brink of making a full confession, which I'm afraid could be very bad news for you, Stephen. And I'm afraid there is even worse news for you. Through that wall there, is Interview Room Three. In Interview Room Three, Gillian McKenzie is waiting for me to interview her, and I have a strong feeling Gillian won't take much persuading to make a full confession either. So, you see, it's like you're in a confession sandwich. Seriously, if I were you, I would get in there first and tell your side of the story. Otherwise, it's almost certain you will never see the outside of a prison cell for the rest of your life.'

'You're bluffing,' said McDonald, his voice cracking.

'Stephen, I have only mentioned a fraction of the evidence we have against you. For instance, we have your phone data from when you were driving to Braemar Woods. Yes, you switched off your phone when you arrived at Umar's flat, but unfortunately, Zach didn't until you arrived at the woods. We even have the tyre tracks leading into the woods, which will undoubtedly match up with Zach's car. I'm sure we will also find DNA of both you and Umar inside Zach's car. I'm also sure that some of those unidentified fingerprints we found in Gideon's flat will be yours, and then there's the damning evidence the fraud squad has uncovered showing the café refurbishment money winding its trail through your numerous offshore accounts to you, and that's just for starters. So, you see, I'm afraid you're bang to rights, as they say. The only hope you have is to make a full confession now and hope the judge looks upon it favourably. Anyway, you think about it, talk to your lawyer, and I'll see you in a bit.' Patterson stood up. 'Oh, if you want a tea or coffee, by the way, just ask the officer by the door.'

With that, Patterson left the room.

CHAPTER 53

A Confession in Three Parts: Part Three

Patterson entered Interview Room Three to see Gillian McKenzie sitting nervously next to her lawyer, a woman in a smart business suit, who was eyeing Patterson with justified suspicion. She twiddled a pen between two fingers over some papers as if she were trying to cast a spell.

'Sorry to have kept you,' said Patterson, sitting down.

As Patterson expected, McKenzie was completely different from the confident, brazen woman who had walked into Dunard's office a few weeks ago, insisting that far-right extremists had murdered Gideon. This was a much humbler woman who made no pretence of bravado.

Patterson went through the formalities of the interview and then began.

'Gillian, the reason I have brought you in for an interview is that there have been some new developments concerning the murder investigation I'm conducting, and I'm hoping you can shed some light on what I've discovered.'

'I don't see how I can help,' said McKenzie.

'You will,' said Patterson. 'As you're aware, my investigation is regarding the murders of Gideon Semanyo and Umar Olowe.'

'Murders? I thought Umar committed suicide.'

'Yes, that's what we believed at first. However, we now know Umar was murdered, forcibly hanged from a tree.'

'Forcibly hanged?' McKenzie looked shocked. 'But you must have made a mistake.'

'Why do you think that? I thought you would have said that Umar being hanged from a tree is proof that it was far-right extremists who murdered him, that this was a lynching, maybe even that the Ku Klux Klan was behind it.'

'Well, yes, of course, you're right. It must have been the far-right, then. Yet…didn't Umar confess to murdering Gideon? I'm sorry, I'm confused.'

'I'll explain everything in good time, but first, if you'll indulge me, I'd like to begin by telling you just how Umar died.'

McKenzie's lawyer eyed Patterson with even more suspicion as he continued.

'Last Sunday, Umar was seen leaving his block of flats at 5:15 pm. We believe Umar was picked up by two men who drove him to Braemar Woods, near East Kilbride. In some respects, we can only speculate about what was said to Umar to persuade him to accompany these two men. However, as you may know, Umar was a vulnerable individual who was very easily manipulated. So, it's possible that the two men simply promised to help Umar in some way. Take him to better accommodation, for example. Who knows? Regardless of that, the end result is that somewhere on the way to Braemar Woods, these two men managed to overpower and restrain Umar, led him into woodland, tied his arms and legs together and put a rope around his neck.'

McKenzie shook her head. 'That's horrific.'

'It is. You know, one of the saddest things I learned at Umar's autopsy was the pathologist saying that just before he died, Umar was crying his eyes out, no doubt pleading for his life, before the two men put masking tape over his mouth. Then, after throwing one end of a rope over a thick tree branch, they hauled Umar up into the air. He—'

'Inspector,' the lawyer said in a tired voice. 'I don't really see the point of this.'

'I assure you, there is a reason I'm telling you this. As I was saying, Umar was hauled up into the air; he would have been choking at this point, well aware he was going to die and there was nothing he could do about it. The pathologist was able to determine, by the marks the cord made on Umar's neck, that one or possibly both men pulled downwards on Umar's legs as he was strung up into the air. I often wonder what poor Umar's last thoughts would have been. He must have been so frightened, absolutely petrified. We know Umar still fought for his life until he couldn't fight any longer. There are signs of a prolonged struggle; Umar fighting, struggling until the last breath left his body.'

The lawyer spoke. 'Inspector, once again, is this really necessary?'

Patterson could see tears forming in McKenzie's eyes, and he knew it was.

'I'd just like Gillian to know, as someone who cares so passionately about refugees and asylum seekers, just how sad and barbaric Umar's murder was.'

Patterson watched as McKenzie wiped tears from her eyes.

'You know the other truly tragic thing about Umar's death? We contacted the Home Office to learn more about Umar's life back in Nigeria. If anyone deserved to be described as an asylum seeker, it was Umar. Yet, Umar didn't like to talk about his past, probably because he was still traumatised by it. You see, Umar had managed to escape a genocide taking place in Nigeria in which his whole family—practically his whole village—was massacred. Yet, incredibly, Umar had the courage and fortitude to make it all the way to the UK by himself, which is truly remarkable. Then, when Umar believed he had finally found sanctuary, here, in Glasgow, our city, believing it to be a forever safe home, he was brutally murdered.'

McKenzie was still in tears as she listened, and the lawyer interrupted Patterson again in a bored, unemotional voice. 'Inspector, as sad as this story is, I really don't see that it has any relevance to why Mrs McKenzie has been brought here today.'

'You're right. I'll tell you the relevance. We now know the two men who murdered Umar are Zach Andrews and Stephen McDonald.'

'What? No! But that's impossible!' Gillian exclaimed, still wiping her eyes.

'Why is that impossible?' Patterson asked.

'They just, they would never do such a thing.'

'So you know Zach Andrews and Stephen McDonald, then?

'Yes, I mean, well, no, I know them a little. They're involved with the café.'

'Gillian, there is no doubt about their guilt. We have proof, including their phone data, which shows that Stephen McDonald drove to Umar's address to pick up Umar, and then Andrews drove Umar and McDonald to Braemar Woods.'

McKenzie shook her head. 'I can't believe that.'

'I'm afraid it's true,' continued Patterson, 'and for the record, the reason I told you about how Umar died and his situation back in Nigeria is because I think it's important to know to what extent Umar was betrayed; betrayed by Gideon, who he believed was his good friend, but who constantly used and abused him, betrayed by Zach Andrews, betrayed by Stephen McDonald... and betrayed by you.

'What do you mean, betrayed by me?'

'Gillian, I first had my suspicions about you when it seemed that no sooner had Gideon been found, than you rushed into Chief Superintendent Dunard's office, saying how shocked you were by his murder and that the far-right were behind it. Of course, I didn't realise at the time that it had all been planned in advance. First, the threatening letters, then you, along with Andrews and McDonald, all insisting it was far-right extremists who murdered Gideon. Then, when you all realised I wasn't going to go along with your far-right narrative, you immediately pressed for me to be removed from the investigation.'

Gillian shook her head. 'You've got it all wrong. I genuinely thought it was the far-right who murdered Gideon. I always knew sooner or later, far-right extremists would start murdering refugees.'

'No, Gillian. When you entered this station, that very first morning, you already knew it was Umar who murdered Gideon, and it was Andrews and McDonald who made him do it.'

'That's not true. You know it's not true.'

'No, it is true. You already knew Andrews and McDonald forced Umar to murder Gideon, and yet you still chose to use Gideon's murder for your own agenda, namely to make out that the far-right were a major force operating in Glasgow. You saw Gideon's murder as a great opportunity to further your own cause, and in turn, your own career. In fact, you couldn't get enough of the interviews. When I saw you on TV, you were practically jumping up and down with glee at the publicity you were getting, and you couldn't organise that protest march fast enough. Isn't that the case?'

'That's a disgusting thing to say!'

Patterson brought out a bank statement. 'I have evidence to support everything I say. For instance, you made a cash deposit of £5,000 on the afternoon of March the twelfth. That same morning, McDonald, out of funds that were, by the way, meant for the café's refurbishment, withdrew £5,000 from one of his many accounts to give to you. You knew exactly what Andrews and McDonald had done, and yet you didn't report it. You didn't just use Gideon's murder to further your own agenda and career, you took payments into the bargain.'

Gillian became tearful once again. 'You're wrong…it wasn't like that.'

'Wasn't it? Then tell me, what was it like?'

McKenzie continued to cry, gulping, not speaking, as if she were unable to do so.

'Gillian, we have proof of everything. We have your bank account transactions. We are aware of your meetings with Andrews and McDonald. I also know it was you, along with Andrews and McDonald, who were briefing journalists against me. We know everything, Gillian. You may not have murdered those two young black men with your own hands, but you're just as responsible for their deaths as Andrews and McDonald. There's nothing more you can do; it's over.'

'You're twisting what happened, I—'

'OK. So why don't you tell us what happened in your own words?'

Her lawyer gently put her hand on McKenzie's shoulder. 'Gillian, you're under no obligation to say anything.'

Patterson addressed the lawyer. 'If you really have Gillian's best interests at heart, then I suggest you advise her to tell us everything she knows now. Gillian, I know those letters purporting to be from the far right were either written by Stephen, Zach, or you. Isn't that the truth?'

McKenzie looked down at the table and shook her head again. Patterson saw she appeared to be contemplating her options, so he tried to press home his advantage.

'I'm genuinely trying to help you here, Gillian. You're going to prison for a very long time. Unless…well, there is one thing you can do. Make a full confession now. Telling us everything can only help your situation.'

There was now fear etched on McKenzie's face, which was what Patterson wanted to see. Her lawyer leaned over and whispered something into McKenzie's ear before McKenzie said, 'I want to have a moment to speak with my lawyer.'

'Of course,' said Patterson. He couldn't help but feel a sense of promise in hearing these words. He paused the interview and gladly left the room. When he re-entered ten minutes later, it was clear McKenzie had been doing a lot more crying.

Patterson sat down, and McKenzie looked at her lawyer again, who nodded.

'Yes, I wrote those letters,' said McKenzie, 'but I honestly didn't know anything about Zach and Stephen being behind the murder of Gideon. I swear the sole motivation I had in writing those letters was to help the fight against racism. If I had realised for one second someone was going to get murdered, I would never have written them.'

'So, whose idea was it to write those letters?'

'Both of them. Zach and Stephen. Zach came and then introduced me to Stephen. They said that because the café was employing new Scots that—'

'New Scots?' asked Patterson.

'Immigrants who had chosen to make Scotland their home. Because the café was employing new Scots, they said it was an ideal opportunity to further the cause of anti-racism, which we were all fully committed to. They said if I wrote letters threatening the café trainees from overseas, then I could go to the press afterwards and say it was proof that the far-right was active in Glasgow. I swear I never knew anything about any murder that would take place!'

'No?' asked Patterson. 'So what did you think when Gideon was murdered? That it was all just a coincidence?'

'I did! I really did! I mean, of course, at first, I was naturally shocked. I immediately contacted Zach and Stephen, and they both said the same thing...that yes, it really was just a coincidence.'

Patterson looked to McKenzie's lawyer, who was decidedly avoiding eye contact.

'And you believed them?'

'Of course, I did. What? You think when I heard Gideon had been murdered, I instantly thought, Oh, it must have been Zach and Stephen who were behind it? Of course I didn't. I genuinely thought it was the far right, and that it actually vindicated me in writing those letters in the first place.'

'Gillian, we know you received another couple of payments from Stephen McDonald after Gideon was murdered.'

'Yes, well...they promised me some extra money if I continued to pressure the police into dropping you from the investigation.'

'Why?'

'Because, as you said, they knew you weren't going along with the far-right theory and wanted you off the case, so they asked me to help pressurise your bosses to get you removed.'

'And you agreed.'

'As I said, at first, I really was convinced it was the far right that murdered Gideon, and you were just being stubborn in not seeing that, so yes, I agreed.'

'Gillian, I understand you're trying to make out you had some noble aim in doing what you did. Maybe you're trying to convince yourself you had some noble aim. Yet, we both know you did it for the money.'

'No! Of course, I didn't do it for the money…well, not just for the money. I told you I've been fighting racism all my life. The money was just like…a bonus.'

'A bonus? A young man was murdered.'

'How many times? I never knew Zach and Stephen were behind Gideon's murder until you told me just now. I mean, OK, yes, it did occur to me later on that it was possible the far right weren't involved, but in that case, I thought it must have been another trainee who had murdered Gideon. You have to believe me, that's the truth.' Gillian broke down crying again.

The lawyer spoke up. 'Inspector, my client has been completely honest with you, as you asked. Now, apart from anything else, you have absolutely no evidence she knew anything about who was behind the murder of Gideon. As Gillian says, she thought she was helping a good cause and nothing more.'

'A good cause? Your client deliberately misled a police investigation. A counter-terrorism officer was brought in, partly because of those threatening letters. It's quite possible I could have found out the real story behind Gideon's murder a lot sooner if I hadn't been deliberately misled. It's also possible that Umar would still be alive today if it weren't for your client.'

McKenzie continued to cry, but Patterson knew they were nothing more than tears of self-pity. Still, he wanted to hear the full story of what McKenzie had done. He still wasn't convinced she was telling the whole truth. More importantly, Patterson wanted to know what McKenzie could tell him about the involvement of Andrews and McDonald in the murders of not just Gideon, but Umar.

'OK. So you admit you sent those letters purporting to be from the far-right. You also want me to believe that when Gideon was murdered, alarm bells didn't start ringing?'

'No! They didn't. Looking back, maybe they should have, but they didn't.'

'I don't believe you, Gillian, and I doubt a jury would either. The best you can do is be completely honest with me now. Tell me the truth. When Gideon was murdered, you really didn't suspect anything?'

'No!'

Patterson thought it was time to try another tactic. 'Gillian, let me tell you something. Through that wall there is Interview Room Two. In Interview Room Two is Stephen McDonald. When I left Stephen earlier, he was on the brink of making a full confession. On the far side of Interview Room Two is Interview Room One. There, Zach Andrews is on the brink of making a full confession. Unfortunately for you, I have no doubt that at least one and probably both men are prepared to throw you under the bus in the hope of getting a lighter sentence. The best thing you can do for yourself is tell me the whole truth now before I revisit those two rooms and get those confessions. Otherwise, you're as good as putting a rope around your own neck. However, if you make a full confession and explain what really happened in your own words, although I cannot promise anything, you may be able to avoid a much longer jail sentence. Gillian, look at me.'

McKenzie didn't move and continued to stare blankly at the table.

'Gillian…'

Slowly, McKenzie looked up.

'When Gideon was murdered,' asked Patterson, 'did you know Zach and Stephen were behind it?'

Gillian hesitated, started to shake her head, but then slowly nodded.

'I need you to say it, Gillian,' said Patterson.

'Yes, I knew Zach and Stephen made Umar murder Gideon. Yes, I knew, I knew all about it from before Gideon was murdered.'

'How did you know?'

'They told me...they told me exactly how they made Umar do it. Umar was petrified of being deported back to Nigeria; they used it to make Umar murder Gideon. Once they told me all about it, they said I had to keep quiet because I was now an accomplice, and they were right. I couldn't tell anyone.'

'What about Umar's murder?'

'Zach and Stephen had to murder Umar to keep him from ever confessing that they made him murder Gideon. It was just as you said. They drove him to the woods and hanged him.'

'OK,' said Patterson with a sigh. I think we'll leave it there for the moment.'

Patterson went to the door and spoke to the policeman standing on duty, who left.

'I'm going to get the testimonies of Zach and Stephen now. With your confession, they won't have a choice but to confess themselves.' The officer on duty returned with Price.

'Gillian, this is DS Price. He's a relatively new recruit to our station, but he's proven to be invaluable since he arrived. In fact, if it wasn't for our eagle-eyed Detective Sergeant here, it's very possible you wouldn't be sitting there right now. Moses, Gillian is ready to make a full confession about her involvement in the murder of Gideon Semanyo and Umar Olowe. She is also prepared to explain exactly how Zach Andrews and Stephen McDonald, in effect, murdered both men. Oh, and make sure she and her lawyer get a tea or coffee, it could be a long night.'

With that, Patterson left the room.

CHAPTER 54

The Partick Bunhouse Café

As Patterson woke up and felt, as always, Stephanie's absence beside him, his first thought of the day evolved into the first question of the day, and the answer to that first question was Friday. It was Friday, and with that, Patterson remembered that he had the day off work.

As Patterson swung his legs out of bed, this happy realisation was accompanied by remembering it was also the last day of June, and that he had said he would go along to an open day at the Partick Bunhouse Café. This open day was somewhat of a misnomer, since it was only for a select group of friends and family associated with the café. The event was, in part, intended to serve as a trial run before the café officially opened the following day on Saturday, July 1.

As Patterson washed, shaved, and dressed,

for some reason, this Friday felt like a holiday in the summer. Looking out the window, seeing clear blue skies and people confident enough to go outside without a jacket on, confirmed this summer holiday vibe.

Later, as Patterson sat at the kitchen table and ate his Shreddies, he thought back to the Bunhouse Investigation. Two weeks had passed since all three main protagonists had confessed to their involvement in the murders of Gideon Semanyo and Umar Olowe. Those confessions had sealed the case, and since then, even more evidence had been gathered that would make the subsequent prosecutions foolproof.

The investigation itself had seemed to last forever, but in reality, it had only lasted a few weeks. Part of the reason the investigation had seemed so prolonged was the constant media scrutiny. Now that the truth of the murders had been revealed, the media had quickly lost interest and moved their short attention span on to the next story.

According to Pettigrew, Inspector Pearce was one of the officers invited to the Bunhouse open day. Patterson didn't know why Pettigrew had told him this, as if he would be interested, although he agreed it would be nice to see Pearce again. Pettigrew was also going, but DS Simpson and DS McKinnon said they had other plans they conveniently couldn't get out of.

Detective Sergeant McKinnon. Patterson was pleased McKinnon had been given his overdue promotion since the Bunhouse investigation had ended. Dunard knew he had to right a wrong, and the sooner he did it, the better.

Patterson thought of Annabelle Pearce again. Yeah, it would actually be good to see her once more. They had just said a perfunctory bye to each other when the Bunhouse investigation ended. He had even considered asking her out for a drink; then he thought...actually, maybe he still could.

'Annabelle, I was just wondering...' or 'Hey Annabelle, if you want some time, we could...'

Yeah, why not? It was settled. He would definitely ask Pearce out for a drink. The fact was, he liked her. Yeah, he definitely liked her. Having determined this, Patterson got up from the table and later that morning headed to the café.

As Patterson got out of his car on Bunhouse Road, he was very surprised at the transformation of the Bunhouse Café. It looked fantastic, all shiny and new, complete with an eye-catching, fancy sign and clean windows. Walking inside, he had a similar impression. The decorators had gone for an alpine feel, and apart from the tartan fabric banquettes, wood was the material of choice. The walls had been layered with wood panelling to complement the wood flooring, tables and chairs. There were images of Glasgow on the walls, Byres Road, The Art Galleries, the view of Glasgow University from Partick Bridge...very original, thought Patterson. Perhaps he had to accept that he would always be a sarcastic old git. In any case, overall, the café wouldn't look out of place atop a Swiss mountain.

There were quite a few people inside the café when Patterson arrived. He noticed Jess Whittaker and Kelly O'Connor, who appeared to be working as waitresses, talking to each other. Andy McLean was at a swanky coffee bar area alongside Tegan Rees. Julie Campbell was sitting at the till, and he spotted Mary McNair disappearing into the kitchen.

Someone tapped Patterson on the shoulder, and he turned round.

'Alistair! Phew, you're still alive.'

'Eh?' said the team leader, confused.

'Well, what with you being Colonel Nicholson...'

' Oh, aye, very good. So, how are ye?'

'Fine, the café's looking great. How are you?'

'Good, busy, just getting everything in place for tomorrow.'

'Aye, well, you seem to be doing a grand job. It's nice to see you again.'

'You too,' said Alistair, a bit more distractedly, as he once more contemplated a shortened lifespan being Colonel Nicholson.

Patterson then saw Pearce in one of the booths talking to Pettigrew, and both looked up as Patterson approached.

'Morning, Claire, Annabelle,' said Patterson cheerfully.

'I was wondering when you were going to appear,' said Pearce.

Patterson smiled at her. She looked radiant. That was the word, radiant, he thought. You would never have guessed she was a counter-terrorism officer.

'I must say,' said Patterson, looking around. 'They've done a great job of doing the place up. It's completely transformed.'

'I know,' said Pettigrew, 'I was just saying the same thing to Annabelle.'

Patterson went to sit down beside Pettigrew, but Pettigrew started to get up.

'Let me get out first,' said Pettigrew. 'I need to go to the toilet.'

Patterson waited for Pettigrew to get up and then sat down next to Pearce.

'So how have you been?' asked Pearce.

'Good,' said Patterson. 'They've fixed the lift.' This was his big news, and he was pleased with Pearce's amplified reaction.

'Really? That's excellent. You'll be pleased about that.'

'I am.' Patterson decided he wouldn't pussyfoot around and that he would ask Pearce straight away if she would like to go for a drink.

'Listen, Annabelle, I was wondering if maybe sometime—'

'Hey, look who it is,' Patterson looked up to see Andy McLean. 'The crime-fighting duo, Patterson and Pearce.'

Patterson and Pearce looked at each other and smiled.

'Inspector,' continued Andy. 'I didn't see you come in. Have you not got a drink? Let me get you one. Jess or Kelly should be taking your order, but as usual, they're too busy nattering to each other. Anyway, I'm one of the designated baristas today, so what will you have?'

'Well,' said Patterson, 'if you're the one making the coffee, then I'll have a coffee.'

'What kind?'

'A cappuccino if you have it.'

'I certainly do, and what about yourself,

madam?'

'The same,' said Pearce. 'I like your apron,' she added.

'Yes, look, it says barista on it. Anyway, I'll go and get your cappuccinos,' said Andy, walking away.

'Nice to see Andy looking so happy. Even if he is a terrorist,' said Patterson.

Pearce playfully punched Patterson on the arm.

'So, what have you been up to?' asked Pearce.

'Nothing special, work, we finally finished the last remnants of the Bunhouse investigation yesterday. Oh, and we found out who the mole was.'

'Who?'

'DS Easdon.'

'Why would he ever do that?'

'Why do you think? Money. He's thrown away his career all for the sake of some extra cash. Still it's no great loss...so anyway, Annabelle, I was wondering, if you want, maybe some time we could—'

'Two cappuccinos!' Patterson looked up to see Andy with two cups on a tray, which he placed on the table.

'That was quick,' said Patterson.

'The quickest and best cappuccinos in Glasgow,' said Andy proudly.

'I'm sure they are,' said Pearce.

'If you want anything else, I'll be at the coffee bar. Otherwise, just ask for the barista,' said Andy, who really did seem exceedingly happy.

To Patterson's surprise, Pearce suddenly put her hand on Patterson's arm. 'Oh, Mike, there's something I need to tell you.'

'Yes?'

'You'll think I'm mad, but I think I've met the one.'

'The one?'

'I met this man who I really think is the guy I've been waiting for. Remember how I was telling you about hoping to find the one, well, this time, I think I've really found him.'

'Really?' said Patterson, taking a sip of his cappuccino. 'Well, that's great news...how... did you meet?'

'Believe it or not, we just got chatting in the supermarket,...isn't it strange the way things work out? Derek is—'

'Derek?'

'Derek, his name, Derek. Derek is so funny.

He has me in stitches sometimes.'

'Not literally, I hope,' said Patterson, as he smiled once more and looked at his cappuccino.

'He's a train driver. Earns an absolute fortune, and he's kind. I mean it, he's kind and funny and...I've already said that, haven't I? Anyway, I'm really hopeful it'll work out this time.'

'Well, I hope it does,' said Patterson quietly, wondering where Pettigrew had got to.

They talked some more, and then Pearce said she had to leave because she was meeting Derek in town. She slid out of the booth.

'It was lovely to see you again, Mike.'

'Lovely to see you too. You'll have to pop by the station sometime, now that the lift is working.'

'I'll do that. Definitely,' said Pearce. Pearce curiously stopped for a moment, looked at Patterson, smiled, then quickly turned and left the café.

Patterson looked at his cappuccino once again. It really did taste quite nice. He wondered if this was down to Andy or the machine. He looked through the window and saw Pearce's car driving away. Ah, well, he thought, that's that. Patterson and Pearce would never get past the pilot episode, and for some reason that Patterson couldn't explain, he suddenly felt an immense sadness. Did it really matter? He asked himself. Who cares?...and yet…anyway, he thought as he tried to shake himself out of his sudden gloom, could he ever be with a woman who said perp? Of course not…and yet….

'Hello,'

Patterson looked up to see Siobhan.

'Hello, Siobhan.'

'I'm not disturbing your thoughts, am I?'

'Eh? No, no…'

'Do you mind if I take a seat?'

'No, not at all, said Patterson, moving across. 'The café is looking great, by the way.'

'It is, isn't it? After all that had been going on, they brought in loads of extra workers to ensure a thorough job was done before it opens tomorrow. I think they are trying to save face, to be honest.'

'Well, they've done an excellent job. You must be excited about tomorrow. Let's hope the murders don't put people off.'

'You're kidding, aren't you? It's brought us publicity we couldn't buy. By the amount of enquiries we've got, we're expecting it to be jam-packed tomorrow.'

'Really? Well, every cloud, as they say,' said Patterson. 'You haven't seen Pettigrew, have you?'

'She's in the kitchen, talking to Mary. Oh, do you want something to eat?' asked Siobhan. 'Remember it's all free today.'

'I know. No, I was just popping by. Unfortunately, I can't stay. So, all the trainees are still here, are they?

'Actually, a few have left once the training program finished. Mohammad, Russell, James, who else...Linh...but some of the others have stayed. Most are in the kitchen making sandwiches.'

'Well, you're doing a great job, Siobhan, but I'm afraid I have to go.' Patterson stood up. 'Like I said, it's nice to see the café looking great, and the trainees looking happy. You should be very proud.'

'Thanks,' said Siobhan, 'Listen...I hope you don't think I'm being forward or anything, but I was wondering if you'd like to go for a drink sometime? Don't feel obliged to say, yes, I just thought...'

Patterson was taken by surprise. 'A drink? Em...actually, yes, I'd be delighted to go for a drink with you, Siobhan.'

Siobhan broke into a big smile. 'Great. Listen, is it OK to call you after and arrange some time for later in the week? Only, I have a feeling this weekend is going to be very busy for me. I still have your mobile number. I'll call you later, if that's OK?'

'Yes, of course,' said Patterson, 'Bye for now, Siobhan. Oh, and say bye to Pettigrew for me.'

'I will. Bye, Mike.'

On the way out, Patterson stopped to say hello to various trainees before heading to his car. Before getting inside, he looked back at the café. It now looked like a place he would definitely stop to have a bite to eat. With the sun shining, it was actually a very pleasant location, situated on the banks of the River Kelvin.

Just as before, when he had felt an immense sadness and didn't know why, now he felt an immense happiness and didn't know why, and yet, perhaps he did. He had a drink with Siobhan to look forward to during the week, and he could also say that the Murder at the Partick Bunhouse Café was finally over.

www.ingramcontent.com/pod-product-compliance
Lightning Source LLC
LaVergne TN
LVHW010554100826
845148LV00014B/2716